Rival – The Complete Series

Rival – The Complete Series is a work of fiction. Names, characters, places, and incidents are either the product of the author's imagination or are used fictitiously. Any resemblance to actual persons or their likeness is entirely coincidental.

Cover design by Cover Shot Creations (covershotcreations.com)

Parts 1-3

RIVAL

MIRANDA DAWSON

Part One

Chapter One

"Who are you, and why are you lying naked in my bed?"

I tried to open my eyes and look up at the figure standing by the bed, but the sun was streaming in through the half-opened blinds limiting my vision and reminding me that I was hung over. Thank God it was a Saturday, because the way I felt right now, I would not be in any shape to go to work. I didn't remember much of last night, and neither did my "date" if he was now standing there surprised to find me in his bed. Some men wanted you out before breakfast, but he hadn't said anything to me at the time.

Or had he? All I could remember was rolling over once we were done and falling asleep soon after.

"Don't panic," I said. "I have no intention on staying and I'm not about to get all clingy." I still couldn't look up at him, but I slung my arm over the edge of the bed and fished around on the floor for my knickers. I grimaced as my hand found last night's used condom that apparently this guy had been unable to throw in the trashcan.

"I take it you don't want my number, then?" I asked. My voice was dripping in sarcasm, but if he was going to act like a dick, then it might be fun to wind him up a bit.

"No, I don't want your number," the man said. "And you still haven't told me why the hell you are in my bed."

My headache was getting worse, but my brain was at least starting to function. There was something not quite right. I had woken up in a stranger's bed completely naked and exposed. There was a sheet somewhere, but I guessed we'd thrown it on the floor during last night's activities. So far, this was all to be expected. I didn't do this sort of thing often. I only ever indulged once a year on the night of July 26th, making today July 27th.

The unusual bit was everything else. The man speaking to me from beside the bed didn't sound like the guy I had gone home with last night. God, what was his name again? This guy's voice was slightly deeper, although that might have been because he sounded mad. I still couldn't bring myself to look straight up into the light, but I could see his legs. The trousers looked like the bottom half of an expensive suit, and while I was not an expert on men's shoes, I would hazard a guess that his cost north of $500.

It seemed odd that this was the same guy I'd screwed. What I did remember about last night involved going to a sleazy bar, not the type usually frequented by people in $500 shoes.

Realizing last night's entertainment was both fully dressed and staring down at my naked body made me feel exposed. I wasn't particularly shy about my body, but being spread-eagled, naked, and sporting bed hair now felt inappropriate.

"If you need me to leave, you can just say," I said. "No need to pretend last night didn't happen. We're both adults, after all."

Each word required more effort and energy than I had available, so I had to speak in short bursts while trying to manage the splitting pain in my head that got worse with even the slightest movement. Something else didn't feel right. The guy I had picked up—well, he picked me up I suppose, but I'd been willing—had been more than a little rough around the edges and I had half-anticipated going back to some dingy loft or apartment he shared with four other people.

But this place was nice. Really nice. I was in a large condo with two floors on the top of a building that must have been in downtown San Francisco, because I remembered that we'd walked back and it hadn't taken long. The bedroom furniture was tasteful and expensive. Even *I* could tell that it hadn't come flat-packed like all of mine.

Finally, I looked up at the man standing by the bed. Even in my condition I could tell that this was not the man I went home with last night. For one thing, this man would never be seen in the type of bar I was in. As my eyes trailed up his body I took in the rest of the suit, which oozed sophistication and money. One of his cufflinks looked like it cost more than any jewelry I had ever owned.

When I saw his face, I knew for sure I had not seen him before. You just didn't forget a face like that. He had a dark, brooding look about him. Maybe that was because he had a strange naked woman in his bed.

I noticed there were some unusual contradictions in his appearance, as well. While his suit was immaculate, tailor-made, and had cost a small fortune, his auburn hair was disheveled and he had the rough stubble of someone who had not shaved for a few days.

"Hello," I said meekly, looking into his eyes for the first time.

He opened his mouth about to say something mean by the look of it, but then he appeared to change his mind. "Hello. Are you going to explain what is going on here? I suppose I shouldn't complain, but I don't usually come home to find strange, naked women in my bed."

He was so easy on the eyes that I was fairly sure he could snap his fingers and a naked woman would appear in his bed. I kept looking at him, but threw my hand behind me to feel the empty space where the guy who'd screwed me last night had been laying. Where the hell was he?

"This is your bed?" I asked, thinking it sounded like a sensible question. My foot found the sheet at the bottom of the bed. I grabbed it between two of my toes and pulled it up, wrapping it around me to cover my chest and everything below it. I thought I saw a slight twinge of disappointment in his eyes, but perhaps I was just seeing what I wanted to see.

"Indeed, it is. This is my condo. I would ask again what you are doing here, but I think I have a fairly good idea at this point." He took his eyes off mine and looked behind me. "James?" he yelled.

I heard a door open behind me. I spun around as fast as the pounding headache behind my eyes would allow and saw the guy—James, presumably—who had brought me home with him last night. I never let myself feel bad for what, or whom, I did on my annual night of freedom, but right now regret was a good word to sum up my feelings. James was not horrendous-looking, but the man on the other side of the bed was in a different league. Sex with James had been functional, but certainly not memorable, and I had not even come close to an orgasm.

"Oh, shit," James said as he walked out of the en-suite bathroom with just a towel around his waist.

"'Oh, shit,' indeed," the other man said.

"You're home early," James said. "I thought you weren't going to be back until tonight."

"Clearly. I got an early flight." He turned from James and looked back at me. "You should get dressed and leave."

I nodded and stood up, walking around the room to gather my clothes while trying not to throw up.

"So, this is what happens when I let you use my condo for the weekend, is it?" the man to James. "Please tell me she's not an escort, or anything like that?"

I retrieved my bra from the floor and stood there open-mouthed, staring at him, but he didn't even turn to look at me. It was as if I wasn't there.

"No," James said. "We met in a bar and had a drink. Then I invited her back. It was as simple as that."

Simple as that? Despite my hangover, I felt the need to defend myself against his accusation of being easy. Not so much because I cared what James thought, but for some reason I didn't want this other man to think of me that way. That seemed to be missing the point, though. Even though I only had casual sex once a year, there was nothing wrong with what I did and I hated the judgment pouring from the stranger right now.

"Just because I hooked up with a guy doesn't make me an escort, thank you very much. I knew what I was doing."

"Well, in that case, you're just stupid," the man said. "Do you have any idea how dangerous it is to go home with random men? You might want to rethink your behavior before it gets you in trouble."

I was silent. Not because I couldn't think of anything to say, but because there were too many things I wanted to blurt out. They all reached the tip of my tongue at the same time, but none of the words could break through into a coherent sentence.

The distinct sound of a woman's heels on a wooden floor came from a nearby hallway. The footsteps got louder as she approached the room.

"Matthew, are you going to make me a drink, or—" The woman froze as she walked into the bedroom and saw the three of us standing there, two of us half-naked.

The woman was as immaculately dressed as this Matthew guy, and the long, red gown she was wearing looked fit for an evening ball. In fact, she and Matthew looked like a couple about to go out for the evening, perhaps to some expensive charity fundraiser. Why the hell were they dressed like this at seven a.m., though?

"Rebecca, sorry, this is not how it looks." Matthew approached her and placed a hand on her back to try to calm her down. I felt a shiver down my spine as I imagined it was my back he had his hand on.

"Really?" she yelled, slapping his hand away. "Because when you invited me back to your place, I assumed it would just be the two of us. What the hell did you have in mind? Were we going to swap partners halfway through? Jesus, Matthew, you can be a real piece of shit sometimes."

"It really isn't how it looks," I said. For some reason I wanted to help Matthew reconcile with this Rebecca woman, even though I was already insanely jealous of her. I stepped forward, but managed to stand on the bottom of the sheet that covered what was left of my modesty. The sheet fell to the floor and

I stumbled forward. I regained my balance and stood up in front of her, completely nude once again.

She looked at me with disgust and quickly turned on her heel and walked away.

"James, get your 'friend' the hell out of here before I throw her out."

Matthew stormed off after Rebecca, leaving me alone with James.

"Uh, sorry about all this," James said. "I guess I may have embellished the truth a little last night."

"Just forget it. I know I soon will."

That was only half true. I would soon forget whatever James and I had done together—already had—but I was hardly likely to forget Matthew in a hurry. I didn't usually take offense easily, but Matthew's words had really stung. I knew I should have ignored him, but what he'd said hurt all the more coming from a man like him.

As I got dressed, I wondered whether I should end my annual one-night stands, but I knew I wouldn't. There were moments where I considered stopping the tradition, but then I remembered *why* I did it and knew I wasn't ready to stop.

Chapter Two

By the time I arrived home to my tiny two-bedroom apartment it was eight in the morning, and that meant I had a chance to sneak into my bedroom before my roommate noticed I had spent the night somewhere else. The last thing I needed was to have to explain my actions to yet another person. My roommate was cool, but in all the time we'd lived together she had never known me to have a one-night stand, and I had no idea how she would react.

I slowly slipped the key into the lock. The sound of metal grinding against metal sounded like a factory floor to my hung-over brain, but logic told me I had hardly made any noise at all. I slipped inside and popped off my shoes before tiptoeing back toward my room. When my bedroom door shut behind me, I breathed a sigh of relief. Walk of shame completed with success. One hundred points!

I didn't even have time to collapse down onto the bed before I heard a knock at my bedroom door.

"Amy?" It was Amanda. "Are you okay? I was worried when you didn't come home last night."

I considered just answering "yes" and staying locked up in my room, but Amanda was a journalist and she had a talent for spotting when someone was hiding something. Besides, I didn't want to hide out in my room all day. That sort of attitude made it look like I was ashamed of my behavior, and I wasn't.

I got up and opened the door. "Hi, Amanda. I'm fine. I just crashed at a friend's house last night. Few too many drinks, you know?"

Amanda nodded, and for a brief second I thought she was going to turn away and leave it at that. I should have known she wouldn't—my luck was not that good.

She bit her lip, and it looked like she was trying to suppress a laugh.

"What is it?" I asked. I tried to sound lighthearted, but I still felt like crap and didn't have the energy for conversation right now.

"If I didn't know you better, Amy, I would swear you hooked up with a guy last night."

"Oh?" I said, raising my eyebrows. Although I didn't like to be the subject of Amanda's suspicion, I did find it amusing watching her tease the truth out of people, even when I was the victim.

"You seem different. You have that glow about you that people get after a night of passion. Plus, I don't know, obviously you look tired, but I think you met a guy. Someone you like."

"Is that all you have to go on? I hope you get more complete evidence before you run your stories."

"I'm ignoring all my journalistic integrity right now and just going with women's intuition. So yeah, I'm going to say you got laid last night and you hope to see him again."

"Well, you're half right." There was really no point in lying to Amanda, but I would have preferred it if she didn't know about the side of me that hooked up with random men once a year. The other 364 days I behaved like the perfect young woman only just out of college and trying to make an impact on the world. July 26th was a different story.

"I did have sex," I admitted. "But not with anyone I want to see again. It was just a bit of fun. A one-night stand." I supposed she was also right about me meeting a man I wanted to see again—it just so happened that man was not the one I screwed. She didn't need to know *everything*, though.

"Really? *You* had a one-night stand? Give me some credit, Amy. I know you well enough to know that you don't do one-night stands. Hell, you don't seem to do relationships full-stop."

"A girl can have fun once in a while, can't she?"

"Of course. I guess it just took me by surprise."

"I don't do it often. Once a year I just like to let my hair down. That's all. Besides, I can't say I've been kept awake by any of your shenanigans recently. And these walls are paper thin, so I would hear. When are you going to get back into the swing of things?"

Amanda sighed. "Once Mr. Perfect comes along, I guess. I've had too many bad relationships these last few years—I'm exhausted. I know this might sound like a cliché, but I'm putting work first for now. Does that make me a bad person?"

"God, no. Why would you say that?"

"Because my mother phones me every other day asking me when I'm going to settle down and have kids. And when she says 'settle down,' what she really means is quit my job and raise babies full time."

"Well, I am hardly in a position to argue with you on that point. There's plenty of time for men later—first I need to get my career up and running."

"Oh, yes. Monday's the big day, isn't it? Isn't that when you get to meet some of the money men?"

"I don't know if 'meet' is the right word," I said. "I'll basically walk into a room and get five, ten, maybe even fifteen minutes, if I'm lucky, to convince them that my business is worth investing in. The odds are stacked against me—only about five percent of people who go in there get an offer, and even then the deal often falls through before any money changes hands."

"It sounds exciting. Like *Shark Tank*, or something. But I guess I can see why you would be terrified. Want to do a practice run of your pitch in front of me later? Might be good to rehearse what you are going to say."

"Oh, thank you. That would be awesome. I don't really have the energy to practice today, but tomorrow would be good, if you have the time."

"No problem. Shall I dress in a swanky suit and try to look all intimidating, as well?"

I laughed, trying to imagine Amanda with her long, blonde hair, slender frame, and generous chest trying to look like one of the intimidating men I would have to perform in front of on Monday.

"Don't worry," I said. "Silicon Valley investors try to pretend they are accommodating to women, so no doubt there'll be a token woman involved. It's bullshit, of course, but I guarantee you that every time a woman like me goes to give the pitch, someone will talk about how good it is to see a strong, female role model leading the way among entrepreneurs. It's a patronizing as hell, but I want the money, so I'll go along with it."

"You can worry about changing the system from the inside once you're there," Amanda agreed. "Besides, I know a woman about your age who has done ridiculously well in this area, so you never know."

"Thanks, Amanda. I'm going to have a shower and then collapse into bed to catch up on my sleep. I really don't know how people have these casual flings on a regular basis. It's exhausting."

That wasn't quite true. After last night—or more accurately, this morning—I knew exactly why people had casual sex. It was because of people like Matthew. Men with some sort of raw magnetism that a girl just couldn't resist. I knew for certain that if Matthew ever propositioned me, any moral compass I thought I had would disappear instantly, even if he did think I was some bimbo who slept around all the time. If I hadn't been so hung-over, I would have subtly told him I was an Ivy League graduate who, with any luck, would be making my mark in the Bay Area soon.

Instead, the impression I left him with was likely one he wished to forget. Especially when he had Rebecca to keep his mind and body occupied.

I was starting to wish I had taken James's number. Not so I could see him again, obviously, but so I could subtly find out some information about Matthew.

As I showered, I imagined all the different ways I could have handled this morning better and prepared silly speeches in my head that I could give if I ever bumped into Matthew again. I knew I cared far too much about someone who hadn't said one nice word to me, but I hadn't been at my best and perhaps neither had he. I was never going to find out what he was really like, so the fantasy seemed harmless enough.

Once I felt vaguely clean again, I settled down to prepare different versions of my speech and think about all the questions I could be asked on Monday. Next week was going to be huge and I couldn't let some stranger distract me. There was plenty of time to think about Matthew after Monday. For now, I had to think about how to satisfy a group of men in exchange for money. Nothing wrong with that, was there?

Chapter Three

In less than thirty minutes' time, I would be asking four investors to purchase a stake in my business for anything north of one million dollars, and I felt woefully unprepared.

The building was surprisingly security-conscious for a private firm and felt more like a branch of the military. I hadn't been allowed to bring in anything, even my laptop, and had to forward a copy of the slides I would use in my presentation via email. That meant I was walking into the biggest business meeting of my life with nothing other than my wits. It didn't seem like nearly enough.

Getting there early had seemed like a good idea, but I now wished I hadn't. As soon as I had sat down in the hall outside the meeting room, a young guy walked out with a massive grin on his face. He had clearly received a promise of investment and was on the phone with his business partner before he'd even stepped into the elevator.

Another guy in his early twenties was up before me. He could have been related to the previous one, but then they all tended to look the same. To get an interview like this in the first place you needed to be connected, and that meant the vast majority of applicants would be typical Ivy League graduates from rich families. Okay, so I was an Ivy League graduate too, but I certainly wasn't from a rich or well-connected family. The reason I was here was because I was a woman. I wasn't naïve enough to think otherwise.

Silicon Valley had a reputation as a boys' club, and that extended well beyond the makeup of the companies themselves. It also extended to the types of companies that got invested in. Whether they did it consciously or not, the vast majority of investors gave their money to companies run by young men. It didn't help that most of the investors themselves were also men. To their credit, there were a few more women investors with the big firms now, but the numbers were still pitiful in comparison.

The real problem I had to overcome, though, was not my gender—rather, I was seeking an investment for a business that wasn't likely to make much money. At least, not for the next few years. My sales to date were a grand total of zero and I had no track record of success. Even *I* wouldn't invest in me.

The sound of laughter came from the meeting room. At first I hoped—in rather mean-spirited fashion—that the investors were laughing *at* the current entrepreneur, but it soon became apparent that they were laughing *with* him. No one would invest in a company just because the founder could crack a few jokes, but it sure did help build a rapport. I would be happy with just getting the words out of my mouth without saying something stupid or making a fool out of myself.

Whenever you wanted time to move fast you could be sure it wouldn't, but right now I wanted as much time as I could get to rehearse the speech in my head. Just my luck that the hands on the clock seemed to be moving impossibly fast. I went to check the time on my phone before remembering that I'd had to leave that behind at reception as part of the insanely high security protocols they had in place.

The door opened and I immediately stood up, pressing down the creases that had formed on my skirt. The founder who had just finished pitching his company came out of the room wearing a grin a mile wide. There was no need to guess how his presentation went. That meant the two people immediately before me had managed to raise some money. Would there even be any left for me?

I took one last look at the invitation in my hand. There was no information of use on there, but it gave me something to occupy my mind. In addition to having the address of the presentation, the paper gave a brief description of each of the investors I would be presenting to. No names or identifying information were included, which made the descriptions all sound generic.

Three out of the four investors were from technology backgrounds, though, so perhaps that would help. The other investor was from the retail industry, so I wouldn't have a chance with him. Three out of four wasn't bad, though.

A woman stepped out of the room. "Ms. Kendrick? They will see you now."

I took a deep breath and followed her into the room. She quickly took a seat to one side and I realized she was just there to take notes or was perhaps someone's PA. The four investors were sat at the far end of the room looking at a blank screen upon which I would give my presentation. None of them greeted me as I walked in, so I kept my head down and walked over to the computer that was set up for me to use.

My presentation was already on the screen and ready to go. With a touch of a button it appeared on the wall over my left shoulder. Before I had even introduced myself to the investors, I caught a mistake on the very first slide. The business logo I had hastily designed just a few weeks ago was misaligned and parts of it had been cut off at the bottom of the slide. What other mistakes had I made in my haste to put this presentation together?

I took another deep breath, but this time I tried to hide the fact that I was doing so. They would soon find out I wasn't a confident speaker, but I hoped to keep up the pretense as long as possible.

Finally, I looked up at the row of four investors in front of me. When I had walked into the room it had seemed big, but now they all looked uncomfortably close to me. On the far left was the token female investor. She looked aggressive, as if she were trying to prove she could be just as harsh as her male counterparts. The two men in the middle looked bored already and I caught one of them looking at his phone, clearly checking the time.

The man on the far end did not look bored. In fact, I had already got his attention as he sat up straight and stared directly at me. Normally an interested investor was a good sign, but not in this case. The investor was interested because he recognized me. We had met before, although last time I saw him, I had been completely naked.

Just two days ago, I had woken up in this man's apartment after a one-night stand. Now Matthew was in a position to decide the future of my business. I didn't like my chances.

Chapter Four

"You can start whenever you're ready, Amy," the man next to Matthew said. According to the card in front of him, his name was William.

How long had I been standing there? Had I been staring at Matthew the entire time? Matthew was certainly still staring at me, but then they all were, so maybe I shouldn't read too much into that. Was he going to blurt out to everyone that I was just some silly little girl who slept with strangers? That didn't seem like a very professional thing to do, but he did look angry, or perhaps "smoldering" was a better word.

His suit was once again immaculate and he was sitting back in his chair examining me with an intense stare. The cuff of his shirt had dropped back to reveal an expensive silver watch that he used to check the time, as if already hoping I would be finished soon. Realistically, the number of people who might invest in my business was now down to two.

"Hello," I said, measuring the strength of my voice and making sure it wouldn't crack. "My name is Amy Kendrick, and I am a twenty-two year-old—"

"We know your name, dear," the woman, Suzanne, said in a tone of voice that sounded like how a patronizing older man would speak to his secretary in the 1950s. "Get on with your proposal. You've wasted enough time as it is."

My natural reaction would be to point out that I had wasted hardly any time at all, but of course you couldn't talk back to these people. "I am a graduate of—" I stopped when I caught Suzanne rolling her eyes. Okay, so no background information, then. So much for being able to milk the fact that I had a decent education behind me.

"My business is going to change the lives of millions of women around the world," I said, pressing a button on my laptop to skip over the first slide of my presentation and onto the slide with my first diagram. The slides weren't exactly works of art, but I liked having them there. They gave me something to look at if I was nervous.

"My company is a software as a service business, with the software in question being a closed communication network that people can use to speak in confidence with those who have been preapproved to enter the network."

"Seriously?" Suzanne asked. "Your big idea is another messaging app? I believe they exist already."

"I don't think that is it," the man next to her said. According to his name card, he was Craig and he had an intriguing demeanor about him. He was attractive, but in a more boyish way than Matthew. Whereas Matthew still had rough stubble on his face, Craig was clean-cut and friendly looking. I wished I had been attracted to people like Craig, but no matter how much I wanted to hate him, Matthew was the one I struggled to keep my eyes off.

"The diagram on your slide looks more like a closed forum," Craig said. "Am I on the right track?"

"Yes," I said. "It is more like an online forum, yes. Except this one is much more private and there is a high barrier to entry."

"So, it's an online forum," Suzanne said. "It's still an old, pointless idea. This has been done before and there is no money in it. Count me out."

The pool of potential investors was down to just three. Two, if you excluded Matthew, who looked like he didn't even want to look at me, let alone invest any money in my business.

"I'm sorry to hear that," I said. Quite frankly, I didn't want her money anyway, but I had to maintain protocol.

"Please, do continue," William said. "How about you focus on the part where this service will help women. I assume that's the way you are differentiating yourself?"

"Thank you," I said. William had just helped me get the presentation back on track. Matthew maintained his silence and continued to stare at me.

"The forum itself is nothing special—that I am more than happy to admit. The user interface is nice to look at, but there are other forums out there like it. This is unique because the forum is specifically designed for victims of rape and domestic abuse. The forum will be a safe place for victims to talk with other victims in private without worrying about who they are speaking to."

"How will you ensure that only victims of abuse will have access?" Craig asked. "Surely, anyone can sign up, including men looking for vulnerable women."

"I am working closely with police departments. The only people who will get access are those who file complaints and who the police think will need extra support outside of what they are able to offer."

"Interesting," Craig said. He was tapping the table with one finger, and if I didn't know better, I would have sworn he was considering investing.

"Why do you think this is important?" William asked. "I don't want to sound heartless, but I feel like there are numerous support groups for people like this. What gap do you see this software plugging?"

"You're right, women do have lots of options, but none of them are perfect. Neither is this one, but it has the potential to help victims stay anonymous and protected. We now take it for granted that you never know who you are speaking to online, but imagine that you knew for sure the person you were speaking to had been through a similar experience to you. You don't know their name or any of their information, but you know they are suffering like you are or once did. It sounds so obvious, but—"

"—but the best ideas often do," William said. "I think this is a great idea."

I sensed a "but" coming.

"But I'm not a computer software guy. I *could* give you the money, but you need an investor you can talk to. Someone who can help you with the business, and I just don't think I can do that. I wish you all the best, but I'm going to sit this one out."

"I understand," I said, turning my attention back to Craig. He was my only hope now. I still hadn't looked Matthew in the eyes, but I could see that he was still staring in my direction and he looked completely unmoved by everything I had said.

"Tell me about the security," Matthew said suddenly, having decided to speak at last. I kept looking at William as I mustered the courage to turn my attention toward Matthew. His voice alone was enough to make me go weak at the knees. I didn't trust myself to maintain my composure if I had to look at him and talk at the same time.

Finally, I faced him. He could have been a model posing in a suit for an expensive fashion label. He sat back in his chair, crossed one leg over the other, and stared at me, awaiting my response.

"The forum is an entirely closed space," I said, surprised I was able to string together a sentence. "Think of it like the software used for exams. When you are on the forum, your computer is locked out from taking screenshots or printing any of the information."

"People can still take photos of the screen," Matthew said. "This idea of yours doesn't work. These women, and some men as well, are in incredibly vulnerable positions. You have to promise them complete security, but you cannot provide that."

"That's what I want the money for," I said. "You're right, this whole thing centers around security and protecting the identities of those involved. And that's exactly what I intend to do. But I will need some help with that, and if you invest in me, my first hire will be a security consultant."

Matthew waved a hand dismissively. It was quite clear he would not be investing in my business. "Even if this works, why on earth would we invest in it? How do you plan to make money? Are you going to charge these women?"

"Of course not. Once the technology is up and running, I plan to license it out to other groups and companies who need a secure method of communication. Even large companies are still operating in the Dark Ages when it comes to electronic communication. Every time a company gets sued, all the emails get searched for useful information. If they use my software, then none of those communications will be saved. That's how I will make money."

Matthew didn't even bother to respond to my answer. I quickly flipped through my slides until I found the one with revenue projections, but he showed no interest in them, either. I felt sure my business was good and I had presented it well today, yet Matthew clearly had no intention of investing in me because he thought I slept around. I hated him almost as much as I wanted to jump on him and rip open that perfect suit.

"I love the idea," Craig said. "I'm still not convinced by the revenue projections, but what you're doing is worthwhile and I'm ready to take a chance on you. I'm going to make you an offer I think you'll really like."

Chapter Five

An offer? The longer my presentation had gone on the more I just wanted to leave in one piece. I'd long since given up on actually getting an offer when Craig decided to speak up. Matthew looked as shocked as I was, and he wasn't about to hide his feelings.

"You're going to invest in her?" Matthew asked. "This whole thing is a waste of time." I could tell he really wanted to say, *Why would you invest your money in this bimbo?*

"I will spend my money how I want," Craig said. "Amy, I have to be honest, I'm not sold on this idea yet. It might work, *might*, but the odds are stacked against you."

"I can make it work," I said fiercely.

"Maybe," Craig said. "But I'm not going to make you an offer for the business. I want to invest in you. Come and work for me and you can work on your project with the help of my team. If you want, you can put your talents to work elsewhere, as well."

I could read between the lines and knew what he was saying. I could go and work for him as a regular engineer. He'd let me work on my "vanity project" for a few months until it petered out, and then I would be just another employee. If I hadn't prepared myself for such an offer, I would have likely rejected it out of hand, but I had thought about how to make it work. I could use all the resources at a company like Craig's and work on this project in my own time, if I had to.

"Well? What do you think?" Craig asked. "We'd have to work out the details, of course, but I can't imagine that being a problem."

Craig had a slight smile on his face that looked gentle and inviting. I looked over at Matthew and he was still staring at me, his index finger pressed against his cheek and the other fingers under his lip. We held eye contact for a few seconds and then there was a slight shake of the head. The movement was minute, but it was a firm "no."

I turned my attention back to Craig. If he was offended by me looking to Matthew for another offer, then he didn't show it. A weight immediately felt like it had been lifted from my shoulders as I made my decision. My idea wasn't one of those billion-dollar stories you read about in the papers, and I knew it. This special forum could help people who really needed it, but that didn't mean it would rake in the money.

"I accept," I said. "I would love to come and work for your company. Can we talk about the terms?"

"You're making a big mistake," Matthew said.

I didn't know whether he was talking to me or Craig, and he didn't look like he was about to elaborate.

Craig led me into a room down the hall where he had lawyers already waiting. He wasn't going to waste any time.

"Gentleman," Craig said to the two lawyers sitting at the table, "I would like to offer this young lady a job as an engineer. Please draw up a contract."

"I don't want to sound too demanding," I said to him, "but I want something in there about being able to work on my project. I want to make this a success."

"Sure, sure," Craig said. "We can include that. You're going to be a real asset to this company."

Without knocking, Matthew opened the door and stepped inside. Craig looked annoyed that he had just burst in on us, but didn't say anything. Matthew looked right past me as if I weren't there.

"Can we talk?" Matthew asked Craig. "Now."

My eyes wandered down from Matthew's face to his chest. There was a gap between the buttons of his shirt and I could see the firm, smooth pecs that lay beneath.

Craig sighed and threw up his arms. "Aren't you glad you're going to be working with me and not with him?" he asked me with a smile.

I was still staring at Matthew's chest and barely heard him. "Huh? Oh, yes, definitely."

The two of them stepped outside the room and left me there with the lawyers. They asked me a few questions—my full name, address, and stuff like that—and were finished with the contract just ten minutes later. They obviously had a template already prepared. *Way to make a girl feel special, guys.*

"We have just emailed you a copy of the contract," the more senior of the two lawyers said. "You should take a day or two to look it over. Maybe show it to another lawyer for a second opinion."

"Thanks," I replied. I had spent all my money trying to put the business together and didn't exactly have the funds for my own lawyer. Still, I would read it over before signing my life away.

The conversation outside the room between Matthew and Craig stopped, but Craig never came back into the room. I hung around for a few more minutes, but it didn't look like he intended on coming back.

I left and started to make my way back to the elevator. I couldn't wait to get my precious possessions back from reception. As I rounded the corner, I got one final glance into the meeting room. Matthew looked less serious now and had a big grin on his face. I thought his smoldering look had been sexy, but seeing that smile full of pearly white teeth was enough to make me weak in the knees. And between the legs.

My stomach sank when I saw why he was smiling. He was sitting on the chair next to Suzanne and was clearly charming the pants off her.

The elevator arrived with a 'ping' and I jumped in as soon as possible. Once the doors shut I would never have to see Matthew again. I would likely picture him when I was alone in bed with the lights off, but there was nothing wrong with a harmless fantasy, and that was all it would ever be.

Chapter Six

"How did it go?" Amanda asked as soon as I got back to our apartment. She looked hard at work on an article judging by the way her fingers were flying all over the keyboard. It couldn't have been all that exciting, though, because she stopped working the second she saw me walk in.

"You know, I'm not entirely sure," I said as I collapsed down onto the sofa. I felt far more tired from the one-mile walk home than I had any right to be. Perhaps the mental exhaustion had seeped into my body somehow.

"Did you get any money?"

"No, but I did get offered a job. That's good, right?"

"I would say so, yes. Who would you be working for?"

"ITC, Inc.," I said, looking at the company name on the contract I had pulled up on my laptop. "They're a big software company with a focus on cloud storage."

"Never heard of them, I'm afraid."

"They aren't that well-known. I think they provide back-end support to a lot of the big name companies, though. Behind the scenes work, but profitable, I guess."

"So, what's with the lack of excitement on your part?" Amanda asked. "Sounds like a good gig for someone who's not long out of college. Are you disappointed no one saw your vision for the business?"

"A little," I admitted. I had felt like I was carrying around my own personal raincloud the entire way home and hadn't been able to pinpoint why. I knew my business idea was no gold mine. It had the potential to be profitable, but not with the kind of money that investors sought. I'd hoped that perhaps one of them would take it on as a charitable project of sorts—it's not like investors were entirely heartless, and the woman at least should have been able to relate to the product.

But I had gotten a job offer out of it. And it wasn't unusual for employees to work on their own projects as part of a bigger company. Hell, some of the biggest software products in the world were created that way. So why did I feel so underwhelmed?

"None of them understood," I said finally. "There was a female investor who thought the whole thing was stupid. Another guy seemed cool, but he wasn't in the software industry so he passed on the idea. Craig was the one who offered me a job, but he said he was investing more in me than in my vision."

"That sucks," Amanda said. "One of the articles I'm working on is about how difficult it is for women to get investment money in this area. Ironically, I can't get anyone to publish it because apparently 'no one wants to read that kind of thing,' according to the *men* I presented it to."

"The whole thing was a long shot, anyway. And you know what? With this job, I don't have to worry about the commercial side of the business. I can build it to work as intended and not worry about stupid licensing deals and that kind of thing."

"Still, if you're not sold on the position, I can still introduce you to the woman I know who is making a big name for herself at the moment. She's in England right now, I think, but she flies back quite often. Want to meet her?"

"No, that's okay. If I'm going to work for someone, it may as well be Craig."

"What's his surname?" Amanda asked. "I want to look him up."

I looked back down at the contract. "Masters. Craig Masters."

"Oh, damn," Amanda said after bringing up Craig's picture in less time than it took me to say his name. "No wonder you don't mind working for him. He's gorgeous."

I gave a lazy shrug. "He's all right, I suppose. Not my type, though."

"Well, he is most definitely my type. Feel free to have us accidentally bump into each other one day, if you like. I mean that literally. I want to press my body up against his."

I didn't see the fascination, myself. Craig was objectively handsome, that much was apparent, but I didn't *desire* him. He wasn't Matthew.

"Wait, didn't you say there were going to be four investors?" Amanda asked. "You only mentioned three. What did the fourth one say?"

"Not a lot," I replied. "He wasn't a fan of me personally."

"What, he didn't like your taste in shoes, or something?"

I told Amanda about Saturday morning and how I had woken up in his apartment when he had come back with a woman. Amanda couldn't hide her amusement and even I cracked a smile. If I made it through all this, then I would one day have a great story to tell my friends.

"You don't have a name for him?" Amanda asked.

"Not a surname. I just know that his first name is Matthew."

"Hmm, I know of a Matthew who is the CEO and founder of DataStore." A few seconds later, she had pulled up a picture. "Is this him?"

It was him, all right. The man of my dreams who also happened to be a total bastard.

"Yes, that's Matthew," I said once I had soaked in the image. Even in such a cheesy, staged photo, he still looked delicious.

"Matthew Bowers," Amanda said matter-of-factly. "He's a big player, and I don't just mean in the corporate world, although he has an impressive record there too. He formed DataStore at nineteen and it was worth a billion dollars by the time he was old enough to drink. He's thirty-one now and has never seen the stock price drop."

"Likes women too, does he?" I asked. I tried to keep my voice calm and detached, but it felt soaked in jealousy.

"I would say so. Check out this page of his photos. Apart from some of the official shots on his company's page, every image online is him with another woman hanging on his arm. I can't find any with the same woman in them, either."

"Sounds about right," I muttered.

My phone vibrated on the table to signify an incoming email. It was from Craig. So much for giving me time to think about the contract.

"Shit," I said, slumping down onto the sofa as I read his message. "Shit."

"Everything okay?" Amanda asked.

"No, not exactly. Craig's withdrawn the job offer. Looks like I'm back to square one."

Chapter Seven

Just as I hadn't known how to react to the job offer in the first place, I didn't really know how to react to losing it, either. In front of Amanda, I pretended not to care and spoke about how I hadn't been looking for a job, anyway. Deep down, I was more concerned about the manner in which I'd lost the job. Why would Craig offer me a job one minute and then withdraw it the next?

Maybe he had done a background check on me and hadn't liked what he'd found. I made sure to search for myself online in case any hint of my secret came up on the first few pages, but perhaps Craig had a more sophisticated way of looking. The past should stay in the past, as far as I was concerned, but the internet tended to have a different way of thinking about things like privacy.

Everything had been going well—I even had a copy of the contract in my inbox by the time I got my phone back from security. What the hell happened? Why did Craig change his mind so quickly?

Maybe someone told him I was a silly little girl who slept around with strangers.

Matthew.

The last time I had seen Craig, Matthew had asked to speak to him. I'd assumed it was business-related, but what if he had told Craig the story about Saturday morning? Those two didn't look like they were close enough that Craig would take Matthew's advice about anything, though. And surely he wouldn't retract a job offer just because of a one-night stand. Were all men really that shallow?

I couldn't take my mind off that moment Matthew asked to speak to Craig. Had there been anything in his voice suggesting he was about to screw me over? I couldn't think of anything, but the more I dwelt on it the more it seemed like the only possible explanation.

By the time the afternoon rolled around, I had completely convinced myself that Matthew was to blame and I was going to do something about it. I could put up with a lot, but this slut-shaming stuff really did my head in.

I pulled up the address for DataStore online. They were located further south in Mountain View, which meant a train ride from San Francisco. I would just about make it there before the end of the work day, although I guessed that Matthew kept longer hours than the average employee, anyway. The train ride would also give me plenty of time to stew on what I would say and let my anger build until I was ready to yell at him.

Visiting Mountain View felt like going to another state. The moderately hectic nature of San Francisco with its tall buildings, hills, and fog gave way to an open, flat place where the temperature was at least ten degrees higher. I needed to consider leaving the city at some point; it was heaven further south.

DataStore didn't have just one building—they had an entire campus. I followed the signs for the corporate office and knew I was in luck when I saw a Tesla in the parking lot. The license plate read "MBOWRS." Not at all subtle, although at least it was a nice car and not some big, obnoxious thing. Maybe he had a conscience, after all.

I strode into the office and walked into a relatively small reception area. The atmosphere could politely be described as informal, but it didn't have quite the same "startup playroom" vibe that some of the other offices probably had. You could tell this was the corporate office because there were actual sofas for visitors to sit on as opposed to beanbags or weird chairs that adorned some of the other offices I had been in.

"Can I help you, miss?" the receptionist asked.

"Yes. I'm here to see Mr. Bowers."

"Do you have an appointment?"

"Yes, at five o'clock. I'm a little early." Hell, it was worth a try.

"Name."

"Amy Kendrick."

"I'm sorry, Miss Kendrick, I don't see your name in his calendar."

"Oh, well, don't worry. Mistakes happen all the time. I'm sure it wasn't *entirely* your fault. Just give him a call and let him know I'm here."

"Mr. Bowers does not accept visitors without appointments, Miss Kendrick," the receptionist said in a much firmer voice. Apparently, she hadn't appreciated my attempt to suggest it might have been her fault.

"But I do have an appointment. Look, just tell him I am here. I can assure you he will want to speak to me."

"That won't be happening. Anyway, it would appear Mr. Bowers has already gone home for the day."

"Oh, really? And how did he get home today? Because his car is in the parking lot and I *know* he doesn't take the train."

"Miss Kendrick, I will call security if I have to."

I looked around and didn't see any security. There was likely a group that roamed the campus, but they were nowhere in sight at the moment. I would have a few moments before they arrived, but that wouldn't help be much because I had no idea where his office was. There were only three floors in this building, but his was unlikely to be on this one. Knowing him, he would have a corner office on the top floor, so I had about a one in four chance of getting to his office before security arrived.

The receptionist didn't give me a chance. "Miss Kendrick, I'm calling security."

"Don't worry about it, Janice," a male voice said. I spun around and came face to face with Matthew, who had come out of nowhere and was now standing just a few feet in front of me. "Miss Kendrick, follow me to my office."

Chapter Eight

I had been right about the location of his office—it was in the corner of the top floor. Neither of us spoke as we walked up the stairs or across the open space. A number of the predominantly male engineers looked up at me as we walked past. I caught a couple grinning and had a good idea what it meant when Matthew brought new women up to his office.

Matthew's office was minimalistic, but it was a lot bigger than it had looked from the outside. He had a desk with a couple of monitors hooked up to a laptop and a separate table with a phone in the middle, presumably set up for conference calls. A leather sofa was pushed up against the wall near the door. The furniture was enough to fill many offices, but this one was left feeling remarkably spacious.

Once the door was closed, I laid into him without a thought to what could be heard by the employees outside.

"How dare you?" I yelled. "You told Craig about what happened on Saturday morning, and now he's cancelled the offer he made me."

"I—" Matthew began.

"I'm not finished. Yes, I made a mistake being in your condo that morning, but it was hardly my fault. That guy I met said he lived there—how was I supposed to know any differently?"

"Who would have thought a stranger you met in a sleazy bar would lie to you?"

The grin on his face was gorgeous and infuriating at the same time. "Do you have a problem with me having casual sex? I find that remarkable, coming from you. You're hardly all that innocent yourself."

Matthew sat down on the sofa and crossed his legs, staring at me the entire time. "Can I speak now?"

I nodded. I needed a moment to catch my breath and collect my thoughts before I resumed yelling at him some more.

"First of all, I didn't tell Craig that I saw you lying naked in my bed."

"Yes, you did. I was there when you asked to speak to him, and then an hour later he withdrew the offer."

"I have no idea why he did that. I promise you, I didn't tell him. Knowing Craig as I do, if I had told him you were keen on one-night stands, that would have only increased his desire to employ you."

Matthew's voice contained a hint of disapproval, but this time it seemed to be aimed more at Craig than me.

"So, what did you tell him, then?" I asked.

"Nothing to do with you," he replied. "You shouldn't go to work for him, anyway."

"What? Why not? You two obviously have some rivalry going on, but I want no part of it."

"Sit down, Amy," Matthew said, motioning for me to take a seat next to him.

Sitting down felt like giving up and admitting that I wasn't mad at him anymore. Had I forgiven him that easily? Still, staying on my feet while he was relaxed on the sofa just made me look stubborn and immature, and behaving like a brat didn't seem the best way to win him over. Oh, God, why was I trying to win him over?

I sat down next to him on the sofa and tried to look as calm as he did. "I shouldn't be apologizing to you after the way you have treated me," I said evenly. "But I'm going to anyway, because you are right about one thing. I shouldn't have been in your apartment that morning. I apologize for my behavior and for spoiling your *date*."

The words felt bitter coming out of my mouth, but this way I could take the moral high ground. I had made a minor mistake and it was only right I apologize for it.

"Okay," Matthew said. "Thank you."

I stared at him, waiting for the full apology I had assumed would be forthcoming any second. Nothing.

"You don't want to say anything to me? You said some cruel things that morning and at the presentation earlier. Or do sluts like me just deserve that kind of thing?"

Matthew raised his eyebrows, but fortunately didn't go so far as to roll his eyes. Things would have gotten nasty had he done that.

"I'm not going to apologize for what I said that morning. You did behave in a reckless manner, and frankly I would expect better from someone like you. I checked out your résumé earlier—it's impressive. You're clever. You should be above hooking up with strangers in bars."

"I do not hook up with strangers," I said, practically spitting the words out through gritted teeth.

43

"Just a one-off, was it?" he asked, knowing it wasn't.

"Once a year," I said.

"Once a year? What does that mean?"

"Never mind. Look, who I sleep with is none of your business, so in the future how about you stay the hell out of it." I stood up to walk away, but Matthew grabbed me by the wrist. Did I imagine it, or were there actual sparks when he touched me? Perhaps it was just a static shock, albeit one that sent my heart pounding.

"Sit down, Amy," he said firmly. "We aren't finished yet."

"I disagree. We are completely finished." I pulled my arm away, but he had a tight hold of my wrist. I didn't want to get free. I wanted him to pull me down on top of him and have his way with me. I'd never felt like that. Not even on my annual evening of casual encounters.

"I want you, Amy," Matthew said.

Did he have any idea how powerful those words were coming from between those lips of his? "You want me?"

"I want you to work for me. Say yes. We can make something special happen."

Chapter Nine

Why on earth would he want to hire me? I had heard him speak about me as if I was beyond contempt, and at the presentation he could not have looked less interested if he'd tried.

"You're offering me a job?" I asked. "Why?"

"For the same reason I offered each of my employees a job. I offer people a job when they can improve my business. It's as simple as that."

"But at the presentation, you clearly didn't think I had anything to offer."

"I never said that. I didn't think your proposal had much merit, but that doesn't mean I'm ready to cut you out completely. You need to have a thick skin to pitch to investors, and I recommend you learn to let criticism wash over you a little bit."

"Was this why you spoke to Craig? Did you want to put him off me just so you could offer me a job yourself?"

"I told you, Amy, when I spoke to Craig, I did not mention you once. That was a separate business conversation and it had nothing to do with you. I don't know why Craig changed his mind, but I intend to take advantage of the situation. Hence, I am offering you a job."

For the second time in the span of less than twelve hours, a billionaire had offered me a job. I was living every young college graduate's dream right now, but for some reason I still wasn't entirely happy. I knew I was being ungrateful, but I felt like I had just traded Craig in for a better-looking model.

"What kind of job?" I asked. I wasn't about to give up my project just to be one of hundreds—no, thousands—of engineers working on commercial projects.

"There's no job title for this one, really," Matthew said. "Every now and again I employ people just so that I have the talent in-house. You can come and go as you please and work on whatever projects you like. You'll even have access to a small team, if you need the help."

"Okay, this sounds almost too good to be true. What's the catch?"

"No catch. You'll want to be paid as much as some of the more senior engineers, of course, but if you prove yourself with a few successful projects then you will be in a position to demand your salary in a year or two. This type of deal doesn't work for everyone. You need to be self-motivated and determined, but I'm a good judge of character and I imagine you fit that model."

"I don't know what to say."

"You can take some time to think about, it if you'd like."

"No," I said, raising my voice and catching Matthew off guard. Craig had offered me time to think about it and look what had happened there. I wasn't about to let another job offer slip through my fingers. "I'll take it. I can start tomorrow."

"Excellent. Glad to hear it."

There didn't seem to be anything left to say, so I smiled and walked toward the exit.

"One more thing," Matthew said, as I was just feet from the door.

I knew it. There was always a catch.

"Obviously, our first meeting was... unusual," he began.

He stood up from the sofa and walked over to me. I could smell a faint whiff of aftershave on his neck. It was subtle, but enough to trigger desires deep inside me. I clenched my fist, digging my nails into the palm of my hand to distract myself from my pleasant, but inappropriate, thoughts.

"I am not going to judge you or treat you any differently because of what I saw that morning."

Was he referring to seeing me in his bed? Or seeing me *naked* in his bed?

"I don't care what you do outside of work, but you should know that this is not the sort of job where sleeping with powerful people will get you to the top. In fact, sleeping with coworkers in general is likely to prove complicated."

Matthew had just offered me one of the best jobs I could have ever hoped to get, so I just about managed to resist the urge to slap him across the face. Just. Job offer or not, I would still give him a piece of my mind.

"I told you," I said, feeling a slight quiver in my voice, "I do not sleep around. That was a one-off. Sort of. I can assure you I have no intention of sleeping with my new colleagues." I was pretty sure I was telling the truth. I wanted to sleep with Matthew, but that didn't mean I had any intention of actually doing so. Besides, Matthew wasn't quite a colleague. He was my boss. So technically, my comments were accurate.

"Good. You're an attractive woman, Amy." Matthew reached out and lightly caressed the palm of my hand with his fingers, taking another step forward as he did so. "A very attractive woman."

"You're incredible, you know that?" I sneered, but without moving my hand away from his.

"I have been told as much, yes, but I have a feeling you didn't mean that in a positive way."

"You just told me I couldn't sleep my way to the top and said I shouldn't sleep with colleagues. For someone who pretends to have such high morals, you are quick to flirt with the new girl."

"I said you couldn't sleep your way *to* the top. I didn't say you couldn't sleep with people *at* the top. Just don't expect it to get you promoted. And it's true, sleeping with colleagues is complicated, but that doesn't mean it's not fun, too."

"Do you do this with all the new girls?" It was a stupid question. If he said yes, then I would just become jealous of every girl in the office. If he said no, then I wouldn't believe him. There was no good answer to the question and I shouldn't have asked it.

"No," Matthew said. "Most of them are fresh out of college like you, and they're not really my type."

I looked up into his eyes, but couldn't think of what to say. I wasn't as young as these other girls, but I was hoping he didn't know about that part of my past. I desperately tried to control the pace of my breathing, but it was impossible. Every breath was so loud. I probably looked like all the other college graduates that he clearly found too immature for him.

The phone on the table rang to break the awkward silence. Matthew stared at me for a few seconds and seemed to contemplate ignoring it, but eventually he sighed and, pulled his hand away from mine, walking over to the table to answer the call.

"Mr. Bowers, I have Senator Jones on the line for you," came the voice of the receptionist from the phone's speaker.

"Amy, I'm sorry. I have to take this."

I waved goodbye and quickly left his office. I had been convinced he was flirting with me, but by the time I got home I had decided he was just testing me. I didn't do relationships anymore and this policy had never been a problem before. But I'd also never met anyone like Matthew before. A guy like him was enough to make me rethink my stance on men altogether.

Chapter Ten

Being able to work on a flexible schedule sounded great in theory, but in practice it seemed to mean working all the normal hours during the day and then the additional ones in the evening too. I had imagined myself drifting into the office when I felt like it and maybe leaving early to miss the rush hour on the train, but after just one day I realized that wasn't going to work.

My first goal was obviously to work on my secure forum project. I needed help, though, and not just with my project, but also with the general day-to-day issues that came up on a regular basis. Plus all the important meetings seemed to take place at lunchtime. On Wednesday, I got very little work done on my project by the end of the day, so I decided to stay late and work on it while the office was half empty. It ended up being a productive day, but I was so exhausted that come five o'clock on Thursday I was one of the first ones out the door. At least it meant I got to see Amanda when I got home.

She could work whenever she liked, but unlike me she would actually take time off during the day and then stay up all night to finish assignments. From the outside her lifestyle looked appealing, but I knew she longed for a job with more regular hours and a steady stream of income.

"So, how have the first few days gone?" she asked. "If this week is anything to go by, I don't think we will see so much of each other anymore."

"Everything's good. It took me a day or two just to get my bearings. I've only ever worked jobs in the service industry before. This is my first real office job. I had completely underestimated the amount of bureaucracy and paperwork involved."

"Let me guess," Amanda said, "you spend more time in meetings talking about what is going to be done than you do actually getting it done?"

"That about sums it up. Still, I did get some time during one of the meetings to talk about my project. A couple of people in the room even managed to look vaguely interested."

"And what about this Matthew guy? Do you see him around much? Is he going to be your mentor, or something?"

"I've not seen him once since I started." That had taken me by surprise. If he had been flirting with me in his office on Monday—and I still wasn't convinced—I would have thought he'd call me into his office again for some alone time. Instead, he was practically a ghost. That might not have been so painful if he were actually out of town or working from home, but he was there in his office the entire time. I had assumed I would be working in another building from Matthew, but the corporate office had some software engineers as well.

Just to really add salt to the wound, I had seen a number of young women enter his office and come out looking rather pleased with themselves. Admittedly some men had gone in there as well, but it was mostly women, which really stood out in an office with so few of them.

"Well, I guess that's to be expected. He didn't get to be a billionaire by micromanaging every one of his thousands of employees. Got any gossip or scandal for me? Or do you need a little more time to figure out who's sleeping with whom?"

I laughed. "I try to stay clear of office gossip. Truth be told, there doesn't seem to be much of that going around, anyway. Everyone is just too serious and too into their own thing. It's hard enough to get someone to look up from their computer screen for a few seconds, let alone actually engage anyone in conversation."

"Sounds boring to me," Amanda said.

"I love it. Besides, even if I did get in on the gossip, I don't think it would be good for my career to go sharing it with a journalist, would it?"

Amanda pursed her lips and grimaced at me. She hated it when I implied that journalists were always after a story. "Fine. In that case, I will just have to get you drunk one day. We journalists always get the story somehow."

"What are you working on at the moment, anyway?" I asked her.

"Ah, it's a secret for the time being, I'm afraid. That's one stereotype of journalists I do fit—I like to keep things secret until they're published. I think it's going to be a good one, though."

On Friday of the first week of my job, I started putting a team together to work on my project. One of the few interested people in the last lunch meeting had been a team leader on a project that was just starting to wind down. He needed somewhere to transfer his employees and said my project would be a good fit. I didn't take all of them on at once because I wasn't sure there was enough work for them to do yet, but I selected six people from the twelve he'd offered.

Four of my team were women and the other two were men. A part of me thought the project should be solely staffed with women, but that type of discrimination seemed almost as bad as the other kind. Men could be victims of abuse too, and even if they weren't they had loved ones who might be. After just a day on the job, it became clear the two men were going to be by far the best of the six.

Three of the women clearly resented being dragged onto this project, which they saw as a complete waste of time. They felt like they were there just because they were women and it was a women's issue. To give them some credit, they were fiercely ambitious and desperately wanted to get ahead and break through the glass ceiling. I couldn't fault them for that, but it didn't help me much.

The other woman complimented me on the work I had done so far and she wanted to help, but her skillset just wasn't quite in the right area to be of any use. She approached me at the end of the day to say that she had asked to be transferred again.

"I hope there are no hard feelings," Sarah said. "I honestly would have liked working with you, but I'll just drag you back on this one."

"It's fine," I told her. "I appreciate your honesty. Maybe we will bump into each other again later down the road."

As Sarah looked away, a man approached who I recognized from one of the meetings this week. I had no idea what his name was, but I was the new girl, I could get away with that for a few weeks.

"Hi, Amy," the man said. "I know it's late, but I just had a meeting with Matthew."

"Mr. Bowers?" I asked, pretending not to know exactly which Matthew he was referring to.

"Yes. He says he wants to see you in his office. Now."

Chapter Eleven

I hated that Matthew felt he could just summon me into his office and I would come running. I wasn't supposed to be his personal assistant or secretary. What could he possibly want to talk about on a Friday evening, anyway? I hadn't made any progress on my project yet, so it couldn't be about that. I suppose he could just be seeing if I was settling in okay, but that was what he had a Human Resources team for.

Matthew couldn't see my desk from his office, so I considered sneaking away, but that would just make my colleagues suspicious. Instead, they would just see yet another woman walking into Matthew's office. That happened far more often than I wanted to think about.

I took a few moments to compose myself once I reached the door and then knocked loudly to announce my arrival.

"Come in."

I walked inside to find Matthew sitting at the table. "Was there something I could help with?"

"I have a conference call starting in a minute," he said as he finished writing an email. "I want you to join me."

"Okay," I said, taking a seat next to him. I made sure to leave an appropriate gap between us, but it was excruciating knowing that if I were to just move my leg an inch or so to the right, I could graze against his. "What's the call about?"

"Just talking about renewing a contract with one of our biggest customers. I expect it'll be boring as hell. They'll pretend they don't need us and can get the services they want elsewhere. We will make a big song and dance about how we're the best around, and then after going back and forth on a few minor points they will finally agree to most, but not all, of our terms. Neither party will be entirely happy with the deal, but it will keep us going for another few years."

"So, what do you need me for?" I asked. I had never read a contract in my life and usually just clicked "accept" whenever presented with the small print on something I've ordered.

"I get really bored on these calls, so by the end of it I lose track of what points we have actually agreed on. I just need you to take notes when something sounds important."

"Don't you have an assistant or someone else a little more suited to the task?"

"It's five o'clock on a Friday afternoon—they're already on their way out the door."

"There are plenty of other engineers left," I said, motioning toward the door. "Why me?"

Matthew shrugged. "Like I said, I get bored. I will be less bored if I have someone nice to look at."

Not only was using me to do secretarial tasks, he was also treating me like some piece of eye candy. Two could play at that game.

"Sounds boring," I said. "I guess I can help, though. I'll be less bored with someone nice to look at sitting next to me, too. I guess you'll do."

He smiled, showing off his perfect teeth. "I guess I deserved that. Okay, let's get this over with."

Matthew hadn't been exaggerating when he said the call was going to be boring. He had started off with some conviction, as had the other participants on the call, but as it dragged on you could tell that everyone just wanted to go home. After forty-five minutes, I still hadn't had to write down a single thing because nothing had been agreed upon.

"Just give me a second, Adam," Matthew said, "I need to check something at this end." He hit a button to mute the call. "You are so fucking gorgeous."

It took me a moment to snap out of the trance I had drifted into and realize he was talking to me.

"I mean it," he said. "You're stunning. Undo some buttons on your blouse."

"What?" I managed to sputter just as Matthew hit the button to rejoin the call.

I didn't move for at least five minutes, but Matthew kept his eyes fixed on me the entire time. His behavior should have made me nervous. Hell, I *was* nervous, but not afraid. More like excited.

Against my better judgment, I opened a button on my blouse to reveal more of my chest and the top of my breasts. It was nothing he couldn't see by browsing my holiday pictures on my social media pages, but it still felt entirely inappropriate and naughty in this context.

He held up one finger and mouthed the words, "one more." Ever so slowly, I opened another button on my blouse, and then one more. I let it hang open so that Matthew could see everything that wasn't covered by my lacy black bra.

He muted the call again. "One day in the near future, I will have those breasts in my hands and your nipples in my mouth." Then he quickly resumed the call as if nothing had happened.

I put the pen down on the table and gave up any pretense of being interested in the topic at hand. I slid my chair closer to Matthew so that our legs touched. The feeling of electricity as our bodies came into contact was just as intense as last time, maybe even more so because having him touch my legs felt far more risqué than him touching my hand.

Matthew didn't look at me, but he put his hand on my thigh and squeezed hard. He kept talking about boring contract terms in a normal tone of voice while his hand crept up my leg. I gripped the edge of the table to resist the urge to whimper as his fingers got ever closer to my sex.

I hitched up my skirt so as not to impede his progress. Still not looking at me, Matthew moved his fingers from the inside of my upper thigh on to the increasingly wet cotton of my panties.

Now I couldn't resist the urge to moan, but I managed to turn it into a cough for the benefit of those on the other end of the line. Both of my hands now gripped the table as I let my ass slip forward so that I could push my aching pussy against Matthew's hand. He took the hint and moved his fingers under my panties, slipping them straight inside me.

I quickly brought my forearm up to my mouth and bit on it to stifle my screams. In just a few seconds he had brought me more pleasure than any man I had been with, and he wasn't even looking in my direction. He moved closer so that his fingers could get deeper inside me. They found the sensual spots that only I had ever touched. My hips reacted to his touch by grinding against his palm in a slow, steady rhythm.

Nothing I did to keep myself quiet seemed to work. Very soon I was going to need to scream as an orgasm washed over me, but Matthew didn't seem at all aware of the embarrassing situation that would soon present itself. When his thumb started rubbing gently against my bud, he sent me over the edge.

"Matthew," I whimpered in between short, shallow breaths.

"Is everything okay?" asked a man on the call, one who was clearly of retirement age.

"Just give me a second," Matthew said as he muted the phone with his free hand while the other one continued to massage my insides to orgasm.

As soon as I saw the red light come on, I let the orgasm take me. I tried to keep my scream as quiet as possible for the benefit of those working in the office, but it came out as a loud growl as my wetness soaked Matthew's fingers.

Finally, Matthew turned around to look at me. I wanted him to take me right there on the table, but instead he just smiled and rejoined the call. The call was still going thirty minutes later and it took me that long to get my breath back and compose myself. I made sure to let Matthew have one last look at my chest before buttoning up my blouse and leaving his office.

I was only a few yards away when someone grabbed me by the forearm. It was Samantha, one of the women who had reluctantly joined my team.

"I want to speak to you," Samantha said.

"It'll have to wait till Monday," I said, as I pulled my arm from her grip.

"No, now. I know what you did in there. We need to talk."

Chapter Twelve

Samantha led me over to an empty corner of the office where we could speak with a degree of discretion. My heart was still racing in my chest and my legs were barely strong enough to support me as I walked. I felt sure the smell of my sex would be obvious to anyone close to me, but maybe I was just being paranoid. I placed a hand to my cheek—it was still hot, but at least I was no longer sweating.

"What was all that about?" Samantha asked.

I tried not to judge people before getting to know them, but nothing Samantha had done so far had endeared her to me. She had shown no interest in helping me with my project, which was bad enough by itself, but even worse, she had brought others down with her. Samantha commanded a lot of respect from the other women here and when she had been rude to me in meetings, the other women on the team had taken that as their cue to dismiss me, as well. It was like being at school all over again.

"Mr. Bowers just wanted me to take notes on a call," I replied. The correct response might have been to keep quiet or tell her it was none of her business. I was supposed to be her boss, or at least her temporary team leader, and she had no real right to demand I account for my whereabouts. Unfortunately, whatever presence Samantha had over other women seemed to extend to me, as well.

I pretended to stifle a yawn in an attempt to look as bored and tired as I should be after a long conference call. The yawn probably didn't look convincing—the orgasm had rejuvenated my entire body and I felt like I had just woken from a twelve-hour nap.

"Yeah, I'll bet. A lot of the women here get summoned to his office for conference calls. I wonder why that is?"

"Maybe because all of the men seemed to have disappeared for the day already," I replied in what I knew was a pathetic attempt at invoking some sort of female camaraderie with her. There weren't many people left in the office now, but a disproportionate number of those remaining were women, so there was a degree of truth to it.

"I know what you're thinking," Samantha said, not reacting to my comment in the slightest. Her stare unnerved me and made me shrink down in my seat. "You think that you're special. You probably can't believe your luck that your talent was spotted by someone like Matthew. And what's more, he seems to be physically attracted to you, as well."

"Samantha, I don't know what the hell—"

"You probably think that he'll start bringing you in on important meetings all the time and that you will be first in line for every promotion. Or maybe you just want to be one of those tarts who hang off his arm at social functions. You aren't the first woman to fool around with Matthew, and you won't be the last. Hell, I doubt you will be the last this week."

"Are you quite finished?" I did my best impression of someone who looked angry, but composed instead of hurt and upset. Samantha's words had struck a nerve. I had seen the parade of women enter his office during the week and yet I'd forgotten, or had chosen to forget, when it was my turn to be in there with him.

"You may not believe me, but I am trying to do you a favor. You should steer clear of him—it never ends well."

"Not that it's any of your business," I said, "but there really is nothing going on between me and Mr. Bowers. There really was a conference call, but before you ask, I am not going to tell you about it. I do not have to prove myself to you. And besides, the details of the call were confidential."

"Whatever," Samantha said. "Don't say I didn't warn you, is all."

"I'm going to take a shot in the dark and guess that you had something with Matthew at one point?" I had only asked to deflect attention from myself, thinking that Samantha would notice my post-orgasmic glow at any minute, but as soon as I asked I regretted the question. She almost certainly had slept with Matthew at some point, but I didn't need to hear her confirmation of it.

"I *thought* we had something," Samantha said. "Sometimes I still think we do, when he decides he wants me again. I'm helpless to resist him, but it's not too late for you. He's like a drug, and I recommend you do what it takes to avoid getting addicted."

Samantha's voice started trembling with the last few words, and against my better judgment I actually began to feel sorry for her. She spun on her heel and tried to storm off as if still angry, but I could tell the overwhelming emotion she was feeling right now was more akin to heartbreak.

Would that be me in a couple of months? Or weeks? I liked to think I had a bit more backbone than that and wouldn't crumble quite so easily just because of a man. After what I had been through in college, I should have been stronger than that. But if any man could make me feel such strong emotions, it was definitely Matthew.

Samantha could have been lying—I desperately wanted to believe she was—but what she'd said and the way she'd acted made sense. I already knew Matthew was a player, and he had just given me a very physical demonstration that he was prepared to dip his pen in the company ink, so to speak.

I'd never taken drugs in college, even though I was offered them on a number of occasions. I knew they could bring about overwhelming highs, but that coming down was twice as bad. The sensible thing to do was not get addicted in the first place. That was the approach I should take with Matthew. Say no, and try not to think about what I might be missing out on. Unfortunately, it might have been too late. I'd already had my first hit and I knew at some point I would have to go back for more.

Chapter Thirteen

My commute was over an hour long, but I was still hot and flustered by the time I arrived home. I had no idea whether that was because of the heated conversation I'd had with Samantha or what I did with Matthew, but either way I just wanted to get home. Every time someone's eyes met mine on the packed commuter train I felt like I was being judged for what I had done. Every laugh I heard I felt sure was directed at me, as if everyone knew what I had just done and how foolish I was for doing it.

I'd been hoping to have the apartment to myself for the evening, but no such luck.

"Evening," Amanda said as soon as I walked in the door.

"Hi, Amanda. Not out tonight?" It wasn't like her to be in on a Friday night unless she had a date over.

"No, I have a deadline and will likely be staying up most of the night to meet it. I'm surprised to see you home so late, actually. I'd have thought they would ease you into things during your first week."

"I had to stay late for a conference call with Matthew." I contemplated telling Amanda what had happened. We hadn't known each other until a few months ago, but living together had a habit of speeding up the process. Within a few weeks roommates would usually know whether they were going to end up hating each other or being close friends. Amanda and I quickly became the latter. I could confide in her about most things—except my past, of course—but it was only last weekend that I had hooked up with a random guy. I didn't want my friend thinking I was that easy, even I had a damn good reason for doing what I did.

"Matthew? As in Matthew Bowers?"

I nodded.

"Oh, wow. You've really jumped in at the deep end, haven't you? You must be important, I guess. I didn't say anything before because I didn't want to burst your bubble, but usually after those pitch presentations you never see the investor again. They're always flying around the world and tend to be too busy for the regular employees. Congratulations, though. If you're in with him, then you should progress up the ladder fast."

"I'm not so sure about that," I said. "I think Matthew may have asked me to join him for reasons other than what I could contribute on the call."

Amanda frowned. "Like what? Are you his good luck charm, or something?"

I told Amanda an edited version of what happened in Matthew's office. I mentioned him flirting with me and said there was a bit of touching. She didn't need to know every detail.

"Holy crap," Amanda exclaimed after a long pause. "That's... It's... Holy crap!"

"Do you have any idea what I should do here?" I asked hopefully.

"I know what you *should* do, but I don't know if it's what you'll *want* to do."

"You think I should stay clear of him and pretend it never happened, don't you?"

Amanda gave an apologetic nod. "I guess that's not what you want to hear, but I think you know it's the right thing to do. This might sound a little harsh, but men like him probably do that sort of thing all the time. You probably aren't the first employee he's flirted with and you might not be the last."

"He's had a stream of women randomly going into his office all week," I said, thinking back to all the pretty girls I had seen come out of his office with big grins on their faces.

"There you go, then. Not to say that you aren't special, of course, and Lord knows you are certainly beautiful, but you deserve more than just a fumble in his office on a Friday night."

"I could just try and keep it casual." I knew I didn't sound at all convincing.

"You don't seem like the type, Amy. No offense."

"I know. You're right," I admitted reluctantly. "It's not just the potential heartbreak, either. If something happens between us then I will be scrutinized by every woman—and man—I work with. None of them will trust me, and with good reason. I've already had a nasty run-in with someone I was supposed to be managing who clearly thinks I'm some silly little slut."

"She was probably just jealous, but that gives you a good idea of what you might encounter if things get more serious. If you've already made some woman mad just by being in his office for a conference call, just imagine what it will be like if two of you have a relationship and it becomes public knowledge."

A relationship with Matthew wouldn't just make me infamous in the office; I might even end up getting attention from the press. An online search for Matthew threw up lots of pictures of him at public functions with women. The lifestyle looked glamorous, but I had never sought or desired fame for myself.

"Do you think I should just quit and get another job?"

"No," Amanda said with a vigorous shake of her head. "You can easily blow this off. It happened late on a Friday night and hardly anyone saw it. If what you said about Matthew having a lot of women is true, then he must be used to them going a little crazy on him. He probably gets people selling stories to the press or stalking him. You're better than that. Go into his office on Monday morning and tell him calmly and plainly that nothing is going to happen. But don't quit. If you quit, then how will I get any gossip for my stories?"

"You're going to have to get me really drunk to get any gossip from me. Thanks, though, Amanda. This has helped a lot. I think I just needed to talk it through with someone. I'm probably being stupid, anyway—it was just a bit of harmless flirting."

"So, you'll go and see him on Monday morning?"

"Do I have to do it in person? He's so goddamn hot. I don't know if I can look at him without getting horny."

Amanda rolled her eyes. "I still don't think he's *that* hot."

There was a loud knock on our door. "Would you mind getting that?" I asked her. "I still haven't had a shower and I'm feeling kind of dirty. From the train," I added quickly.

I heard Amanda call my name as soon as I had locked the bathroom door. "Who is it?" I asked.

"Forget everything I said," Amanda said excitedly. "He is so much better in the flesh. Screw being sensible. Matthew is waiting for you in the living room. If you don't do something wicked with him, then I sure as hell will."

Chapter Fourteen

Amanda quickly shoved some stuff into a bag and left Matthew and I alone in the apartment. I tried to convince her to stay—I didn't trust myself alone in the apartment with him—but she made up some lie about having plans to meet with a friend. I saw her laptop in her bag so I knew she was just going somewhere to work, probably the library, but I could hardly force her to stay.

"What are you doing here?" I asked as soon as Amanda had left. "You can't just turn up to my apartment unannounced."

It felt a little odd to berate Matthew, mostly because the last time he had seen me I had been recovering from the heavy orgasm he'd brought me to with his fingers. I had done a lot of thinking since then, but from his perspective he probably thought I was still into him. Well, I *was* still into him, but I sure as hell wasn't about to admit it.

"You know, most people would offer their guest a drink," Matthew said, relaxing into my sofa as if it were his own. He handed over a bottle of red wine that he'd brought with him. "Here you go. Let's get a glass of wine in our hands and then you can tell me what an awful person I am."

My mouth started salivating as soon as I saw the red wine, so I didn't object to his demanding behavior and poured us a couple of glasses. If he insisted on bossing me around all evening then having some wine in me would make it that much easier to tell him to get stuffed.

"You seem to be expecting me to be mad at you," I said, as I handed him a glass and sat down on the sofa. "I suppose you have been in this position before with your female employees?"

"You think I turn up at my employees' apartments on a regular basis?"

"I'm not naïve enough to think I'm the first. Hell, I doubt I'm even the first this week."

For the first time, Matthew's confident grin slipped a little and he looked confused. "I know I have a bit of a reputation, but I'm not *that* bad. I do still have a business to run, after all. That places some constraints on my evening activities."

He left a great opening for me and I wasn't about to pass it up. "Is that why you entertain so many women in your office during work hours?"

"Ah, now I get it. You think that what happened between us tonight is something I do all the time. I'm guessing you're a little low on self-confidence and choose to believe I'm just fooling around with you?"

"Let me guess: you were a psychology major at college?"

Matthew gave a polite laugh. "No, nothing like that. Although it's something I'm interested in, but that's strictly extracurricular."

"I know you think I'm just some silly girl straight out of college, but I would rather you didn't treat me like an idiot. I've seen you this week. Or rather, I've

70

seen the stream of women going into your office every couple of hours."

Matthew laughed more generously this time. "There have been a lot of women in my office this week, I admit."

"And they all come out looking rather satisfied."

"Like you were when you left my office this evening?"

I didn't respond, but subconsciously I folded my arms across my chest, pushing my breasts up in the process.

Matthew sighed. "You're no fun. Those women were coming into my office for a performance review. They all ended up getting rather generous pay raises, so that's probably why they looked happy when they left."

"Are you just doing performance reviews for the women? Because I didn't see many men go into your office."

"The women were underpaid. A few months back my company completed the acquisition of another company. They had some brilliant software and great talent working for them, but when we brought them on board we found that the women were all being paid less than the men. It was blatant discrimination. Over the last couple of weeks, I've been working frantically to get all the pay packages put together. This week all those women got large pay raises plus a rather generous bonus for their previous efforts. So yes, I had a lot of women come to my office today and most of them left rather satisfied."

"Oh." Damn him, that wasn't a bad excuse. It made a lot of sense, too, because I'd read about DataStore acquiring another company when I'd done some research before starting the job.

"How long do you think I would last as CEO of this company if I went around hitting on all the female members of staff?"

"You own the company, so a long time, I imagine."

Matthew shook his head and let his mouth stretch open into another wide smile. "There are other shareholders, and you'd be amazed at how quickly they take an interest in things when million-dollar sexual harassment lawsuits start getting thrown around."

"So, why are you taking that risk with me? I could sue you, as well."

"You could, yes. But I couldn't help myself. You're a very special woman, Amy, and despite all my better judgment, I just can't keep my hands off you. Even now all I can think about is ripping off that blouse, sliding you out of your skirt, and devouring you."

A heat stirred between my thighs. I crossed my legs and then changed my mind and brought them up onto the sofa, placing the feet underneath my bottom. The fidgeting was likely obvious to Matthew, but I couldn't help it. His eyes remained fixed on mine, and with every second he looked at me, I felt less able to control my reactions.

"You still think I'm beneath you, don't you?" I asked. I was trying to put up imaginary barriers between us as if that would stop the inevitable.

Instead of an instant denial, Matthew appeared to actually give the question some thought. It was hardly the reaction I had been hoping for. "No," he said finally. "I don't. I must admit that my first impression of you was far from flattering, but I'm not going to hold that against you."

"You're too kind," I said, my voice dripping with sarcasm. "May I remind you that you had also come home with a stranger for sex, by the looks of it? You're hardly the picture of innocence."

"At least I knew her name," Matthew replied. "But you're right, I shouldn't have judged you. I'm sorry. I had just come off an overnight flight and was rather tired. You caught me at a bad time."

"I wasn't exactly at my best, either," I replied. "I don't usually do that kind of thing." I hadn't meant to apologize for my behavior that day—again—but I felt the need to be honest.

"I don't want to hear about it. The thought of you with James is not a pleasant one for me."

Matthew put down his glass and my stomach tightened in anticipation of him making a move toward me. It never came. He stayed rooted on the sofa, but his eyes were full of lust. He wanted me as much as I wanted him.

"How can I make it up to you?" I asked, placing my wine down on the floor was well. I let my feet fall and didn't pull my skirt down when it rode a few tantalizing inches up my thighs.

"Come here, Amy. I want to finish what I started in the office."

Chapter Fifteen

For thirty long seconds, my body remained frozen on the sofa. I couldn't move. It was one thing to lie back and let Matthew take me, but he wanted me to go to him. My brain was willing, but nerves had made my body all but useless.

"Amy, come here."

Finally, my legs followed the instructions and I shuffled over to Matthew. My fingers fumbled at a button on my blouse to reveal the chest that had gotten him so aroused back in his office. He made no effort to move, even when I was sat right next to him, so I brought my legs back up on the sofa, got on my knees, and leaned over in front of him. His gaze stayed focused on mine, but I could feel him straining not to glance down at my chest.

"Closer," Matthew whispered. "Closer."

I placed my hands on the sofa either side of him and leaned forward, never once letting my eyes move away from his. When my lips were just inches from his own I waited once more for him to do something. I pressed my sex up against his muscular thigh and eagerly rubbed against him.

"You're so beautiful, Amy." I felt his breath against mine as I parted my lips in anticipation.

Matthew reached out and grabbed hold of my blouse. He pulled me toward him and our lips collided. I collapsed on top of him, his firm chest easily supporting my weight.

"You were so wet for me earlier," he whispered in my ear. "I bet you're dripping now."

"Why don't you find out?" I replied as I started unbuttoning his shirt. His muscles were hard and inviting. I just wanted to dig my nails into flesh, but that felt like something I should save for later.

He quickly sat up, slipped his hands under my thighs, and flipped me onto my back in one smooth motion. I gasped as I hit the leather of the sofa and my legs fell conveniently open, inviting Matthew between them.

He unzipped my skirt and pulled it off while I removed the blouse that had become suffocating.

"I can't wait to taste you," he said as he planted kisses along the insides of my thighs. His mouth moved slowly—far too slowly—toward my wetness. Finally he reached my damp panties and laid a few kisses on the soft cotton before hooking his thumbs underneath the waistband and pulling them off.

My annual one-night stand had only been a week ago, and thankfully I was still immaculately styled down there. If Matthew had seen me naked a month ago it would have been embarrassing. I still wouldn't go as far as to say I had confidence in my body—certainly not with someone like Matthew, who was way out of my league—but I looked as good as I ever would.

His tongue moved slowly into my folds, exploring every nerve-packed bit of flesh. He grabbed my thighs and thrust them up into the air as his tongue reached deep into my tunnel. I arched my back to push my sex hard against his face, making his tongue slip even deeper inside me.

"You're so sweet, Amy. I've never known anyone to taste this good."

"Don't stop," I moaned as he resumed licking every exposed piece of my skin. His tongue continued exploring my chasm until he came to rest on my clit. His lips formed a seal around my swollen bud and sucked gently while the tongue flicked against it in a slow, rhythmic manner.

"Oh, God," I whimpered. My fingers wound their way through his hair and I held him tight against my wetness so that he couldn't move, even if he'd wanted to. My hips swayed in time with the movement of his tongue as I came ever closer to coming. "Keep going. Just like that. Suck my clit."

I had no control over my body now. My feet had clamped down against his muscular back and I kept hold of his head, thrusting my sex against his lips. "I'm coming!" I moaned as I lost what little control of my body remained. My back arched up into the air, but Matthew's firm grip on my thighs made sure his lips never left my clit.

An orgasm came over me like a violent wave, forcing a scream from my lungs that would have been audible to everyone on this floor of my apartment building. I felt my wetness gushing between my legs as Matthew did his best to absorb every bit of my pleasure. My hands and legs no longer had the strength to hold Matthew against me as they spasmed in the aftershock of my orgasm.

"God, you get so wet," Matthew praised as he lifted his face up from between my legs. Seeing my juices still glistening on his stubble stoked the desire within me as if I hadn't just had the hardest orgasm of my life.

"Fuck me," I murmured. "Please, fuck me. I need you inside me."

Matthew slipped off his pants, then removed a foil packet from his pocket and sheathed his throbbing shaft.

"You're... you're big," I stuttered, unable to take my eyes from his cock. I'd never had one that size before. He was more than seven inches long, but it was the thickness that had my sex throbbing.

"It's a good thing you're wet enough to take it," he replied as he crawled between my legs.

When his face reached mine—close enough that I could smell my essence on his skin—he spread my legs and pushed his girth against my opening. I held his face in my hands as he pushed himself inside. I winced as he reached parts of me that had never been explored, but our bodies soon merged.

"You're so tight, Amy. I can feel your cunt clenching onto me, as if you're trying to pull me in and keep me there."

"I am," I replied. "My pussy wants you so bad right now. No—it *needs* you."

With every stroke he worked his way deeper inside me, exploring uncharted territory until finally I took his entire length. My legs were still weak, but I wrapped them around him and tried to keep his cock lodged inside me as much as possible. I didn't want our flesh to ever part. My fingers tried to grip his back, but the solid muscle gave me little to grab hold of. I dug my nails into his skin instead, but he seemed to barely feel them.

Matthew picked up the pace and I knew he was close. "Harder, Matthew," I whispered in his ear. "My pussy needs a good, hard pounding. Fuck me, Matthew."

He pressed his wet lips against mine and shook hard as he came to a finish inside me.

"So, when were you going to tell me?" he asked.

"Tell you what?" I replied, still bathing in the afterglow of my orgasm. I'd spent the last twenty minutes resting on Matthew's shoulder without a word said between us. It hadn't been awkward—we were both far too exhausted for conversation, anyway—but I was still relieved when he broke the silence by saying something other than, "So, I had better get going. Catch you later."

"That you were a fan of manga," Matthew said.

I closed my eyes tightly, and not for the first time in my life—and probably not the last—I thought about how stupid I had been to get that tattoo.

"I guess you got a good view of it while you were... down there. I'm surprised you didn't notice last week."

For some reason known only to a very drunk version of my eighteen-year-old self, I had decided to get a tattoo of one of my favorite manga characters. Getting that tattoo was a stupid enough decision by itself, but I doubled down on the stupidity front by getting the tattoo on the inside of my upper thigh. The fact that so few men had commented on it over the last few years spoke a lot to how unsuccessful my annual hook-ups were.

"I was trying not to look at your body last week. Didn't seem like the gentlemanly thing to do. The tattoo is... interesting," Matthew said as his fingers danced down the side of my naked, sticky body. "I take it there's a story behind that?"

"Not a good one," I said truthfully.

"I didn't recognize the character. Maybe I should take a closer look." His hand started to part my legs, but I slapped him on the wrist.

"My body can't handle any more," I said. "You're going to have to let me recover. Anyway, next time it's my turn to get my lips around you. I want to see just how much of that hunk of meat I can suck on."

"I have a feeling this mouth can work wonders," he said, touching my lips before joining them to his for a long, sensual kiss.

Chapter Sixteen

Outside of my annual one-night stands, I'd kept physical contact with men at a bare minimum, so at first I was not surprised or disappointed when Matthew got called away on business and didn't return all weekend. Unlike my other sexual experiences, though, I actually wanted him to return.

My body missed the crushing orgasms he brought me to with apparent ease, but my mind missed him as well. Amanda was fun to talk to, but I still found myself wishing Matthew was there. He'd said his fair share of mean and inappropriate things to me, but now that we'd gotten past that, there was a dark sense of humor that I found irresistible.

When getting ready for work on Monday, I was determined not to make any special effort in terms of what I wore or how I acted. That meant I ended up spending more time getting ready than usual, because I had to determine what I *would have* worn if I was just going to a regular job with a regular boss. I settled for jeans instead of a skirt—even though I liked to wear skirts to work in the summer—but sexed the upper half up a little bit with a revealing and tight-fitting top. Overall, it was nothing that would stand out in a normal workplace, but it was tough for a woman to blend in among all the male engineers wearing jeans and hoodies.

Last week I had been on time every day, but on Monday morning I got my first taste of how unreliable public transport could be in Northern California.

"Sorry I'm late, guys," I said as I arrived at my desk at nine-thirty. I wasn't really late, as such; I could come and go as I pleased, and to a certain extent so could everyone else. Still, there was an unwritten rule of sorts that most people would be in around nine o'clock, and being the team leader, I didn't want to set a bad example.

"Late train?" Nigel asked. Nigel has been an absolute gem of a team member ever since I had started, and he made me feel bad for showing a preference to women.

"Yeah, some problem with a train in front of me which caused mine to slow down."

"There's always something. I gave up with the train in the end. You're lucky you manage to go a whole week without any problems."

"I have considered getting a car," I said. "But I have nowhere to park it at home. Do you live near here?"

"I live down near San Jose," Nigel replied. "It's not far, but to and from work the traffic is horrendous. I've tried doing the whole 'come in early, leave early' thing, but it's still bad."

"Looks like Samantha got caught in it, as well," I said, noticing the empty space that Samantha usually occupied.

"Samantha's not coming back," Claire said. "I got an email from her over the weekend. Apparently, she has been reassigned."

I had received no such email, but Claire and Samantha were close so Claire would likely know before I did.

"Oh. Okay, then. I guess we will have to make do without her."

"We're getting a little low on numbers," Nigel said. "Any chance you could ask for some additional resources?"

"Sure, I can try, I suppose," I answered. "I'm not sure who to ask, though. I'll see what I can do."

"Why don't you just ask Matthew?" Claire sneered.

It was obvious to me, and likely everyone else, what Claire was implying. "I can hardly just go up to the CEO and asked for help. There are about fifty people above me in the hierarchy before you get to Mr. Bowers."

"He does respect you, though," Nigel said tactfully.

"He respects all of us, otherwise we wouldn't be here. Sorry, but I can't just walk into his office and—"

"Amy?" A quiet male voice said from behind me. I didn't recognize him, but from the way he was juggling two cups of coffee and what looked like breakfast sandwiches, I guessed he was somebody's assistant. "Mr. Bowers would like to see you in his office."

"Thank you," I muttered. I didn't look back at Nigel and Claire, because I knew exactly how they would be looking at me right now. "While I'm there, I will ask for some help," I said over my shoulder as I walked over to Matthew's office.

Matthew was sitting at his desk typing when I walked in. He acknowledged me with a vague nod toward a chair but didn't stop what he was working on. I had a feeling this was going to be "the talk." This was where he would explain that Friday night had been a mistake and it was not going to happen again.

"About the other night," Matthew began, not looking away from his screen.

"Let me guess: it shouldn't have happened, it won't happened again, and I should just forget all about it. Maybe you would even like to just go whole hog and fire me so that your embarrassing little mistake isn't sitting on the same floor as you?"

"You do like to jump to conclusions don't you?" Matthew said. "You should stop overthinking things."

I shrugged. "I'm not overthinking it. Experience has led me to believe this is how these things usually go."

"All I wanted to say was that we need to keep the relationship professional in the office. If we keep seeing each other, then at some point the news will spread—quickly, in my experience—and that's fine, I can live with people knowing. But I don't want to shove it in people's faces, so we need to be discreet. Is that okay with you?"

Not only was it okay, it was exactly what I wanted, as well. Even ignoring the fact that he was my boss, workplace relationships always looked awkward. I had seen a number of couples getting overly affectionate in the cafeteria and it was painful to look at.

"I'm definitely on board with that. Does this mean we will see each other again? Outside of work, I mean."

Matthew looked confused and finally glanced away from his computer screen. "I can't imagine the circumstances that would keep me away. In case you didn't notice, I had a lot of fun with you on Friday night. And judging by your... reaction, I think you rather enjoyed yourself, too."

I bit my lip and looked down at my lap, unable to hold eye contact with him while I thought back to how greedily he'd licked me between my legs. "I enjoyed myself a couple more times after you left, as well. I *definitely* want more."

"Good. One other thing, though," Matthew said. "As part of a professional relationship at work, I have to treat you like I would any other employee. I may need to make some tough decisions, and those decisions can't be swayed by my feelings for you."

His words didn't worry me so much as his tone of voice as he delivered them. He sounded almost somber as he spoke, and I had a bad feeling his warning was not entirely hypothetical. Next time Matthew called me into his office, it wasn't going to be to discuss our relationship.

Chapter Seventeen

The next day, I made sure to be the first of my team at the office. That required getting up before six a.m.—the first time I had done so in many years—but I wanted to do my bit for the team. I only beat Nigel to the office by about ten minutes, but it was a good hour before anyone else showed up. Getting an early start really helped my productivity. With fewer distractions, I got more done in those first few hours than I usually did in an entire day.

"Where's Claire?" Nigel asked at about ten o'clock. "She usually comes in with Sanjit, but he's been here for an hour now."

"No idea," I said. As team leader I should probably have cared more about where she was when she was supposed to be working for me, but to be honest she served as more of a distraction than a help. I knew from what she had achieved already that she was talented, but she had one hell of an attitude. That would eventually help her get to the top, but she would piss a lot of people off along the way.

The answer to Nigel's question came through a few minutes later via email.

"She's being reassigned," I said as I read the message. My team of six was now down to three, and while those who left were not my favorites, I was not going to achieve much with such a small team.

"Can't say I'm too surprised," Nigel said. "Do you think she put in a request for a transfer?"

"Actually," I said, reading the email through again, "it sounds like the decision came from higher up. She may not have had much of a say in the matter. In fact, her new job looks like one she'll hate— working on apps that specifically target the female audience. God, she's going to despise that."

"Can't say I feel sorry for her," Nigel said. "I do feel sorry for us, though. Any news on replacements? Nothing of note can be achieved with just us. We'll create bugs quicker than we can solve them."

I shook my head. "No news." I felt guilty for dragging Nigel onto a project that already looked like it was on its last legs.

"I take it yesterday's meeting with Matthew didn't go too well, then?"

"I made some requests," I lied. After what Matthew had said about keeping it professional, it didn't feel at all appropriate to ask him for help. Someone in my position would not ask the CEO for additional support, so I shouldn't have, either.

"Look on the bright side," Nigel said. "This will likely put those rumors about you and Matthew to bed pretty quick. After all, if there were something going on, then this probably wouldn't be happening."

"Rumors? What rumors? No, wait I don't care about that. What do you mean 'this probably wouldn't be happening?' What do you think is going on?" I sounded desperate, but I had confidence that Nigel would respect me, regardless.

"I've seen this kind of thing a lot. Huge companies like this allow their employees to experiment with all these weird and wacky ideas, which is great, but if it starts to look like those ideas won't pan out then they get shut down. The first clue is usually when people leave the team and aren't replaced. I'm sorry. You don't deserve this and neither does the project. It's a noble cause that could really help people, but sometimes the higher-ups let money dictate what people spend their time on."

"Do you think that could be happening so quickly? I knew that would be an issue at some point, but I assumed I would get some time to prove that the project could work. We still don't even have a build ready. If Matthew—I mean, Mr. Bowers—didn't think this was a good idea, then why would he let me start in the first place? I need more than a week."

"You're preaching to the choir, but who the hell knows? I'd like to think all decisions are based on the merits, but let's face it: most of them are based on spreadsheets. I'll stick around until I'm made to go elsewhere, so you don't need to worry about me."

"Thanks, Nigel. That means a lot."

The morning's high level of productivity soon petered out once I had to start worrying about the future of the project. That kept me distracted until lunch, and the afternoon wasn't much better because I was worried my meeting this evening. I hadn't been to a support meeting for a while, but lately I felt like I needed to talk to someone about my past. I could have told Amanda, but friendships always changed once I revealed my secret, and she was someone I had to live with for the foreseeable future.

I snuck out of work a little early to make sure I arrived on time even if there were some issues with the train. Sure enough, even though I should have been there thirty minutes beforehand, I only just arrived on time because the train's horn wasn't working. It sounded like the sort of excuse a child would give to a teacher—almost too ridiculous to be true.

The meeting took place in a rundown community hall in one of the more intimidating parts of San Francisco. At least at the moment it was still light outside, but by the time the meeting had finished it would be dark. It was hardly the most appropriate meeting place for our group and was a great example of why I needed my project to work.

I recognized some of the people from previous meetings and we shared nervous smiles. There were plenty of new faces, as well. I never knew whether to feel happy that they had come here to seek support, or sad that they needed it in the first place.

I helped myself to some cheap coffee and took a seat in one of the middle rows, hoping to become part of the crowd. I didn't plan to speak tonight. I was just here to listen to the problems of others and remember how fortunate I was to be where I was today. Many of those around me looked like they had sunk so low that they probably thought there was no way back. I had been in their shoes once, just a couple of years ago, but I was proof that no one should ever give up. No one should give up on their dreams, even if someone tried to take those dreams from you. The best achievements in life were the ones that were hardest to achieve at all, and I wanted to pass that message on to as many people as possible.

Chapter Eighteen

Spending a few hours with the people you were trying to help was a great way to get a renewed sense of purpose and enthusiasm. I went into work early again the next day, except this time it didn't feel early at all because I wanted to be there. If necessary, I would be the one to push this project to completion, even if I had to do it all by myself. The parking lot was noticeably emptier than I'd ever seen it before and I even managed to beat Matthew to the office.

Once again, I found myself able to work more efficiently in a quiet space. When the entire floor was empty it wasn't so noticeable that my team had been transferred elsewhere. At the meeting last night I had struck up a conversation with a couple of women who agreed to test the product once it was ready. I didn't go to the meeting to seek them out, but they recognized me from previous meetings where I had been more vocal about my desire to set up a system to help women who had been abused.

In such a quiet office I should have heard every noise, but somehow Matthew was able to sneak up on me and perch on the edge of my desk before I noticed him.

"Good morning," he said. He had heavy bags under his eyes and looked like he should have slept for a few more hours.

"Hello, Mr. Bowers." My eyes darted from side to side and I chanced a quick look over my shoulder. There were a couple of people who might be able to hear our conversation, so we would have to keep it clean.

"You disappeared early last night," he said.

I couldn't tell if that was just a statement or an accusation. His voice was weary and it was impossible to pick out the meaning. Was he just curious, like a boyfriend? Or was he annoyed, like a boss? As my boss, he shouldn't have cared; part of our deal was that I could come and go as I pleased.

"I had a meeting to go to," I replied. "It was in the city, so I had to leave a little earlier than usual."

"Meeting? Not with Craig, I hope?"

My face twisted in confusion. "Craig?" Why was that the first thought that came to his mind? "No, not Craig. It was a personal meeting, not business-related. That's why I came in early yesterday and today."

"I needed you last night," Matthew said.

"Oh, I'm sorry, Mr. Bowers. Is it something I can still help with? What do you need?"

"I was working late last night on a press release," Matthew explained. "By around eight, I desperately needed to get a *release* out. By nine, I was fit to burst. Like I said, I could have really used you there to help me out."

He exaggerated the word "release" every time he said it, just in case I didn't quite get his meaning. I completely understood and was more concerned with what those around us had heard. More people were trickling in now and there were three or four within a short distance of our conversation. Rumors were already flying about us, so even subtle innuendo like that could get picked up by someone.

"Did you manage to get the release out?"

"No. Like I said, you weren't around to help me and I hate working on my own press releases. The ones I do are never as good as the ones you do."

"Well, I'm not too busy now, if you need some help."

I was busy. I had a million and one things I could be doing, but right now his groin was almost at my eye level and it was all I could do not to stare at his bulge. I gripped the armrests on my chair as I fought the urge to reach out and touch him.

"That sounds like a fantastic idea, Amy. Please, come to my office."

Matthew insisted I walk in front of him, so I made sure my hips swung a little more than usual. I heard a quiet murmur of appreciation from behind me and knew he was getting as excited as I was.

As soon as the door was closed, Matthew grabbed hold of me by the wrist and pulled me over to his desk. His strong hands clasped around my waist as he lifted me up and dropped me back down on his desk.

"I can't wait to taste you again. I wasn't able to focus all weekend because all I could think about was how sweet your cunt tastes and how tight it feels around my cock."

"Sorry to disappoint you, but you're going to have to keep thinking about it for a while. You're not tasting me or fucking my pussy today."

Before Matthew could argue, I pushed him away, clambered off the desk, and pulled him over to the sofa. He sat down and I dropped to my knees between his legs. My hands fumbled at the buckle on his belt, but finally managed to open up his pants and boxers enough to free his bulging member.

His cock had been straining to be set free and it stiffened within seconds of me taking hold of it in my hands. No one had ever accused me of having dainty hands before, but they certainly felt that way now as I struggled to get my fingers around his thick shaft. I placed a hand at the base and felt blood pumping through the prominent vein strengthening his erection.

I looked up at Matthew and gave him my best innocent young girl look as I licked my lips in anticipation. I bent down to within a few inches of his tip and then extended my tongue far enough to flick the end. The slightly salty taste on the end of his cock told me all I needed to know about how much he needed this.

I teased him with a few more gentle flicks of my tongue against his head before moving on to taking long licks up and down the shaft until the entire thing was wet. Matthew kept tensing and he gripped the back of my head. The anticipation was killing him almost as much as it was me. Finally, I opened wide and placed my lips over the entire head before pushing down another couple of inches.

The largest man I had ever sucked off was about six inches when erect, and I had managed to take him almost the entire way into my mouth. Matthew was a good inch more than that, but the bigger problem was his girth. My lips were stretched wide around his cock and it took me a while to get into a rhythm. My hands worked up and down the base so that my mouth could focus on the top half until finally I was limber enough to push my lips down to the base of his cock.

"Shit, Amy. How are you doing that? I've never had anyone able to take it all the way before."

I wasn't exactly in a position to respond. Instead I just sucked harder, making a loud slurping noise as my lips came back up to the tip. My head soon bobbed up and down in a steady rhythm as my throat opened up to take him all the way back.

"Keep going. I'm close…"

That was all the extra motivation I needed. I placed my palms on his thighs and sucked even harder on his shaft. Matthew moaned and placed both hands on the back of my head before sending a hot, sticky stream of his release into my mouth. I swallowed most of it as it hit the back of my throat, but there wasn't a lot of room in my mouth and some of it escaped my lips and dribbled down his length.

"That was amazing, Amy. You're incredible."

Matthew sagged into the sofa as I licked up the last drops of his bliss. I'd always avoided swallowing if at all possible, but Matthew's cum was a taste I could get used to. It was less bitter than usual which, if the articles in women's magazines were anything to go by, meant he didn't drink too much beer and kept in good shape.

"When do I get to taste you again?" he asked, as I made sure I looked presentable enough to go back into the office. "Are you free on Friday night?"

"I can do Friday," I said, leaving out the fact that I could do any night of the week. He didn't need to know about my lack of a social life.

"Come to my condo. I promise you will have a better time there than you did last week."

Chapter Nineteen

A remarkable number of people managed to get work done on the train, but I had never been one of them. On a good day my train journey was only about forty minutes, which was long enough to do something productive, but not so long that I felt guilty if I chose to just read a book instead. That was on a good day, though. More and more, it seemed that the train would take closer to an hour. One morning the entire journey lasted ninety minutes, and while I enjoyed reading a bit of steamy romance before work, that time could have been better spent getting something done on my project.

On Friday, I decided to bring my laptop with me and take a seat where I would have a degree of privacy. There wasn't exactly a lot of elbowroom, but my laptop was tiny and at the very least I would be able to clear my inbox before getting to work. I plugged my headphones into my phone and put on some Taylor Swift. I knew the words a little too well and found it difficult to resist mouthing along to the songs, but replying to emails wasn't exactly the most taxing of work, so I didn't need my brain in full gear.

The office must have been busy last night, because a lot of emails were time stamped between eight in the evening and midnight. They didn't look particularly important, at least not to me, so I was able to delete them fairly quickly. They were the typical bureaucratic emails about nothing and were probably just sent to keep the in-house lawyers happy.

I was making good progress and inbox zero was in sight when a new one popped in from Nigel. I knew he made a special effort to get to work early on Friday, so I wasn't surprised to see such an early message from him. However, I was surprised to see it flagged as urgent. Nigel was calm and laid back, and not at all the type to demand focus on his emails by flagging them with a big red exclamation mark.

By the time I finished reading his email, my heart was pounding in my chest and I was sweating despite the air-conditioning roaring through the train.

Amy, something is going down here in the office. I got in early, but there were already a load of Human Resources people here moving computers and desks. They aren't doing it for the entire floor—looks like it's just us. All they are telling me is that we are being moved to new projects. Please get here as soon as possible. Nigel

His email was short, but it still took me three reads before I completely understood what he was saying. Being a technology company, DataStore's offices were set up so that people could be flexible with where and when they worked. Despite that, teams still tended to be grouped by project because some people preferred the element of human interaction. We could all work from home if we wanted to, but apparently studies showed that we were better off being able to see each other in person. If Human

Resources people were moving our desks—and presumably our belongings—then that meant the team was being split up.

What made it sound even worse was that this was happening in the early hours of the morning. Why not just call a meeting at ten o'clock when we were all present and explain it to us like adults? The circumstances made me suspicious.

I sent a quick reply to Nigel so that he knew I had read the message at least, although there was not much I could do to speed up my arrival at the office.

I wished I knew what it was about, but I am as in the dark as you are. Stay calm; I will be there as soon as I can. Amy

Another email came seconds later.

I heard them talk about where we are being moved to, which at least means we still have jobs, I suppose. I think the decision came from Matthew. I've seen him talking with the HR people this morning.

Surely, Matthew wouldn't have anything to do with this? I was supposed to be going to his apartment this evening for dinner and… other things. He'd have said something if this was in the pipeline. Wouldn't he?

As CEO, he must have known this was happening—nothing important happened in this company without him knowing about it. That meant even if it hadn't been his idea, he hadn't stopped it from happening, either. He could have put his foot down if he'd wanted to, and it wasn't like he was scared of confrontation. But if Matthew was being consulted on this, then that meant he had agreed to it.

I'd only been on the job a week. If he had that little faith in my project, then why the hell did he hire me? Was it just so I didn't go and work for Craig? If he wanted to keep me away from him, then closing down my project was hardly the way to go about it. At this rate, he was going to drive me straight to Craig's company.

The office was close to the train station but I still ran there, not wanting to leave Nigel by himself for a second longer than I had to. Everyone was arriving about this time, so there was a large group standing outside the elevator. My office was only on the third floor and I always felt guilty and lazy for taking the elevator anyway, so I headed to the staircase and ran up.

As I burst through onto the third floor I saw everyone turn to look at me. Most of them had the decency to look like they pitied me, but I saw more than one smirk. Poor Nigel was sitting on his old desk, which was now stripped of all his possessions.

"I got here as fast as I could," I said as I jogged up to him.

"It's okay. It's not like there's anything you could have done. I'm now going to be working in another building as part of the advertising team. It's a good job, I guess, but I was enjoying working on something with a little more social meaning behind it. I can't say for certain, but I think I heard them say you are going to be working as part of the security team."

Security and advertising were two huge parts of DataStore's business and working on those teams was something most people would kill for. But Nigel's skillset wasn't a great fit for advertising, and mine certainly wasn't for a security team. One of the reasons I came to DataStore was to get security experts to help with the backend of my software. I couldn't do that myself, so I didn't see what I could add to part of the larger security team.

"This is fucked up," I yelled. "Who is in charge of all this?"

"I'm the manager in charge of your relocation, Miss Kendrick," said a man to my right. I hadn't even noticed him standing there, but he had overheard our conversation. "As your colleague said, you will be working in the security division now. Your possessions have already been moved to the appropriate building. Follow me and I will show you to your new desk."

Matthew had promised me a job where I would have complete freedom to come and go as I pleased and work on whatever projects appealed to me. That was just two weeks ago. Now I was being treated like just another cog in the machine. This wasn't part of the deal.

"To hell with this," I said, as I pushed passed the Human Resources guy and stormed into Matthew's office without knocking.

"Amy, close the door," Matthew said as soon as I walked in. He'd clearly been expecting me.

I slammed the door behind me, no longer caring about whether or not I made the scene. "What the hell is going on?"

Chapter Twenty

"You need to calm down," Matthew said as if I were just annoyed at someone cutting in front of me in traffic.

"Calm down?" I yelled. "You've completely screwed me over. I know you gave the order to shut down my project. Why even bring me in to work on it if you were just going to close it a week later?"

I knew the answer, but just needed to hear the words from his mouth. Matthew had hired me just to get one over on his rival, Craig. I was still none the wiser about what Matthew said to him that day to cause him to withdraw my job offer, but I knew he'd had something to do with it.

"I'm not firing you," Matthew said. "Your project has just been shut down. You still have one of the best jobs in the country for someone your age."

"You don't understand at all, do you? I didn't come here for a job. I came here to build my project and to help vulnerable women. You've dismantled the entire thing after a couple of weeks."

Anger had been dominating my words and actions, but as I described the downfall of my project that anger gave way to guilt. By failing with my project I had let so many women down, including the ones I had met just a couple of days ago. Worst of all, I had let myself down. This project was partly about me and, as much as I tried to forget, I needed it to be a success as much as anyone else.

"Your project couldn't work," Matthew said. He went to place a hand on my arm, but I pushed it away. I didn't want him touching me right now. "I had my legal team do their due diligence and they found loads of legal headaches that will present themselves the second we try to make any money from this. I tried to think of a way around it, but it's a no go. I'm sorry."

"There would have been another way," I said. My voice was cracking now and it was becoming harder to hide the tears that kept appearing in the corners of my eyes. "The technology wasn't the important part—it was what the technology could have achieved."

"Listen, Amy, I told you I was going to have to make tough decisions and that I wouldn't let our relationship affect those decisions. If this project were being run by anyone else then I would have shut it down, so I had to do the same for you."

"Why even bring me into the company?" I asked. "If you knew the project was a waste of time, then why offer me the job? You just wanted to get one over on Craig, didn't you?"

Matthew glanced down and shook his head slowly. "That's not it at all. I hired you because I knew I wanted you as part of the team no matter how successful the project was. You're incredibly talented and passionate—that's important for any company."

"What did you tell Craig to put him off hiring me? Did you tell him about my one-night stand?"

"For fuck's sake Amy, I'm telling you, I had nothing to do with Craig's decision. Frankly, I'm as surprised by that as you are. He was crazy to withdraw that job offer."

Against my better judgment, I actually believed him, although I wasn't about to tell him that. Matthew had a way of conveying a look of complete honesty with his eyes—if he was lying, then he sure was one hell of an actor.

My legs were feeling weak now and I desperately wanted to sit down, but that would look like I was conceding defeat and I wasn't ready yet. Matthew wasn't lying to me directly, but there was something else, something he wasn't telling me.

"I can't work here," I said. "I know something else is happening and you're not being completely honest with me. I can't work for someone I don't trust."

"You're right," Matthew said. "There is a problem with honesty here, but the problem isn't with me. You've been lying to me from the start."

"What are you talking about?" I asked, trying desperately to sound shocked at his accusation. Had he found out?

"How old are you, Amy?"

"Twenty-two," I lied.

"No, you're not."

He knew.

"How long did it take you to complete your degree?"

"Four years," I lied again. There was no conviction in my voice. If he hadn't already known I was lying, he sure as hell would now.

"Didn't you realize I would do a background check?" Matthew asked. It was now his turn to look angry. "I am well-connected at all the Ivy League schools. It didn't take a lot of effort to find out that you actually took six years to complete the degree. And you're twenty-four, not twenty-two."

"So what? What difference does two years make?" It made all the difference to me, of course; those two years had been the most painful of my entire life.

"It means you lied. It means you dropped out of college at some point. So, what was the problem? Drugs? Alcohol? That would explain why you sleep around, I suppose. Once you hit rock bottom, you lost all self-respect and—"

I slapped Matthew as hard as I could across the face. I heard him take a deep breath to collect his composure, but he didn't raise a hand to me.

"I never had a drug or an alcohol problem. And for the last time, I do not sleep around. Every year on July 26th, I hook up with a random guy and fuck him. Once a year. That is all."

"Once a year? Why? Why on July 26th?"

I shrugged. I knew the answer, but even after spending years talking about it to professionals, I still couldn't say I truly knew *why* I did it.

"Because I can. I fuck a random guy because it reminds me that I can control who I have sex with."

Matthew hadn't looked stunned when I had slapped him, but he did now. There was shock, then anger, and then pity. It was the typical mix of emotions people felt when they found out. He had put two and two together and arrived at four.

"You were... someone..." Matthew couldn't bring himself to say the word.

"Yes," I said, summoning the last shred of strength left inside me. "Five years ago, on July 26th, my college boyfriend raped me and destroyed my life forever."

Part Two

Chapter One

"So, what do you think?" I asked Amanda. "Should I quit?"

"You're going to have to give me a minute to process all this," Amanda replied. She briefly touched my hand in a show of solidarity. "I still can't quite believe everything you just told me."

"It's okay," I said, waving my hand as if the rape I'd endured at college had been as inconsequential as a late bus. I didn't know why I always acted as if it were nothing; maybe it was my way of trying to make other people feel less awkward.

After telling Matthew I had been raped, there was an uncomfortable silence between us. He tried to apologize for how he had acted, but I hadn't been able to stop shaking. When he tried to hug me, I panicked and fled his office before heading straight back home to Amanda.

For all of five minutes, I had done a decent job of acting like everything was fine, but when Amanda asked me if I was seeing Matthew on Friday night I collapsed onto the sofa in tears. This was usually the point where I fled to my room for privacy, but I had already told one person about my past today—might as well make it two.

I also had no intention of letting Amanda think I was some silly little girl who'd been left heartbroken by a playboy billionaire I had just met. The only way for her to know what I was going through was to tell her the whole story. Outside of the private meetings I went to with other victims, I hadn't told that story to anyone else. I still left out a few details, but she knew enough now.

"I honestly don't know what to say," she murmured, looking more lost for words than I had ever seen any journalist. "I had no idea you went through that at college. What happened after? I mean, you told me you were... you know…"

"Raped?"

Amanda nodded, unable to bring herself to say the word.

"I don't really want to talk about that right now," I said. What happened after the rape was almost as painful as the event itself. "That's all in the past. But I would like to know what you think about the job."

Amanda looked a little shocked at the change of topic, but she was clearly relieved to talk about something less awkward. "I think you should stay there and try to work on your other project in your spare time."

"But he spied on me," I said. "I don't see how I can trust Matthew anymore."

"Do you need to trust him?" Amanda asked. "He's the CEO of the company and you'll be working lower down the food chain. I don't even know who the people in charge are at the companies I sell my writing to, let alone trust them."

"You're right," I agreed. "If I was offered this job without ever having met Matthew, then I probably would have taken it all the same. It means accepting I failed with my project, though, and that's hard to stomach."

"It doesn't mean that at all," Amanda said, shaking her head. "You have DataStore on your résumé and you're going to learn a lot working there. Didn't you say that one of your weak areas was security? Just imagine how much you will learn if you stay there for a year. Next time you go and ask venture capitalists for money, you will be going there as an experienced employee of one of the biggest software firms in Silicon Valley, not just as a recent college graduate. They'll be falling all over themselves to give you money."

"Thanks, Amanda. I needed to hear that. I probably sound like an ungrateful brat for complaining when I have such a good job. I know it doesn't make a lot of sense to outsiders, but something just wasn't sitting right with me."

"That's understandable. You felt betrayed."

"I'm still pissed at him for looking into my past like that," I said. "It's annoying to think that I'm going to be making money for him now."

"Without wanting to sound like I'm taking his side," Amanda said, "can you even blame him for this?"

"He investigated me behind my back. Wouldn't you be pissed if a guy you were seeing did that?" I nearly called Matthew my boyfriend, but that would have been a stupid move. We had barely lasted a week together.

"Promise you won't hate me for saying this?" she asked.

I rolled my eyes. "I promise."

"Okay, well, he didn't know what happened to you. He was—is—your boss and you lied about your background. I've known people who got in big trouble for that, and it's certainly a terminable offense."

"Dammit. I wish you didn't speak so much sense."

"You're annoyed at me now, aren't you?"

"No, no. I'm not. I'm annoyed at myself. I want to hate him because that would make things easier."

"You can be *mad* at him," Amanda said. "He still acted like a jerk, considering you two were supposed to be... intimate. I can excuse his behavior as a boss, but going behind your back is still a good reason to be pissed at him."

"Thank God for that," I sighed. "Because I need to hate him right now, and I'll feel better if there is some valid reason for that. So, you think I should keep the job and just try to ignore Matthew?"

"Well, I didn't say you *had* to ignore him, but I guess it would be for the best. Just let this one play out for a bit, and if in a few weeks you decide it won't work, then quit. I can still put you in touch with that other hotshot engineer I know. She's awesome, and I'm sure you'd be a great fit for her business."

"Thanks, but I think you're right. I should stick it out at DataStore for a bit and see how it goes. Meeting your friend might just serve as a distraction."

"Let me know if you change your mind," Amanda said as she checked the time on her phone. "You know, it's a Friday night, and for once I'm not going to be working late on a deadline. Why don't we go grab a few drinks in a bar somewhere?"

I pursed my lips and ran through a list of possible excuses in my head. A few good ones did come to mind, however much to my own surprise—and Amanda's—I didn't want to use any of them.

"All right, I can get on board with that. Nowhere too fancy, though," I added. "Somewhere that plays pop music."

"In other words, you want to dance to some Taylor Swift, as per usual?"

"You know you love her too," I said, as I subtly moved toward the bathroom to claim first shower rights. "Thanks, Amanda. For everything."

She smiled and nodded as I closed the bathroom door and stripped off my clothes. I needed a night out and a few overpriced cocktails. Tomorrow would be a busy day. If I couldn't work on my project at DataStore, then I was damn sure going to spend every waking minute of the weekend working on it.

Just as I was about to step into the shower, my phone vibrated by the sink. I leaned over, one foot already in the stall, and grabbed my phone. There was a message from Matthew.

When can we talk?

Chapter Two

I didn't reply to Matthew. I turned my phone off and refused to look at it all night. I knew that if I sent one reply to him I would be checking my phone every five minutes, and that didn't seem fair to Amanda.

I contemplated replying as I lay in bed, waiting to sober up before going to sleep, but drunk-texting him sounded like a truly awful idea.

My thumbs remained poised over my phone for what felt like all of Saturday, but I still never replied. The longer I went without sending him a message, the harder it became to send one. I couldn't ignore Matthew forever. If he still wanted to speak to me on Monday, then he could just summon me to his office and I would be helpless to refuse.

Finally, I found the courage to send a message, but not to Matthew.

When is the next meeting?

I sent it to Karen, a woman I had met at previous support meetings. She didn't need to go to meetings any more—at least, that was the impression she gave—but she still went to every meeting she could in order to offer support to others. If I were going to talk about what had happened to me, then the best place I could do it would be at a support group.

There's one tonight at City Hall. You okay?

I replied to let her know everything was okay and then knuckled down to get some work done. Knowing that I could go to a meeting in the evening helped me take my mind off my problems and focus on making some progress with my project. It took me a while to get used to working on it by myself, but by six o'clock, I had made some tangible progress by implementing a large button that could be pressed to immediately close and logout of the website. It was a safety button, of sorts. If the women using the site suddenly felt uncomfortable, or if perhaps someone came by and was able to view their monitor, it would let them sign off in one quick, easy step.

The meeting place was once again in a bad spot. Not because the neighborhood was sketchy, but because the building was surrounded by bars and nightclubs which were starting to get busy. The last thing most women wanted on their way to one of these meetings was to be harassed by drunk men. Still, there was safety in numbers, so while there was a risk of verbal abuse, it was unlikely there'd be any physical threat.

I spotted two women I knew, but other than that, the group was comprised of strangers. As soon as I sat down, I made the decision to speak tonight. New visitors always got offered the chance to speak first, so it wasn't long before I was standing at a podium and looking out at rows of chairs filled with at least forty women.

"Hi, my name is Amy. I was raped five years ago by my boyfriend at college, but I'm not really here to talk about that today. For the most part, I have moved on from that incident. But recently, I started getting frustrated with myself. I think my past is affecting my current relationships."

There was something awe-inspiring about how every single member of the audience was giving me their complete attention. No one was sat there playing on their phone or yawning. I couldn't think of any other place where such a large group of people would sit there respectfully and listen to another person's problems.

"I have always been a driven and determined person," I continued. "I got it from my parents—my father, mainly. He made me study as much as possible and instilled a great work ethic in me. They wanted me to have more than they did. Neither my mom nor my dad graduated high school, so they always worked low-paying jobs to support me. I love them for that, of course, but recently I have found myself wondering whether my drive to succeed is actually making things worse for me."

I wasn't blaming my parents, although I suspected it might have sounded like that to some people in the audience. "I have a great job, and as you can imagine, my parents are rather proud." I smiled as I remembered their faces when I told them the news of my job at DataStore. "Unfortunately, my past has come back to haunt me and I may have to get a job somewhere else. I'm worried they will be disappointed in me after all they suffered through to put me through college and all the support they offered me after the incident."

I didn't say too much more; I hadn't come here to badmouth my parents or blame them in any way. I just wanted to talk about the pressure I was under. It helped a bit, although not as much as I had hoped. The first time I'd talked to a group about the rape, I had left feeling emotionally wrecked. People talked about it being like a weight lifting off your shoulders, but for me I just felt faint and exhausted. But the next day, I felt like a new woman, and that was when I'd made the decision to go back to college and finish my degree.

The meeting went on for another hour after I had finished speaking. There was free coffee and an opportunity to talk afterwards, but I didn't feel like staying today. I slipped out into the street, which was now a busy hub of people moving from one bar to another. I knew the city like the back of my hand, but when I was sober and surrounded by people who were drunk, I felt like a stranger in a place I didn't belong. I darted between groups of people not looking where they were going and headed for the nearby bus station.

"Amy!" I heard a man yell from behind me. Soon after, a hand grabbed my forearm. My momentum spun me around and brought me face to face with Matthew.

"What the hell are you doing here?" I asked, trying to keep my voice down.

"You didn't reply to my message."

"How did you know I was here? Oh, God, please don't tell me you followed me here."

"No, of course not," he replied. "I was having a drink with a friend in the bar just over there, and I saw you walk past an hour or so ago. I tried to get your attention before you entered the building, but you couldn't hear me."

"I was meeting a friend," I lied.

"It's okay, I know what you were in there for. I accidentally followed you in before I realized what was going on in there."

"Those meetings are supposed to be a sacred place for me. You shouldn't have been there."

"It was an accident," Matthew insisted. "Look, I just want to talk to you. You left so quickly after telling me about your past that we haven't had a chance to speak. At least let me apologize."

I shrugged and tried to look like I didn't care. "Go on, then. Apologize and then leave."

"I'm sorry for invading your privacy. Obviously, if I had known, then I never would have acted the way I did. But you have to admit that lying on your résumé made you look somewhat suspicious."

"You would have done it anyway."

"Maybe," he admitted. "I guess I am a little hyper-vigilant. But I have my reasons. In the past, some women have… Well, let's just say they have tried to get my attention through means other than their work performance."

"Perhaps if you didn't screw your employees, you wouldn't have so many problems." The words felt bitter and I immediately regretted saying them. I had no right to accuse him of that, and I liked to think I was above such petty comments. "Sorry. I didn't mean that. Look, I'm not in the mood to talk right now. I'm going home."

"Will you be at work on Monday?" Matthew asked as I walked away.

I turned around to look back at him. "I'll be there."

Matthew smiled with that annoyingly perfect grin which still made me weak in the knees. It was an image that stayed with me for the rest of the night until I drifted off into a blissful sleep.

Chapter Three

When I showed up to work on Monday, it felt like I had a new job at a completely different company. The atmosphere and my colleagues couldn't have been more different. When I started at DataStore, I was given my own team of people and had free reign to do my own thing. Admittedly, that didn't go too well, but it was still miles better than the job I walked into that morning.

Instead of a degree of independence, this role required me to be part of a large team and it was made clear that I would be starting from the bottom. The security team had an entire floor to themselves and they had certainly made their mark on it. Everywhere you looked there were weirdly-shaped seats, beanbags, and even napping pods where people went to sleep in the afternoon.

The vibe on the floor was energetic, but unfortunately it was not a positive energy. At first glance it looked fun, but after an hour I soon realized that working with so many young people has its drawbacks. Eighty percent of the people in the security team were my age or younger, and even my boss and my boss'

boss were under thirty. In theory, it should have been a lot of fun with mutual respect between us all, but it didn't work out like that. Everyone was trying to push themselves to the head of the pack. The dynamic wasn't just competitive—it was downright violent.

As per usual, men significantly outnumbered the women, and the women that were there showed no interest in talking to me. Some of the men made an effort, but they tended to fit into one of three categories. The first were the men who, upon seeing a new women arrive, immediately started bragging about their credentials in the hope that it would somehow score them a date. I could handle them. I'd gone to university with enough of those entitled brats to know how to deal with them.

The second category of guys was really nice to me, and for a moment I foolishly thought some of them would make good friends. But after just a short conversation with them, it became clear they were only being nice to me because they thought I was stupid and needed help. Their patronizing tone of voice as they explained everything to me soon began to grate on my ears. I did actually need help with this stuff, but only because I hadn't worked in security before. I wasn't stupid. This just wasn't my area.

The third group of men were the ones who really got on my nerves. Those guys were just outright hostile to me. The way they saw it, every time a woman got a job like this despite being under-qualified, one of their male friends had been rejected just to meet some arbitrary quota. At first, I tried to make a point of how much experience I had with other areas, and I even referenced my Ivy League degree more than once. It made no difference. They just assumed I'd only gotten into a good college because they needed women in the engineering courses.

After a couple of hours trying to figure out my new responsibilities, I soon got the hang of it. There wasn't much to understand. The work I had been given was boring and repetitive and felt more like data entry—albeit the data in this instance was code—and I wasn't creating anything of note.

Once the working day got underway, the only sounds in the room were those of fingers gently tapping keys and the occasional snicker from those involved in conversations over the internal messaging system. Nearly everyone here was multitasking in some way. While they banged out code they would listen to music on their headphones, watch TV shows on a tablet next to the screen, or send messages to each other.

When I got stuck, I had no obvious place to turn for help. I didn't really want to make the long walk over to my boss. I was trying to look halfway competent, so announcing to the entire room that I was already in over my head was not part of my plan. I sent a message to one of the girls who had helped me get set up in the morning, but she just replied to say she was too busy. I could see her screen from where I sat and she certainly didn't look that busy, not unless you counted engaging in three different conversations at once as being busy. She certainly wasn't editing the code on her screen.

I spent another thirty minutes trying to figure it out, but eventually realized I would have to suck it up and ask my boss. I knew our productivity was monitored, so while it might have been admirable to figure it out myself, I would end up looking like I didn't get any work done. Although judging by what a number of my colleagues were doing, perhaps productivity was not monitored as closely as I had been led to believe.

My immediate manager was Christine, and to say she had taken an instant dislike to me would have been a huge understatement. Much like how Samantha had resented being put on my team because she was a woman, Christine seemed to resent getting all the female employees as her underlings. I was just another useless woman they had saddled her with, as far she was concerned.

"What is it, Amy?" she asked as I walked up behind her. She must have been able to see my reflection in her monitor. "Stuck already?"

"Yes," I admitted. "I'm trying to match those two pieces of legacy code together as you requested. I know which pieces of code I am supposed to keep from each project, but they are not playing nice with each other."

"So fix it," Christine said. "Write some new code. I assume you can do that."

"Of course, but the guidelines specifically say that no new code should be used. If I add new code, it has to go through a load more testing procedures which I guess we are trying to avoid. I can write new code, but is going to cause problems down the road."

"Yes, I had a feeling you might cause problems."

I gritted my teeth, closed my eyes, and took in a long, deep breath. Only a few people had heard; most of them were too preoccupied with working or pretending to work to listen to our conversation, and I wasn't about to yell at my boss on my first day.

"So, you are okay with me writing new code?"

"You can do what you want. It's not like you can be punished. You'd just go running to Matthew. Just keep your head down and try not to cause us any problems."

"Jesus Christ, why the hell does everyone think I'm close to Mr. Bowers? I barely know him, and—"

Someone cleared her throat behind me. I let out a low groan as I saw one of Matthew's assistants standing there. Not again. Every time I tried to convince people I wasn't in Matthew's pocket, evidence to the contrary would immediately make itself apparent.

"Amy, Matthew would like to see you in his office."

Chapter Four

"You've got really crappy timing, you know that?"

"Good morning, Amy. Nice to see you, too."

"I might not mind you summoning me to your office quite so much if you didn't do it at the worst possible times."

"I'm fine, Amy. Thank you for asking."

"Today is my first day on my new job," I said. "You remember? The job I didn't ask for, but you forced on me anyway? I'm trying to make a good impression down there and could do without being summoned to your office. You do realize most of the people at this company think we are sleeping together?"

"We *are* sleeping together. Well, we were. And I hope we will be again. I'm guessing that this morning hasn't gone so well?"

"I've had better mornings," I sighed. "How can I help you, *Mr. Bowers*?"

"There's no need to be so formal, for one thing."

"We agreed that at work we would keep things professional," I reminded him. That was true—we'd had that conversation at one point—but that hadn't stopped me from sucking his cock in this office. I couldn't exactly claim to have played by all the rules myself.

"Fair point. I just wanted to apologize again for Saturday night. I promise I wasn't following you from your home or anything creepy like that, and I certainly wouldn't have walked into that building had I known what you were going there for."

"It's not really a big secret that I go to those meetings," I said, trying to put Matthew out of his misery. "But I certainly don't want everyone to know about my past."

"And they won't. I swear, I haven't told a soul. There was one person helping me out with the… research I was doing on you, but I made it clear they were to forget about it. You're safe, I promise."

"Thank you. Sounds like it was just one big coincidence. Was there anything else I could help you with?"

I desperately wanted to leave his office. Given how bad the morning had been so far, I was seriously contemplating quitting and getting another job. That decision was hard enough to make without being swayed by such a gorgeous specimen of a man standing right in front of me.

I had taken Amanda's advice and was going to make one decision at a time. First, I would make a decision about where I was going to work. Then, once I had made my mind up, I would think about what the hell I was going to do with Matthew. I got the distinct impression that me quitting this job would not mean he would be out of my life, and I wasn't sure I wanted him to be.

"How is the new job going?" Matthew asked. "I'm assuming from the way you came storming in here that you're not enjoying it?"

"It's not exactly my area of expertise," I said. "But then, you already knew that, so I'm wondering why you sent me to work there. Since I started here, you have promised me as much time as I needed to work my project and even given me a team to help me do it. Then you started stripping me of my team members, and finally you sent me to work somewhere I'm not qualified. And that is all in the space for a couple of weeks. I dread to think what I will be doing in a month's time."

"I explained all this to you," Matthew said. "I promise, I'm trying to help you."

"How does sending me to work with a load of arrogant young men help me, exactly?"

"Your project can't be successful while it is being controlled by DataStore. When I offered you the job, I honestly thought I would be able to help you complete the project, but it just can't work. Sure, you might be able to get it up and running, but it doesn't fit within the rest of the company's portfolio and I won't be able to find the resources to support it long-term."

"So why didn't you just say that? I can quit and work on the project by myself."

"That's exactly why I didn't tell you. I don't want you to quit, and that's not just me being selfish and wanting you around here more often. You can work on the project on your own time, and while you are here, you can learn the skills you need to fill in the blanks you were missing before."

"You sent me to work with your security team so that I could learn about security?"

Matthew nodded. "There are other areas you will need to work on, as well, but we can deal with them as they arise. The important thing is that when you develop this project, it should be yours and yours alone. It's not right that DataStore take control of it. For one thing, do you really think you can get women to trust the software if they know there is a big corporation behind it?"

Matthew had a point, and it was something I'd been aware of from the beginning. Some people took comfort from knowing that a big company with a lot of money was in control of their security, but others thought differently and would be deterred from using the forum if they thought a company like DataStore was going to mine the information and use it to send them ads. In the end, I had decided to seek help because regardless of privacy issues that might arise, I would never even get the project off the ground without help from someone with the resources to make up for what I lacked.

"I'm not sure how long I will be able to stick it out down there," I said, sitting down in one of the chairs at Matthew's table. "Have you spent much time down there? It's horrendous."

"Yeah, it's not exactly how I like to work, either, but that is the sort of setup people like around here. You have to offer that or you won't get the best talent to come work for you."

"Unfortunately, the best talent consists of a bunch of assholes."

Matthew laughed and sat down next to me. "I can't argue with that, I suppose. Just give it to the end of the week and see how you get on. If you really want to move, then I will sort something out."

"Thank you. I should get back to work."

"There was one other thing," Matthew said. "It's what I asked you up here for really. I know you like to appear brave and strong all the time, but you can talk to me. I'm worried about you. I know I'm going to sound selfish again, but I don't want July twenty-sixth to roll around next year and have you feel like you need to have another one-night stand. Please, Amy. Let me help you."

Chapter Five

"You're not going to let it go, are you?" I asked. "One night of the year I do the same thing that you do every weekend: I pick up a random stranger. Is that really such a big deal?"

"Of course it is," Matthew replied.

"So it's one rule for you, and another rule for me?"

"That's not what I meant at all. I don't have a problem with you having casual sex. Well, obviously I'm hoping to be the *only* one you have sex with, but you know what I mean."

"What is the problem, then? Why do you keep bringing this up?"

I didn't take Matthew for the jealous type. As far as I could tell from online research, he hadn't had any steady girlfriends since he became famous, but he had certainly been seen with his fair share of women. Surely someone like that would be more understanding of the odd night of sex with a stranger.

"If you were just having a bit of fun, I would never have said anything. But you told me *why* you do this, so you can't blame me for being worried about you."

"It's one night a year," I said. I wished he would drop it. "And I'm always safe. You have no right to criticize me for what I do."

"That's exactly why I'm *not* criticizing you. I'm worried. I'm trying to help you. Look, you have these nights of casual sex to try to forget about what happened to you, but you shouldn't need to do that."

"You can't tell me how I should feel about all this. Do you have any idea what it feels like to be raped?"

Matthew reached out and took my hand in his. "No, I have no idea. Why don't you tell me? I want to help you move on so that you don't feel you have to do anything you don't want to do this time next year."

"I *have* moved on," I said. "It took me two long years, but finally I came to terms with what happened to me. Three hundred and sixty-four days of the year, I push it to the back of my mind. On just one day of the year, I take back the control I didn't have that night. All in all, I think I'm handling it pretty damn well."

My words were coming out strained and I was starting to lose control of my voice. I wasn't crying—not yet—but I soon would if I spoke for much longer. I couldn't cry in front of Matthew. I didn't want him to see me as someone who needed his help. I wasn't some project deserving of his charity.

"Have you ever talked to anyone about it?" Matthew asked me.

"About what? The rape? Or the fact that I have casual sex once a year?"

"Both."

"A few people know about what happened that day. My parents. Some of the administrators at my college. And of course, I had to go to a psychiatrist."

"And did you tell any of them about how you deal with the issue now?"

"No." I hadn't told anyone because I knew exactly what they would say. I could hardly tell my parents. They wouldn't want to know their daughter was out there picking up strange guys. My psychiatrist had been a complete prick, and I could just imagine how he would look at me if I told him. No one knew except for Matthew.

"I know as your boss I have betrayed your trust, but outside of the workplace, I have been completely honest with you. You can talk to me about it, if you want to. You can trust me."

"Fine," I said, snatching my hand away from his grasp. "You really want all the details? You can have them. The first time was on the one-year anniversary. I hadn't even made the decision on purpose. I just went out and got absolutely wasted. Guys were hitting on me all night and I loved the feeling of being in control, being able to choose which guy I went home with. It didn't help, and the next day I still felt like shit. The next year things were a little bit better, and that time I decided to go and pick up a guy to prove to myself how much better I felt. I don't remember anything about the first guy I picked up, but the one on the second anniversary was pretty memorable. God, the things he did to me, you should've seen it. He flipped me over onto my belly, grabbed my ass and pulled it up into the air before really going at me—"

"Okay, okay. I've heard enough."

I was glad for the interruption. I was completely losing control of my emotions and I was lying anyway. I couldn't ever remember much about any of my encounters. I always had to get drunk before I could muster the confidence to go home with a guy, so by the time we would get back to his place, the sex wouldn't be much more than a drunken fumble.

Even as I lied to Matthew, I was thinking about him doing those things to me. Even now, as I stood in his office on the verge of tears, I wanted him to take me in his arms and have his way with me.

"Maybe I don't need all the details about your sex life," Matthew said. "Sometimes, it's best that stays in the past. I'm sure you don't want to hear about mine."

"No, I'd like to get home from work in time for dinner."

Matthew laughed and ran his fingers through my hair. His thumb brushed away the tears that had trickled down the inside of my cheek without me even realizing.

"If you ever want to talk to anyone about what happened, then I will always be here for you, Amy. If you like, I could accompany you to one of those meetings. They allow men in there sometimes, right?"

"No. I mean, yes, they do let men in, but I don't want you to go with me. I know you say I can trust you, but I'm still mad at you for screwing up my project." Matthew tried to interrupt, but I carried on. "I know, I know, I need to separate you as a boss from you as... well, whatever you are to me. But that is easier said than done."

"I had a bad feeling you would say that." Matthew sighed and stepped back a few paces. "You're going to hate me for what I'm about to do, but I really think it is for the best. Being your boss is great, but I'd rather be your boyfriend. Amy—you're fired."

Chapter Six

Apparently, I couldn't even keep hold of a job when I was sleeping with the boss. Of all the things Matthew could have said to me right then, firing me from the job he had given me just a few weeks ago seemed pretty far down the list.

"You're firing me?" I asked incredulously. I laughed. I couldn't help it. At least I was no longer crying. The situation just seemed surreal now and I had no clue what was going on. Laughing felt like the only option.

"Yes," Matthew said. "I want you to work here because I know you will do phenomenal things for this company, but I also want to see you outside of work. I'm getting the distinct impression that those two things cannot coexist."

"Well, I'm glad you cleared that up, because for a moment there it sounded like you were firing me so we can keep having sex."

Matthew tilted his head to the side and smiled. "You look gorgeous when you're angry, you know that?"

"This is serious," I said in my best "I mean business" tone of voice. It was serious, but for some reason I felt happy. Not just happy—I felt relieved, like that big, metaphorical weight really had been lifted off my shoulders. I didn't want to work here anyway. I'd spent the entire weekend agonizing over it, and based on the morning I'd had so far, coming to work had been a big mistake.

"Damn right it's serious," Matthew said. His voice was stern, but the smile that still graced his lips made it clear he was enjoying this. "If the other shareholders ever find out I fired a star employee because I wanted to date her, then I'll be in a whole world of trouble."

"Would you lose your job, as well?"

"Oh, God, no. But it would make for some rather unpleasant phone calls."

He wanted to date me. Matthew, a handsome billionaire who could have anyone he wanted, had just told me he wanted to date me. That was an effective way to cushion the blow of losing a great job, but the realization hit me that once again I would be going around trying to convince investors to take on my project. Getting the meeting with Matthew and the other investors had taken months. Who knew how long it would take to get another?

"I'm back to square one," I said. "No job and no money."

"I'll make sure you're okay for a few months. How about I arrange for a generous severance package? You won't need it, but it'll help take the pressure off."

"No," I said firmly. "I don't want any handouts. My roommate has been trying to set me up with a contact of hers for the last couple of weeks, so that's the first place I will look."

"As long as you don't end up working for Craig," Matthew said. His face turned instantly sour as if merely speaking the name was uncomfortable for him.

"What is it between you two?" I asked. "You're both mega-successful billionaires. Do you really need to have some silly feud?"

"It's not a silly feud. He's just bad news. Nothing I can prove, but let's just say some of his business practices leave a lot to be desired. Just promise me you won't go and work for him."

I shook my head. "No way. I'm not promising anything. If I need a job and he offers me one, I'm at least going to hear him out unless you give me a reason not to."

"How's this for a reason?" Matthew said as he grabbed the back of my head and pulled me in close for a firm kiss.

His stubble was rough against my skin and he needed a shave, but as his tongue forced my lips open, I felt my legs spread for him. It took all my willpower to press my hand against his chest and push him away from me.

"Don't think you can win me over that easily," I said. "I'm not just going to follow your commands because you happen to be a good kisser."

"Do you know how rare it is for a woman to push me away when I kiss them?"

"I can imagine. I'm guessing you don't usually try it on with women right after you've fired them."

My smile felt forced as I thought back to him flirting with Suzanne immediately after our presentation. Matthew was far too smooth for his own good, and I would have to try hard not to get jealous every time I saw him chatting to someone far sexier than I was.

"Good point. Tell you what—I can arrange a meeting with a woman I know who would love to hire you. She's a CEO at a big company, probably even bigger than DataStore. You may be slightly predisposed against her, but you should meet her anyway."

"You mean there's a woman with a bigger company than yours?" I asked. "That must be tough for you to live with."

"I'm not a complete dinosaur you know," Matthew said. "Just because I don't want you sleeping around doesn't mean I'm against equality. Anyway, are you interested?"

"This woman—it's not Suzanne, is it?" He had said I might be 'predisposed' against her, and that would certainly be the case with Suzanne.

Matthew laughed. "No, no, it's not Suzanne. No offense, but I don't think she would have you. Besides, she's nowhere near as successful as she likes to think she is. Just let me know if you want the meeting, okay?"

"Okay."

Matthew leaned forward, again closing the gap between us. "Now then, where were we?"

"Not here," I said, putting a finger against his lips as he moved his head toward mine.

"When?" he growled.

My eyes flicked down to his crotch where I spotted his shaft straining to be set free. It would be so easy for me to just pull down his zipper. After that, everything would happen naturally.

"Dinner. Friday night," I said, standing up to leave. "At your place. I want to see if you cook as good as you... eat."

"I'll send a car," Matthew called out as I left his office.

I took great satisfaction from knowing I had left Matthew as horny as I now felt. It would do him good to have to wait for a woman for once, although I had no intention of making a habit of this. If I was going to be unemployed, then that meant spending a lot of time at home with nothing to think about but Matthew between my legs.

I spent the entire commute home in a daydream. It was a minor miracle I even managed to get on the correct train. When I got back to my apartment, there was a man leaning against my door checking messages on his phone. I had been so out of it my first thought was that perhaps I was on the wrong floor or even in the wrong building.

Then the man heard me approach and looked up. It was Craig.

"Hello, Amy. Can we talk?"

Chapter Seven

"Craig is here?" Amanda asked. "The ridiculously good looking guy who runs ITC?"

When I told Amanda I had lost my job, she made me a cup of coffee and listened intently to every word I said about what happened between Matthew and me. She thought the whole situation was great news if it meant Matthew and I could date normally from now on. Well, as normal as it ever could be to date a billionaire. But she lost all interest in Matthew when I told her who I'd run into in the corridor.

"He *was*," I said. "He was waiting just outside the door when I returned home."

"Outside the door? Oh, shit."

"What's wrong?"

Amanda cringed and dropped her head into her hands. "I was singing earlier. Oh, God. He probably heard me."

"If he had heard you singing, then he wouldn't have hung around for long," I said. "No offense." I'd heard Amanda's singing, and it wasn't exactly easy on the ears.

"Why didn't you invite him in?" she asked. "You remember me saying he was sex on legs, right?"

"I'm not inviting some strange guy into my apartment. Don't you think it was a little creepy that he was waiting for me here in the first place?"

Amanda shrugged. "Creepy, passionate—there's a fine line between the two. What did he want?"

"To offer me a job. Again. Apparently, he won't withdraw this one at short notice."

"Oh. That's a little weird, I guess. What did you say?"

"I told him I would think about it. I'm going to go to his office tomorrow for a more formal interview. Assuming he doesn't rescind the offer before then, that is."

"Are you going to take it?"

"I have no idea. Matthew is pretty dead set against me going to work for Craig, but he's not in a position to tell me what to do with my life. I'm going to hear Craig out. If he can give me a good explanation for the way he fucked up the last offer, then I will consider it."

"You're in control this time, Amy. He came after you, which means you have some power in the negotiation. Don't accept any old offer."

"Oh, I won't. If he doesn't meet my terms, I won't take it."

"Good to hear. I'm still going to introduce you to my friend Emily, though, and I won't take no for an answer."

Craig's company had one big advantage that was apparent before I even stepped through the door. The ITC, Inc. office was right in the heart of San Francisco's financial district and was just a short bus ride away from where I lived—or a two-mile walk, if I was feeling more active. No more dealing with the awful San Francisco train network. That was worth pissing off Matthew for. Instead of owning a campus of buildings with a chill, laid-back vibe, Craig's setup was in a tall skyscraper that enjoyed views of the marina.

The differences extended to the atmosphere in the building. I stepped off the street into the reception area and was greeted by a silence that made me think I had gone temporarily deaf. This was definitely a formal place of business and there were plenty of law firms and investors on the upper floors. The only noises were the clicking of heels and receptionists answering phones. I suddenly felt rather underdressed in my jeans. It wasn't typical job interview attire, but then it wasn't typical for the person interviewing you to show up at your house, either.

"Amy, I'm so glad you came," Craig said as I walked into his office. "I was starting to think you might stand me up."

"You would have deserved it," I said, taking a seat opposite his desk.

"Fair enough. Listen, you know I want you to come and work here. What do I have to do to convince you?"

Craig was letting me state my terms, and I wasn't about to pass up the opportunity to see what I could get away with.

"You won't be surprised to hear that I want to keep working on my project. I didn't get very far with it working for Matth—I mean, Mr. Bowers."

"Done. But you give me two days a week to work on ITC projects."

"Agreed." I could give up two days a week, and with any luck, I could use those days to learn things useful. Matthew had been onto something with that idea. "I also want to hand pick a team to work with me. I don't just want a list of candidates. I want to put the word out about what I'm doing and let people put in requests to work for me."

"Okay, but no more than five people," Craig said. "Engineers are expensive, and this project of yours still doesn't show much profit potential."

"Five is acceptable." That would be more than enough, if they were enthusiastic. "One more thing," I added. "I want to know why you withdrew the offer after the initial meeting. And why do you now want me here?"

Craig grimaced and leaned back in his chair. "I had a bad feeling you would ask that. Look, I can't tell you all the details, but the gist of it is that someone passed me information about you that sounded... well, if that had been correct, then I couldn't have employed you."

"Matthew?" I asked. Despite his protestations to the contrary, I had been sure he was the one who had caused Craig to withdraw the offer. Now I was starting to have doubts. Matthew hadn't found out about my past until much later, and then he had confronted me about it. Besides, Craig probably wouldn't trust anything Matthew told him, anyway.

"No," Craig said. "Not Matthew. I can't say who, but the important thing is the same person admitted that the information was incorrect. Unfortunately, by that point, you were working for Matthew. As soon as I heard you had left DataStore, I went straight to your apartment."

"You heard the news quickly," I said.

"I have my sources," he replied with a grin. "And I'm sure Matthew has some within my company, too. Why did you leave DataStore, though? That much I don't know."

Craig might have been testing me to see if I would tell him the truth. Even if he didn't know about Matthew and me yet, he would soon find out.

"Mr. Bowers... Matthew and I are kind of a thing," I said, unable to stop my blood from rushing to my cheeks as I spoke.

"Oh," Craig said. "Wow, so you're the next woman to try to tame Matthew, eh? Well, good luck. I mean that."

"Uh, thanks. I guess." An awkward silence fell over us, so I let my eyes wander around his office. Craig had plenty of personal items on the shelves, and it looked like he spent more time reading for fun than work. "You like manga?" I asked, spotting some volumes of *B.L.E.A.C.H.*

"Yes. It's a big weakness of mine. What about you?"

"I'm a fan," I said, being careful not to elaborate. I couldn't mention the tattoo—he would ask to see it and that would be far too embarrassing, even for this unusual job interview. "I'm reading a lot of *Black Butler* at the moment. Have you seen the anime for *B.L.E.A.C.H?*"

"Huh? Oh, no, not yet. I'm not a fan of reading the subtitles if I'm honest."

I was fairly sure *B.L.E.A.C.H* was dubbed into English, so there weren't any subtitles, but I couldn't be bothered to question him on it. The rest of the interview was relaxed and I was relieved to note there was no attraction whatsoever. The feeling seemed to be mutual.

I accepted the job offer and spent the entire walk home contemplating how I was going to tell Matthew. He was not going to be pleased. I started typing a message to him as I walked down the hall toward my apartment. For the second time in two days, there was a man waiting for me outside. This time, it was Matthew.

Chapter Eight

My body reacted to seeing Matthew before my mind could process what was in front of me. Thoughts of an afternoon of passion immediately overwhelmed me and it was all I could do not to run up to him and drag him inside my apartment. I felt the heat begin to build between my legs as I smiled at him. Matthew didn't smile back.

Then my mind caught up. Matthew didn't look at all pleased to see me. He knew.

"You took a job with *him,* didn't you?" he asked.

"Hello Matthew. Nice to see you, too," I replied, unlocking the door and walking inside. I left it open so Matthew could follow me through. I had a feeling this was not a conversation we should have in the hallway. "How the hell do you know about that already?"

"I have sources who work in his office," Matthew replied with a hint of shame. Only a hint, though.

"Holy shit, you two are as bad as each other," I said. "If you could put your silly little rivalry aside then you would probably be good friends."

"That sounds boring. Competing with Craig is my main motivation these days. I'm not exactly short on money, so our little feud keeps me on my toes."

"Men," I muttered under my breath.

"How did it go?" he asked as I passed him a glass of water. "With Craig, I mean."

"I'm not telling you a thing," I replied. "Look, you're the one who fired me, remember? I know you did it for a good reason, but the consequence of that is me going to work for Craig."

"I don't trust him around you. He's got a reputation with women."

"So do you," I reminded him. "I don't think Craig is like that, anyway. His office certainly didn't scream 'ladies' man' as much as yours does. Do you not read all those stories about you?"

"I try not to read what the press says about me. Anyway, I'm not that bad. I'm a one-woman man now."

"You had better be. I know it's fashionable to date lots of people at the same time these days, but I don't have the energy for that."

"So we're officially dating, then?" Matthew asked. "I mean, I hope we are, but I wasn't sure. I know I still need to earn your trust after what I did."

"You've never been dishonest in our relationship. Not that I know of, anyway."

"I want you to trust me, Amy," he said. "I'm not saying you need to suddenly tell me all about what happened to you, but I want you to know that you can. What can I do to help you have complete confidence in me?"

"Trust doesn't work like that," I said. "You have to earn it. Tell me something I don't know about you, a secret that you wouldn't want getting out."

"That's tough. So much about me is public."

"Don't pretend you don't have any secrets," I said. "If you don't have any, then I'm going to assume you're boring."

Matthew laughed. "People don't call me boring often. All right, I can think of one thing very few people know. When you were at my condo that night, did you go in the recreation room?"

"Honestly, I remember very little about that night. The only place I remember going is the bedroom."

"I shouldn't have asked—I don't want those details."

"What's the recreation room? Sounds kind of kinky."

Matthew raised his eyebrows. "I'll have you know it's an actual recreation room. Video games and fitness stuff."

"Sounds like a man cave."

"That's the plan," Matthew said. "I have friends over, and they love it. But there's a dark secret to my playroom. Something I don't let any of my friends know about."

"Are you sure it isn't a sex dungeon? Come on, spill the beans."

"Under the sofa, I keep a secret. Something I only bring out when I'm alone." Matthew took a deep breath. "It's a yoga mat." He buried his head in his hands in mock shame. "Amy, I have a confession. I do yoga. And I *enjoy* it."

He raised his head back up and looked at me. I pursed my lips, trying to hold back the laughter, but eventually I had to let it out. He didn't look like the stereotypical yogi. I'd always assumed his firm, toned arms came from weights, but yoga could be good for building muscle too if you did the more adventurous positions.

"Please don't spoil this and tell me you just like looking at women in skin-tight clothing."

"Well, that can be a distraction sometimes, but no. I do it because it's a great way to relax and exercise at the same time. Do you think less of me now?"

"If that's the worst secret you have in your closet, then I think we're good. You want a drink?"

I disappeared to the kitchen to make some tea and made sure to walk past Amanda's room. She wasn't home. We had the place to ourselves. Matthew and I had a date planned for Friday, so it felt wrong to fool around before that. But we'd already screwed once, so would it really do any harm to spend the afternoon in bed with him? I could think of worse ways to celebrate my new job.

While the kettle was boiling, I slipped into my bedroom and changed into some yoga pants and a strappy top. Usually to feel sexy I would have to spend hours squeezing myself into some slutty outfit, but if Matthew liked yoga, then there might be an easier way to get him in the mood.

The outfit worked like a charm.

"How am I supposed to resist you when you're dressed like that?" Matthew asked as I sat down next to him.

"You're not."

Chapter Nine

My stomach froze as Matthew leaned in toward me. I closed my eyes, hoping that not being able to see his gorgeous face would help me relax. My lips parted in anticipation for a kiss that didn't arrive.

"You're so beautiful," he whispered, his face so close I could feel his breath on my cheeks.

"I'm not," I replied, my eyes still closed as I took in his scent. "Not compared to those other women you date."

"Trust me, they have nothing on you."

Finally his lips pressed against mine, and every worry and doubt in my life disappeared. I felt lightheaded as he pushed me down onto my back. I parted my legs for him, but instead he lay next to me, his hand running up and down the smooth fabric of my pants.

Our tongues tangled and fought for dominance as I allowed him to pull me close. I could feel his cock stiffening and straining under his jeans, pushing into my thigh. My fingers shook as I tried to unbutton his shirt, desperate to get at his chest as we squirmed against each other.

Wearing tight yoga pants had been a great way to get Matthew in the mood, but now they felt suffocating and I couldn't wait for him to peel them off my legs. He slipped his hand down inside the front of my pants and under the thin cotton of my panties. Then he gracefully slid his fingers between my slick folds as he massaged my growing clit and engorged lips.

"You're so wet," he said. "How long have you been waiting for this? For me?" He pressed two of his fingers inside my dripping hole.

"Since the last time," I murmured as I pushed myself against his fingers, sending them deep up inside me. "I need you so much."

"You like that?" he said, looking into my eyes as his fingers worked magic inside my sex.

"Keep going," I moaned, writhing in pleasure against his hand.

"I love watching you squirm. I can feel you getting wetter—my hand is soaked."

"Oh, God," I groaned as I tried to get a grip on the leather sofa. It felt so weird to come while fully clothed. I was desperate for Matthew to undress me, but didn't want him to take his fingers out of my channel.

"I can feel you coming," he said, quickening his pace. "Your cunt is tightening up around my fingers. Come on my hand, Amy. I want your cum all over me."

"I'm coming," I whined. "Oh, God, I'm coming so hard."

"I can feel it. Oh, Jesus, you're so fucking wet."

I tried desperately to undo the buttons on his shirt, but my orgasm overpowered me and I lost all control. I grabbed hold of him and pulled him in toward me. I came hard onto his hand as I pressed my chest against his.

"Fuck me, Matthew. I need you to fuck me right now."

Matthew pulled his fingers out of my pussy and slipped them straight under the waistline of my pants.

141

They came off in one swift motion and my top quickly followed.

He put his fingers, still dripping wet with my essence, into his mouth and sucked hard.

"I'd forgotten how good you taste. I need to eat your pussy again."

"Not now," I said. "I can't wait any longer. Let's go to the bedroom. I need your cock inside me."

"No. I want to take you right here."

Matthew removed his shirt and pants and stood before me, completely naked. I couldn't take my eyes of his shaft, fully erect in front of me. It still looked too big to fit inside me and I had no idea how I had fit so much of it in my mouth. He slipped a condom over it as I opened my legs for him. I'd never felt so comfortable naked in front of a man. Before Matthew, I had never let a man look at me like this while sober. Now I was lying on a sofa with my pussy dripping and my nipples pointing up at the ceiling, begging for his touch.

He climbed onto the sofa and knelt between my knees. He stared at my sex, and I could see he desperately wanted to go down on me. I knew he'd be able to make me come once more with his tongue, but that wasn't what I needed right now. I had to have his cock inside me. I needed to feel it pulse against my flesh.

"You look so beautiful down there," he said. "Even with that tattoo. You're gorgeous all over, Amy."

He lowered himself on top of me and I wrapped my arms around him, feeling the smooth skin of his back stretched over his rippling muscles. There was no way he got all of those from yoga.

He cupped my breast in his hand and gave it a firm squeeze before pinching my nipple between his thumb and forefinger. I winced as it hardened under his grip.

"I could hold these breasts all day," he said before letting his tongue twirl around my areola, which was now covered in little goosebumps. He bit down on

142

the nipple and pulled away, stretching my breast. I gasped and dug my nails into his back until he let go.

"Too much?" he asked.

I shook my head and pulled him toward my other breast, which he took firmly between his teeth. I wrapped my feet around his ass and lifted my pussy into his crotch. The tip of his penis brushed against my folds, coming agonizingly close to slipping inside.

"You're getting impatient," he said. "Maybe I should tease you some more."

"Don't you dare," I moaned. "Get inside me, now."

Matthew pushed himself back up onto his knees and lifted my legs up into the air. He thrust his cock down toward my sex and let his thick head spread my hole open wide. He grasped me under my knees and pushed them back toward my chest.

"Oh, shit," I moaned. "That's it. Oh, that's the spot." Matthew had my knees pressed back by my ears while his cock pounded against every nerve inside my chasm. I could already feel a wet patch forming on the leather sofa.

He leaned forward and put his weight on my thighs, pushing them back even further against my chest.

"You're flexible," he remarked. "I like that in a woman."

"You're big," I replied. "And I like a man with a big cock. Fuck me, Matthew. *Hard.*"

Matthew planted a gentle kiss on my lips and leaned into me further. He pulled his cock out all the way to the tip. Just as I thought he was going to slide out his shaft completely, he plunged forward until his balls slammed against my ass.

I screamed as I felt his meat fill and stretch my insides. "Again!" I demanded. "Keep going."

He kept ploughing his cock into my aching pussy, letting the pace get faster with each thrust. His tip was angled to hit the rough spot on the top of my tunnel that quickly drove me to orgasm.

"I'm coming again," I murmured. I'd never known my orgasms to come this quickly and easily.

"I love watching you come, Amy. Look at me. Look me in the eyes as you cover my cock in your juices."

I held his gaze for as long as possible until my orgasm shook my core and forced my head back so that I could let out another wail.

"Oh, Jesus. That's so hot," Matthew said. "You're bringing me to the edge. I can't last much longer."

"Come on me," I moaned, still out of breath from my orgasm. "I want you to come all over my breasts."

"You sure?"

I nodded. Matthew instantly pulled his member out of my aching hole and whipped off the condom. He took hold of his shaft and tugged hard until a hot jet of cum splattered all over my chest. I was soon covered in Matthew's jizz, which I rubbed into my chest. It was supposed to be good for the skin, after all.

I felt like a hot mess. My body was covered in sweat and my chest was sticky. Matthew, on the other hand, looked frustratingly immaculate, as if he hadn't been the one doing all the work.

He looked down at me and smiled. "I have never seen any woman look as stunning as you do right now."

Chapter Ten

Living so close to the office made it harder to be late to work than to be on time, but somehow I still managed it. The gym I was a member of—and occasionally even went to—was located close to ITC's office, so I was sure I knew exactly how long it would take me to get there. I planned to walk on my first day, so it never occurred to me to take traffic into account. Unfortunately, I had underestimated how long it took to walk around the city streets early in the morning. People packed the sidewalks and cars blocked the pedestrian crossings, adding about ten minutes to my trip.

By the time I reached the reception desk, I was out of breath after having run the last few blocks. I really needed to start going to the gym more often. A receptionist—who was much more polite than the one at DataStore—invited me to take a seat while she called the HR manager. This was promising. At DataStore, I had dealt with Matthew far more than was appropriate for a normal employee. In my new job, I intended to see Craig as little as possible.

"Amy?"

I looked up to see an enthusiastic young man in a sharp suit and tie. His outfit made him stand out in the more relaxed setting typical of offices in San Francisco. I hazarded a guess that he was from the East Coast, somewhere like New York City probably, or that he'd at least gone to school there.

"Hi," I said, standing up and shaking his hand.

"I'm Jason, the HR manager here. I'll be giving you a tour of the building, showing you your workspace, and getting you sorted out with some paperwork. I must say, we are delighted to have you. Your résumé is impressive, even by the high standards we set for our employees."

"Thank you. Given how many résumés you must see every day, that is particularly flattering."

"I meant every word. Now, as I understand it, you basically have your pick of work and will also be working on a project of your own."

"Yes. Two days a week I work on internal projects, and the other three days I work on a business proposal of my own. Craig—I mean, Mr. Masters—said I could canvass employees to see if they wanted to work on my project."

"Certainly," Jason replied.

He had a constant smile on his face, but it wasn't fake or arrogant in any way. He seemed to genuinely enjoy his job and was definitely a people person. I could tell already he made a great HR manager.

"May I make a recommendation?" he asked.

"Of course. I listen to anyone who has advice to offer."

"Don't start your project for another week or two. Spend that time working in as many different departments as you can. Just go in there and do basic stuff, squashing bugs, editing code, whatever you want. Just be part of the team."

"I kind of want to get my project started as soon as possible, though. It's had a number of setbacks already."

"I heard. I'm sure a number of people will want to work with you, but how will you know who you want to work with? If you spend some time working in large teams, you might find people you like, but even if you don't you will get a better idea of what skillset each employee has. It will help you make better hiring decisions."

That made a lot of sense. The truth was that while I knew I had talent at coding, I didn't have a great idea what went on in large companies like this. If someone applied to work for me with experience building mobile apps, I wouldn't know how useful that would be.

"That's actually a great idea. Thank you."

"Where would you like to start?" Jason asked.

"You know what? You choose for me. Just stick me in any old department for two days and then move me somewhere else for another three. At the end of the week, I'll see how it's going."

Jason's permanent grin stretched even wider. "I can see why he hired you, Amy."

By the time I was done with the tour and signing all the paperwork, it was nearly lunchtime. The first department Jason assigned me to was a group designing a new app for smart watches. The app itself looked relatively basic, but there had been a number of problems working with new software and the limited processing capability of such a small piece of hardware.

My job was essentially to find bugs and suggest solutions. It was generally considered boring work, but I tried to enjoy it. I liked to think of myself as a detective hunting down clues and trying to solve mysteries, and there was a definite sense of satisfaction when you found a problem that had been plaguing other talented engineers.

At around midday, people started disappearing for lunch, but a few colleagues hung around and ate lunch at their desks, chatting quietly amongst themselves. I didn't bother trying to strike up a conversation because I thought I would learn more just listening in on them talking. Okay, so it was eavesdropping, but I wanted to be sure I didn't end up hiring more people like Samantha to work on my project.

The three men, two of them Indian and the other Chinese, spent the entire time talking about how they compared to other colleagues in terms of what contributions they were making. At first it just sounded like typical male bravado with everyone wanting to be the best, but their voices lacked the usual confidence associated with cocky young men. Instead of talking about reaching the top, they just said they didn't want to be considered in the bottom third of employees. The same date kept coming up—September 30th. The Chinese guy made some comments about how he only had a month to drastically improve his performance.

My first thought was that a round of redundancies could be coming, but ITC, Inc. was far too financially secure for that. In addition, doing something so drastic would be awful for the company's public image and they would struggle to recruit engineers in the future. But if it wasn't that, then what was it?

I was lost in my thoughts when I heard one of the Indian men use the word "merger." I completely missed the context, but the topic of conversation was still firmly on ITC, Inc. and not any other company. That meant they thought—or perhaps even *knew*—that a merger was in the cards.

ITC was a huge company. It acquired other companies all the time, but when that happened the ITC employees weren't worried about their jobs. If these three were concerned, then it meant ITC was merging with the company of similar size, or perhaps even being bought by a bigger company. But who could that be? There were very few companies in the software space that were anywhere near as big as ITC. DataStore was one of them, but given Matthew's hatred for Craig, that hardly seemed likely.

Matthew would love to have this information, and a part of me even wanted to tell him. He would know straightaway who the likely suspects were. Was my project safe? Tech companies in Northern California were known to be trigger-happy and quick to implement changes. If the other company involved in the deal didn't like my project, then I would be out by the end of the day.

There was another problem, too. I trusted Craig just enough to have my project be part of his company, but what if I didn't trust the new people who came in? They could take the intellectual property for my project and do what they wanted with it. Fortunately, I'd taken Jason's suggestion and would not be starting anything for at least two weeks. That meant I had two weeks to figure out what was going on before it was too late.

Chapter Eleven

"How does it feel to be back?" Matthew asked me.

"Are you going to tease me about that this the whole evening?"

He shrugged. "Maybe. I find that making light of the situation makes me less jealous."

Being back in Matthew's condo felt strange. The reception area of his building looked vaguely familiar, but that was because I was at least partly sober when I'd left the day we met. I could have sworn one of his doormen looked at me as if he recognized me, but I tried to ignore it.

Matthew's apartment brought back a strange sense of déjà vu, as if I were returning to a hotel I had stayed at a few years ago on vacation. My eyes knew that the scenery looked familiar, but my brain could not remember it clearly. To be fair, the only room I had spent any real time and was the bedroom. The huge TV on the wall looked even more spectacular to my sober brain, but the kitchen and huge dining table didn't even ring a bell.

"What's upstairs?" I asked, noticing the stairway at the far end of the apartment. The bedroom definitely wasn't up there, because I would have remembered it from when I'd left that Saturday morning.

"That's the playroom I told you about."

"Oh, I remember—your little yoga studio."

"Playroom," Matthew said sternly. He looked serious at first, but a smile appeared on his lips eventually.

"So, what are you making me for dinner?"

"Nothing. Trust me, you don't want me cooking for you. I'm not exactly a natural in the kitchen."

"Take-out?"

"I've ordered some food to be delivered. The chef is a close friend of mine and often caters for DataStore functions. He's hooking us up with a kind of Asian fusion thing."

"Sounds good," I said, relieved that Matthew had avoided ordering Indian food. I loved that stuff, but it didn't love me.

"How were your first few days at the new job?" he asked.

To his credit, he was making an effort to keep the snarkiness out of his tone, but there was still a slight edge that reminded me he was less than pleased at my choice of employer.

"Good, although a little boring. I'm taking it slow this time and not starting the project for a few weeks." I had resolved not to tell Matthew about the merger, but I planned to drop a few hints to see if he would volunteer any information. "There's a lot of excitement among the employees. At first I thought I was just working with people who were new to the company, but that wasn't the case. They all seem to be on their toes and keen to do a good job."

"I like to think my employees are too," Matthew said defensively. "Craig is a good manager. I have to admit that much, although it pains me to say it. I still

151

don't trust him and would rather you weren't working there, though."

"Sorry, but it seems like a good place to be at the moment. Unless you know something I don't, then I intend to stay there."

If Matthew knew anything, he was doing a damn good job of hiding it. He didn't even flinch.

"Just keep your wits about you, okay? And don't take what he says at face value."

"Fine," I said, disappointed I wasn't getting any information from him. "When will the food make it here? I'm starving."

"Should be here in about five or ten minutes. Actually, there is something I wanted to talk to you about, first. It's a little awkward, so I would rather get it out of the way before dinner."

"Why do I get a feeling that by 'awkward,' you mean an ex-girlfriend?"

Matthew laughed. "No, it's not that bad. I'm going to a charity function on Saturday night. I'd much rather spend the evening with you, of course, but I made the commitment months ago and I don't want to back out."

"That's fine," I said. "No offense, but I do have a life outside of you. I'm sure I can handle a Saturday night by myself or with some friends."

"That wasn't the bad bit."

"You're going with someone, aren't you? A woman."

Matthew nodded, but didn't look away. "It's not a date. Well, technically she is my date for the evening, but that just means we show up together and link arms occasionally. We're just friends. This is not a woman I have ever slept with, nor will I ever do so."

"Why are you going to this function together, then? I'm not saying I have a huge problem with it, but I struggle to understand why you always have to show up with some glamorous woman on your arm."

"It's for the benefit of the charity. The woman in question is running the fundraiser, and if I go with her it makes my involvement look more official. If people see me there spending money, then they are more likely to open their wallets. Plus, she genuinely is a friend. A good one, as well. I'm not going to make some empty gesture where I offer to pull out, because I really don't want to do that."

"No, you're right. I don't particularly like seeing women with their hands all over you, but we've only just become an item and I'm not quite at the insane, jealous girlfriend stage yet."

"Next time one of these events is on my calendar, you can be my date. How does that sound?"

"I guess I had better start saving for a dress. Something tells me you can't show up to these things in jeans and a t-shirt. What are these charity fundraisers you always go to, anyway? Do you have any particular charities you sponsor?"

Matthew attempted to give a casual shrug, but this time he looked away and I had a feeling he was hiding something. "Nothing special. I just like to try to do my bit. This might sound like bragging, but I have more money than I can spend, so I feel obliged to spread it out to worthy causes."

I had a feeling the lie was just a small one, but I couldn't for the life of me figure out why he would be dishonest about what he did for charity. Maybe he was just being modest and didn't want me to know the extent of his charitable work. I made a mental note to ask Amanda to look into some of these events he attended. I could do it myself easily enough, but didn't really want to see all the pictures of him with other women.

The food arrived ready to eat, but instead of sitting down at the dining room table we put the exquisite entrées on trays and ate in front of the TV. Even *Jeopardy!* looked better on a screen that big.

After dinner, Matthew let me choose something to watch. I was so desperate to avoid putting some cheesy date movie on that I ended up selecting an episode of a crime procedural. We didn't take it too seriously and both had a good laugh pointing out all the flaws in the show's depiction of hacking and how computer software works. It always seemed strange to me that the television networks didn't just hire consultants who could explain that stuff.

It wasn't until near the end of the show that things started to get awkward. The killer had also committed a lot of sexual assaults and some of his victims came forward to help the prosecution. The topic was far too close to home for my comfort and Matthew immediately switched it off.

"You didn't have to do that," I said, although I was relieved he had.

"I did so for my benefit as much as yours. I can't handle the thought of you going through something like that. It drives me crazy to think you were abused in that way. My brain keeps putting images in my head that I can't shake out."

Matthew had clenched his hands into fists and I could see he was straining to keep his anger under control.

"Do you want me to tell you?" I asked.

"Tell me what?"

"Tell you what happened to me that day. It sounds like you're driving yourself insane thinking about it, anyway."

"You should only talk to me about it when you are ready."

"I'm ready," I said. "I'm ready to tell you what happened the day that changed my life forever."

Chapter Twelve

"Are you sure?" Matthew asked. "I'm glad you feel you can trust me enough to talk to me about this, but if this is going to cause you any pain, I would rather you just not tell me."

"It's never easy to talk about, but it doesn't make the pain any worse. Other than my therapist, you will be the first person to hear the entire story. You're going to get mad at some point, I'm sure, but I need you to just listen and try to keep the interruptions to a minimum. You took psychology classes in college. Pretend you're a therapist."

"Okay. I'll listen and do my best to keep my feelings to myself."

"As you may have guessed, I wasn't exactly one of the popular girls in high school. Girls who are into computer programming, manga, and geeky TV shows tend to get lost in the shuffle."

"Boys must have liked you, though," Matthew said. "There's no hiding that beauty."

"I suppose, but not the popular boys. I didn't really fit into any stereotypes. Even though I was a little nerdy, I still fooled around with guys after a few drinks. By the time I went off to college, I was good at giving head but was still a virgin.

"Obviously, I didn't go near sororities or fraternities, but I made friends and was having a good time until near the end of spring semester. One of the guys in my computer science class took an interest in me. Most people in those classes were doing it as part of their major, but he had enrolled to get a few extra credits."

"Don't people usually take easy classes when they just need extra credits?"

"Yes, but he wasn't exactly lacking in confidence and he figured it would come easy enough to him. It didn't, so he started asking me for help after class. He wasn't my usual type, but he wasn't some uber-aggressive meathead, either. After a while, we started dating, but took things really slow by college standards. Most couples would spend days in bed doing nothing but screwing once they got together. I knew he had been with other women before and I was nervous about losing my virginity."

"So he decided to force the issue?" Matthew asked.

"You know, you're not doing very well with this 'not interrupting' thing."

"Sorry. Carry on."

"He didn't, actually. Not at first. He was pretty cool about the whole thing, although now I look back on it, I imagine he probably had other women on the side. Anyway, he always got invited to frat parties and he started taking me along with him. I know it sounds shallow and stupid, but it was so refreshing to be a part of the 'in crowd' for once. I even found myself starting to like some of the people I'd always assumed I would hate.

"The trouble was, once he had a few drinks he would start trying to... persuade me. He never got overly aggressive or physical, but I could always see the frustration in his eyes. Typically we'd slip up to a bedroom and I would suck him off, but he clearly wanted more. To be honest, so did I. I wanted to have sex, but I was nervous about doing it for the first time.

"One night, I wasn't so nervous. I had only had a few drinks, but when he started groping at me in the corner of the room, I didn't push his hands away like I usually did. My memory is hazy, but I cringe thinking back to what people saw us doing. At least one of my breasts were showing and he had his hand up my skirt, fingering me in full view of everyone.

"I'll skip some of the details, but basically we went upstairs and had sex. I knew something wasn't right, but I didn't have the willpower to stop it. I can still remember the act, but God, I wish I couldn't. It's so weird to think back on it; I couldn't really feel anything, so it was like I was in someone else's body looking through their eyes.

"I felt rough as hell the next morning, even though I'd only had a few drinks. I knew what had happened; they gave lots of talks about that kind of thing when we first started college. Someone had slipped something into my drink. That was why I went along with all of his suggestions."

"What did you do when you found out?" Matthew asked.

"I felt sorry for him." The look of confusion that came across Matthew's face was the exact one my therapist had when I'd said the same thing to him. "I know it sounds stupid now, but you have to remember he was my boyfriend and I trusted him. I knew someone had spiked my drink, but I had assumed it was one of the other people at the party. I felt bad for him because I would have to tell him the special moment he thought we had shared was actually the result of me being drugged.

"The creep pulled off quite the act, convincing me that he was angry. He started talking about how he was going to question everyone at the party and how he would find out who did it. He even managed to fake

157

tears. Or maybe they were real and he just felt bad about what he did.

"I was devastated to have lost my virginity in such a harsh way, but there was a small part of me that was relieved because at least now it was over and done with. I considered going to the police or reporting it to the administration, but I knew they would blame my boyfriend. There wouldn't be any evidence, but he would have that stigma hanging over him for the rest of his time at college.

"Later that day, he popped out to get something from the campus store and I went into his backpack to borrow his textbook because I had left mine at home. That was when I found the pills and everything fell into place. At first I think I was angrier at how much he had lied to me the following morning than I was about the actual rape. I went straight to the police and told them what had happened."

"Thank God," Matthew said, visibly relieved. "I had a bad feeling this story was going to end with him getting away with it."

"The police worked with the college to gather evidence and take the appropriate statements. I had been worried that people would accuse me of just having regrets over drunken sex, but everyone I spoke to took the whole thing really seriously. But then his family stepped in.

"I'd never met them before, but I knew he was well-off. I would carefully weigh every spending decision and buy used textbooks where possible, but he would throw money around without a second thought. As it turned out, his family wasn't just wealthy—they were powerful, too. His father was a huge donor to the college, which was likely how my ex had gotten in, since he wasn't that bright."

"I can see where this is going," Matthew said.

"The administration soon gave up any attempts to find out what went on and he was allowed back to school without so much as a slap on the wrist, let alone any kind of permanent mark on his record. To their credit, the police kept their investigation up for a few more weeks, but his family retained expensive lawyers who filed lawsuits every time the police went anywhere near him."

"He got away with it," Matthew said. "You're telling me that he is out there somewhere getting on with his life as if nothing ever happened?"

I nodded. I had managed to tell my entire story without crying, but now that I was finished talking the emotions came flooding over me. Matthew pulled me to him as tears started streaming down my cheeks. He held me until I stopped crying, either because I had regained my composure or just run out of tears.

Matthew didn't say a word, but his reaction wasn't hard to gauge. My ear was resting against his chest and I could feel his heart was beating a mile a minute. His arms held me tight and the pressure of his fingers digging into my skin were a physical sign of just how angry he was right now.

My ex-boyfriend had destroyed my life, and if I wanted to, I could now destroy his. If I said two words right now to Matthew, then the man who raped me would get his punishment. If I told Matthew his name, he would make it his life's mission to find him and ruin him. I could get my revenge.

Chapter Thirteen

"You can talk now, if you like," I said, trying to force a laugh although I was still crying.

"I don't know what to say," he murmured.

He released his grip on me and I sat back up and looked him in the eyes. He wasn't crying, but he looked tired. The story hadn't been easy for me to tell, but it hadn't been any easier for him to listen to.

"You never told me his name," Matthew said at last.

"And I'm not going to. If I give you his name, you will go out there and do something stupid. I'm not going to let him ruin your life, too."

"It's not right. He shouldn't be able to get away with this."

"Having you go over there and kick the shit with him would be nice and might make me feel better for a day or two, but it's not a solution."

"At least let me fuck up his career," Matthew said. "I know his type, and I bet he's landed on his feet in a big job somewhere. Someone like him would be miserable if they were poor. I can make that happen, if you just give me his name."

"I don't doubt it. But I'm not giving you his name. Don't ask me again." My voice sounded firm, but I was already wavering. If he asked me again, I might not have the strength to stop myself from letting it slip. It was true that I would only feel better for a day or two, but what a couple days those would be.

"He might do this again to other women," Matthew said. "Doesn't that worry you?"

"Of course it does, but I don't think he'll do it again. He got away with it, but he's just about clever enough to realize how lucky he was. I like to think he was scared straight. I know it's a risk, but I did try to have him punished through legal means. I'm not going to take some kind of vigilante justice against him. That's not how I want to move on from this."

"Your way of moving on isn't exactly perfect, though."

"Don't you dare bring that up. It's one night a year, and you are not in a position to judge me for having casual sex, anyway. If I want to get drunk and screw someone, I will."

Matthew immediately held up his hands in a sign of defeat. I knew he hadn't accepted my reasoning, but he at least accepted my request not to discuss it again.

"As long as you are careful and don't still do it while we are together, I can't complain, I suppose."

I still found Matthew's obsession with my one-night stands to be rather unusual and hypocritical. In all other ways he was a modern man, and I had never known him to judge women based on what they wore or how they acted. For some reason, he seemed to think it was dangerous. Certainly going back to a stranger's apartment carried some risks, but so did everything in life, and I was hardly the only one in the city having casual sex.

"What happened next?" he asked me. "Is that when you left college for two years?"

"Yes. I got behind on exams while the investigation was ongoing, so I either had to accept getting bad grades or take the rest of the semester off. I only intended to be away for a few weeks, but I started seeing a therapist and things got worse before they got better. I was in no shape to go back to school. Not while he was still there."

"Did you consider changing schools?"

"Yes. But I really liked where I was and that felt far too much like giving in to him. I waited until he graduated and then went back. In some ways, it all worked out for the best. While I was taking time off, I held down some part-time jobs and earned enough to make a serious dent in my student loans. I still have some debts, but it's nowhere near as much as most people my age have."

"Well, you've achieved one thing I never did: you graduated college."

I gave him a playful smack on his firm chest. It probably hurt my hand more than it did him. "Yes I'm sure you're absolutely devastated to have not graduated college. All those billions of dollars help you get by, I'm guessing?"

"I'm serious. It's still kind of bugs me that I didn't stick it out for the final year. I'm not saying I would necessarily change anything about what I did, but it's something that eats at me from time to time."

"Until I start a company worth ten billion dollars, I think you still have the upper hand on me."

"You don't want to start a company worth ten billion dollars."

I frowned, but he was right. I wanted to make my mark on the world, but I had no intention of building some huge entity like DataStore. I admired Matthew for what he had accomplished, but I was not looking to replicate it.

"Why do you say that?" I asked anyway.

"Do you know what people usually do when they come to this apartment?"

"I'm guessing you take them straight to the bedroom, and I'd rather not think about what happens in there."

"Very funny. Usually I have to give them the tour, and they walk around commenting on how amazing everything is. It doesn't take long before they ask me to buy them something."

"I did ask you to invest in my business," I pointed out.

"Some women have asked me to buy them a house. Just like that. The thing is, I could do it at a snap of my fingers and I wouldn't even notice, but I never wanted to. With you, I just want to buy you everything—especially necklaces, for some reason. I've seen some beautiful pieces that would suit you. The only reason I haven't so far is that I know you would think I was trying to buy your affection."

"Thank God for that. I wouldn't know what to do with an expensive piece of jewelry, and there is no way you are buying me a house. I do have one thing I'd like you to buy, though."

"Anything."

"If I'm going to spend more time here, then I'm going to need you to expand your taste in music a bit."

"Oh, God. What crap are you going to make me buy?"

"Only the very best. I hope you like Taylor Swift, because you're going to be hearing a lot of her."

Chapter Fourteen

When I'd sent the e-mail to Amanda's friend Emily, I never actually expected to get a response. I only sent it to keep Amanda from bugging me about it. Despite being part of the tech community myself, I wasn't well-versed in who was who, so I didn't recognize the name Emily Saunders. After doing some basic research on her, I realized I probably should know who she was. She had hit the big time in a major way, but she made an effort to stay under the radar where possible. Still, I knew she likely got inundated with e-mails, so when she replied to mine, I had to do a double take.

Not only did she reply, but she said she wanted to meet me and even proposed we get together the coming Saturday. I replied immediately to say I was available, and we arranged to meet in the morning at a coffee shop she suggested called The Station. I'd never heard of it, but it was only a ten-minute walk from work, so it was easy enough to get to.

Emily's company was huge, so I was sure she must have a big office somewhere nearby, but from the looks of her as I walked in to the coffee shop, she had been there for some time working on her laptop. I suppose a change of scenery helped productivity, sometimes.

"Emily?" I asked as if I wasn't sure it was her. I knew exactly what she looked like, and she was easily the most beautiful woman in the entire place.

"Amy, hi. I'm so glad you could come," she said as she closed her laptop. "What would you like to drink?"

"Oh, it's okay. Please, let me get them. It's the least I can do for taking up your time."

"Nonsense," she said as she got the attention of one of the waiters. "I'm in this place so often that they actually give me table service. What will it be?"

"In that case, I'll get an Americana."

The drinks came quickly and Emily also ordered a couple of muffins, which was a relief. I was starving.

"Amanda told me all about your project," Emily said. "I must say, I'm really impressed. Not just at what you are doing, but that you managed to get the biggest software companies fighting over you for a project that probably won't make much money. How the hell did you manage that?"

I laughed and shook my head. "I wish I knew. I wouldn't say they are fighting for me, though. I only spent a couple of weeks at DataStore, and it didn't work out. I'm at ITC now, and it's going to bit better. I'm only working on the project a couple of days a week. That seemed like a sensible way to handle it."

"That's a good arrangement. They get your skills for whatever it is they are up to, and you get the resources to complete a personal project. I like it."

"That means a lot, coming from you," I said, blushing. Emily deserved the praise, but I felt a little like I was sucking up to her.

"I'm nothing special. In the end, a lot of my success came down to luck, really. Or at least, the stupidity of others. If PharmaTech hadn't tried to screw me over, then I wouldn't be where I am today. Still, we'll need a bit of luck in this business, especially since we're women."

"Tell me about it," I sighed. "Everywhere I go, it's all some big boys' club. When I have had the opportunity to work with women, they want to make me suffer even more than the men."

"Is that a problem at ITC, as well?" Emily asked.

"Kind of," I said with a shrug. "But this time, I'm trying not to let it bother me. I know Amanda probably told you I was looking for a job, but I think I'm going to stick it out at ITC."

"Good idea. From what I know, you would be a great fit at my company and I would take you in a second, but you can learn a lot at ITC."

"You don't have to answer this if you don't want to," I said, "but do you know Craig Masters personally? I'm hearing mixed things about him and don't know what to think."

"I have met him, yes, but I'm not sure I could vouch for him. That said, what I do know is positive, even if he does have a reputation as a ladies' man."

"They all do, it seems."

"Yes, I did hear about you and Matthew Bowers."

"Is that public information already?" I asked. I had hoped we would stay out of the limelight.

"No, not public, but I'm sure I don't need to tell you that Amanda likes to gossip."

"How could I forget?"

I looked past Emily toward a man who had just walked into the coffee shop. He seemed to be coming directly toward us, but I had never seen him before. A number of heads turned in his direction—mainly women's, but some men's as well—and took a good, long look at him as he walked past. He was tall and attractive, although like Craig, he was a little more clean-cut than I liked. Judging by the reaction of the other women around us, I was in the minority.

"Hi, babe," the man said as he reached our table. For half a second I thought he was talking to me, but Emily quickly got up and kissed him on the cheek.

"Amy, this is Carter, my boyfriend. You don't mind if he joins us, do you?"

"Of course not. Nice to meet you, Carter."

Emily filled Carter in on me and what I was trying to accomplish. I had no idea what Carter did for a living, but judging by the comments he made, I could tell he had a business brain but wasn't so clued up on the software stuff. Between him and Emily, they must have made a good team.

Carter was enthusiastic and asked me lots of questions, but I couldn't help noticing that he was silent when I mentioned I worked for ITC. He nodded, but it looked like he was holding something back. Emily noticed, as well.

"You know something," she said to Carter. "Is ITC not a good company to work for? I know from a software side it is, but I know nothing about their financials."

"It's a good company," Carter said.

"Come on," Emily pleaded. "What you holding back?"

I could tell Carter was reluctant to speak in front of me, but Emily was right—he definitely knew something.

"There is a big deal in the cards, isn't there?" I asked. "A merger?"

"I can't really say much because I honestly don't know, but I am hearing talk in that space. It would make sense. ITC and DataStore are huge companies, but to a certain extent, they still loom in the shadow of VirtualCore Technologies. Maybe they want to create a bigger and better company?"

Carter did his best to talk in a casual manner as if he was just speculating, but it was clear he knew more than he let on. This was not just idle speculation, and that meant there was a real chance Matthew's company could merge with Craig's. But what worried me was what would happen after such a merger took place. Would Craig and Matthew be able to work together? My gut told me there would only be room for one of them at the top, and I just hoped it was Matthew.

Chapter Fifteen

Amanda was supposed to join us in the coffee shop for a drink, but she didn't show up until I was already on my way out door, and Emily and Carter had left ten minutes before.

"Sorry I'm late," Amanda said between heavy breaths. "I completely lost track of time working on something, and then had to run all the way here. Did I miss Emily?"

"Yes, I'm afraid so. They left about ten minutes ago."

"They? Oh, God, was Carter here too?"

"He showed up about halfway through our meeting. Do you know him?"

"I've met him a few times. Not as much as I'd like to, though."

"You're a member of the fan club, huh?"

"Don't tell me you aren't attracted to him. I'm not going to tell Matthew. You can admit it."

"What can I say? He just doesn't do it for me. And speaking of which, I don't trust you not to tell Matthew anything. Emily knew about Matthew, and it doesn't take a genius to work out who told her."

"She won't tell anyone," Amanda said, as if that were a good excuse. "Damn, I can't believe I missed Carter."

"Does Emily know you have a crush on her boyfriend?"

"Everyone has a crush on her boyfriend. She's used to it, and you should get used to it too. Matthew isn't my usual type, but even I think he's dreamy. You're going to have to get used to seeing other women throw themselves at him."

So far, I had managed to avoid seeing Matthew with other women except for in photos. I knew at some point I would have to deal with that, but as long as our relationship was strong, I didn't think it would be a huge problem. Matthew was honest with me about having to go to a charity function with another woman tonight, and once I had gotten over the initial weirdness of it all, I had decided I could live with it. I hated the thought of having photographs of me and Matthew put up online and wouldn't have wanted to go with him tonight anyway, so his "date" worked out quite well for me.

Amanda popped inside to grab a coffee to go and then we decided to take a walk while the sun was shining. Today was a rare day in San Francisco where there was no chill in the air, so I was able to walk around with bare shoulders and my jacket in my hand.

"Were you supposed to be meeting Matthew today?" Amanda asked.

"No, not today. He has some charity thing to go to and he's taking another woman. Which is fine," I added before she could ask any questions. "They aren't on a date, or anything."

"Oh, good. I'm glad you know, because he's over there with another woman and I was worried you would see him."

Amanda pointed toward the entrance of a shopping mall where Matthew was standing talking to another woman. My heart stopped for a split second, but I managed to get myself under control and not overreact. There was no touching and the conversation looked entirely platonic.

"The charity thing isn't until tonight," I said. "But maybe they're meeting beforehand to discuss planning, or maybe she still needs to buy a dress."

"As long as you're okay with it," Amanda said. "You *are* okay with it, right? You seem a little... off."

I nodded. I had no issue with Matthew hanging out with a friend, regardless of whether they were going to some dinner function together. That wasn't why I was quiet. I didn't have a great view of the woman and people kept walking between us, but I could have sworn I recognized her from somewhere. If she was hosting a charity function, she was likely a public figure of some kind. Maybe she had been on TV.

I knew the more I thought about her, the less I would be able to figure out where I recognized her from, so I tried to put it to the back of my mind and let my subconscious work on it. By the time I got back home I was none the wiser, so I went online to figure out where Matthew was going tonight and with whom.

He had never told me exactly what the event was for, so I had to search through all the various fundraisers that were going on in the city tonight. Most of them were only charity events in the loosest sense of the word. When you looked closer, they were predominantly about networking. No doubt the charity did get some financial benefit from the arrangement, but the participants were hardly acting out of a sense of generosity.

Finally I found the function Matthew was attending. His name was plastered all over the website and the invitations. The other name mentioned prominently was Francine Mahoney. There was one picture of her, and while the quality was poor, it was enough to confirm that she was the one I'd seen Matthew speaking to earlier. Even knowing her name, I still couldn't place how I knew her.

171

I nearly closed the browser when I caught sight of what the evening was raising money for. The name of the charity was nondescript, but according to the website, the evening was designed to raise money for victims of domestic violence and sexual assault.

I was pleased to see Matthew fundraising for such a noble cause, but something was bothering me. Why hadn't he told me? He had been planning to go to this event since before he met me—the invitations were dated months ago and still available on the website—so it had nothing to do with me. I could see why he wouldn't invite me to go, but surely he could have told me what the event was for?

The whole thing seemed a little odd, but I loved that Matthew didn't try to impress me or win me over by talking about his charity work. It would've been easy for him to mention it all those times he'd tried to get me to talk about the rape. The fact that he never brought it up spoke highly of his character.

The thing bugging me more than anything else had nothing to do with him. It was this Francine Mahoney woman. I knew her from somewhere, and I knew I wouldn't be able to rest until I figured out where from.

Chapter Sixteen

Between Tuesday and Wednesday of that week, Jason assigned me to work closely with the marketing team. That proved to be an interesting, but rather negative experience. The marketing guys worked closely with clients and test groups, so they knew what people wanted from our products. In their view, improving the search functionality of one of the software databases "to make it more Google-y" was something that should be quite straightforward to implement. After all, Google had been around for years. Couldn't we just implement something like that so clients could easily search their internal information?

The entire week I found myself saying "no" to people and generally sounding rather incompetent as if I did not know what I was doing. I promised to take all their suggestions back to the programmers, but the programmers would just laugh them off. What the company really needed was for the marketing team to spend some time with the programmers to get a better idea of how tough the job was, not the other way around.

When I got an invitation to go for drinks after work, every part of my body wanted to reject it in favor of going home and curling up in my pajamas for a few hours. I was exhausted and still had one more day to get through before the weekend. The thought of spending hours drinking with people I barely knew and probably wouldn't like anyway didn't exactly inspire me. I wanted to give some excuse, but I was so tired I couldn't think of one. In the end I agreed to go out, but I said I needed to go home to change first. If I arrived late and left early, I would only need to be there for about two drinks, at most.

I ducked out of the office as soon as everyone started to gather and debate where to go for drinks. I made it out of the building and onto the busy streets without anyone noticing, but just when I thought I was safe, I heard someone call out my name.

"Amy."

"Matthew?" I said loud enough to attract a few startled looks from passersby.

He stood on the other side of the road from the ITC building and was motioning for me to come over to him.

"What are you doing here?" I asked after making my way over.

"Waiting for you after work," he said, kissing me on the cheek. "I'm going to take you to dinner."

"I'm supposed to be going out for drinks with people from work."

"Oh. Well, some other time, then."

"No, no, it's fine. I was looking for an excuse not to go. Now I have a good one. Why were you standing all the way over here? You could have just waited for me in reception."

"I don't think Craig would appreciate it if I was in his building. Besides, it's not a good idea for me to be seen around there. That's how rumors start."

I didn't see how being in the same building as Craig would start rumors unless there was something more going on. All the little signs were pointing toward a business deal involving those two companies, but I didn't bother to ask Matthew about it. I wanted him to be honest with me, but leaking secrets about business activities like that was a big deal. Hell, that was how insider trading often started.

Even though we were already in the city and surrounded by everything from top class restaurants to cheap food trucks, Matthew insisted on driving back down to Palo Alto. For the first twenty minutes we sat in traffic, but once we were out of the city he was able to show me what an electric car was capable of these days.

I knew nothing about cars. I knew some were bigger than others and that was about it, but even I was impressed by the Tesla. It probably wasn't that much faster than other cars, but it just felt different being in a car that barely made a noise and had no engine. I felt like I was floating above the road rather than driving on it.

"You're going to have to let me drive this one day," I said as we pulled up to the restaurant's valet parking. The parking attendants fought over who had the pleasure of parking the car in the same way that women would fight over Matthew.

"Only if you promise to go gentle with her," Matthew said as he held the restaurant door open for me.

"Her? Don't tell me you've named your car."

"No," he replied after a long pause that gave away his lie. "Come on, let's get our table and order. I'm starving."

I didn't give Matthew much choice over the shared appetizer—I loved bacon-wrapped asparagus—and then I went with a chicken breast stuffed with feta cheese and wrapped in prosciutto. Under normal circumstances I would have been completely happy with my meal, which was cooked to perfection, but Matthew had ordered a steak that looked so juicy I actually took my eyes off of Matthew occasionally to stare at it. I'd only ever eaten steak well-done, but now I could see why people liked it a little redder.

"How was your 'date' Saturday night?" I asked Matthew in my best disapproving voice.

"My evening was just fine, thank you," he responded, not taking the bait. "Lots of money was raised in the auction. Some people had too much to drink, and then lots of money was raised again when they were writing checks near the end of the evening."

"Why don't you like to talk about your charity work?" I asked. "It sounds like something you should be proud of, but I never hear you mention it and there's nothing on the company website about it."

"Have you been researching me?"

"Maybe," I replied, biting my lip and looking up at him through my lashes.

"I seem to recall getting in a lot of trouble when I did that to you."

"That was different. I only looked at public information."

"Fair point. I don't mention the charities on the company website because they have nothing to do with the company. I don't want the board of directors having to approve every large donation I make, so I prefer to do that personally. And I don't go to any effort to disclose my activities because I would then have any halfway benevolent organization trying to hit me up for money all the time."

We were ordering our deserts when Matthew's phone vibrated. I was actually surprised we had managed to go so long without an interruption.

"Shit," he said before even reading the message. Whoever it was from, he wasn't happy to see the e-mail. "I have to go back to the office."

"Oh. Well, that's okay. This is still better than what I was originally going to be doing this evening. Just drop me off at the train station."

176

"Nonsense. I'm not done with you yet. You're coming back to the office with me."

Chapter Seventeen

The last time I worked late in Matthew's office, he had seen to my needs while he was busy on a conference call. This time, it looked like he actually intended to work. The office was far busier than it should have been at eight in the evening, and the lack of curious stares I got on the way to Matthew's office either meant that everyone was too busy to care or they already knew we were a couple. I suspected it was a combination of the two.

"Are you okay just waiting here for a bit?" he asked as we reached his office.

"That's fine. Lucky for you, I bring my e-reader to work with me."

"Don't ever let it be said I don't know how to show a girl a good time," he quipped, grinning as he slipped out of the office.

I pulled out my e-reader, and for a few minutes I made a genuine attempt to read my book. I had a couple on the go at the moment, but I settled for a light romance. I'd had a drink at dinner and wasn't in the mood for anything too taxing. I quickly got to a steamy part of the book and had to put it down. I didn't trust myself to get horny with Matthew in such close proximity.

I peeked through the blinds covering Matthew's office windows and saw him engaged in conversation with three other senior members of staff. From my limited time at the company, I recognized one of them as an accountant and I was fairly sure the other was a lawyer, but I had no idea who the third one was.

By itself this was nothing to be suspicious about, but heading back into the office late at night—and interrupting a date to do so—did seem out of the ordinary.

I went back to my book, but after having to read the same paragraph four times, I just gave up. My phone only kept me amused for the length of time it took me to find out that none of my friends had been up to anything interesting since the last time I checked at lunch. I tried to use Matthew's computer, but it was asleep and required a password to wake it up, which was hardly a surprise for a company that specialized in computer security.

Matthew never struck me as someone who read a lot of books, but there was an e-reader lying on his desk and I couldn't resist snooping. Looking at someone's collection of books wasn't really spying anyway, in my opinion. If he had physical books, then I wouldn't hesitate to look at them on a bookshelf, so why should it be any different with e-books? That was what I'd say if he caught me, anyway.

His e-reader was not password protected—very sloppy, Matthew—but there was nothing interesting on there, either. All he had were business books: *How to Launch a Startup in 30 Days, Effective Employee Management*—that kind of thing. One thing was for sure: we wouldn't be one of those couples who read the same books. I couldn't resist going to the online store and downloading a couple of erotic novels with shameless and revealing covers. That would teach him not to password protect his electronics.

"That grin on your face worries me," Matthew said from the doorway.

I dropped the e-reader in shock and swore. Either he could move like a ninja, or I had been so obsessed with my little practical joke that I didn't notice.

"I was just amused at how boring your taste in books is," I said, picking up the device and checking for scratches or dents. Thankfully, there were none.

"I don't read a lot," he admitted. "I spend all day reading things at work and don't have the mental energy for it when I get home. But if you're judging my taste in books based on this," he picked up the e-reader, "then you're mistaken. This isn't mine."

Shit. "Whose is it?" I asked.

"The CFO's. She was in here earlier showing me something and left it behind."

"She?"

"Yes, the CFO is a woman. Why?"

Double shit. "Um, tell her I may have pressed a few buttons by mistake."

"Is my CFO about to sue me for sexual harassment?"

"Not if she has a sense of humor. Anyway, just because you're a big hotshot doesn't mean you can't find time to read. I'll have you know Craig reads a lot and is a huge fan of manga."

I probably shouldn't have mentioned Craig, but it would be interesting to see if Matthew's opinion of Craig was changing now that their companies were probably going to merge. I thought he might go quiet or get mad, but instead he laughed.

"Manga? Are you kidding?"

"No, I saw the books in his office. He has loads of them."

"Okay, I know Craig better than most, and I can tell you there is no way he reads manga. He's not a fan of genre fiction at all. He's one of those incredibly serious types who only reads the award-winning stuff.

Trust me, if he told you he reads manga, then he was just trying to impress you because he knows you like it."

"You're so skeptical," I replied, though my tone had certainty wavered. Craig had made an odd comment about manga when I was at the interview, but surely he couldn't have just been trying to impress me. For one thing, how would he even know I liked manga? It wasn't something I talked about a lot, and I certainly hadn't shared that information before the interview. He had the books on his shelf, so that would have been a lot of effort just to convince me he liked manga.

"And you're too nice," Matthew said. "In business, you need to develop a nasty edge."

"I'm not always nice," I said, licking my lips seductively. "I can be nasty, too. You know that. Don't you remember what we've done in this office?"

"I'm hardly like to forget."

I leaned in and let my tongue slide slowly up his cheek while I cupped him between his legs. I could feel his length pulsing through his pants and I knew I had to set it free. I unbuckled his belt and opened his slacks.

"Amy, I can't. I have to get back out there and speak to the legal team."

"Sounds like you need to relieve some stress first, then."

I dropped to my knees before Matthew had time to protest and pulled his stiffening meat from his boxers. He hardened in my hand and was solid by the time I closed my lips around his head.

"Oh, Amy," he moaned as bobbled along his shaft.

I lifted my head back up slowly until just his head was left in my mouth, and then used my tongue to flick and caress his tip. I sucked hard and released with a loud slurp, then clamped my mouth back around it instantly.

"I want to fuck your mouth," he said.

I nodded with my mouth still full of his cock. He grabbed hold of my hair and slowly thrust himself in my mouth. I used one free hand to steady myself against his thigh while I opened my pants with the other hand, reaching down to my sex.

Occasionally I nearly gagged as Matthew's tip hit the back of my throat, but he controlled his thrusts and stopped before going too far. My body didn't know how to handle having a cock fuck my mouth while my fingers worked away at my clit. I rubbed at myself furiously in time with Matthew's movements. Within a couple of minutes I had come hard, digging my nails into Matthew's thigh, unable to scream with my mouth full.

"This is so good, baby," he moaned. "Your mouth is almost as hot and wet as your pussy. I'm so close. I'm about to finish."

I quickly yanked his hands away from my head and pulled myself away from his cock.

"On my face," I said, gasping for air now that I could finally breathe through my mouth. "I want your load all over me."

"I'm going to cover that pretty little face of yours," he said as he took hold of his hard cock. The spurt came seconds later, splattering over my face and only just missing my eyes. I stopped his cum from dribbling down my chin as I scooped it up and into my mouth.

"Damn you look beautiful," he said as I sucked the last drops from his tip.

"Go speak to the lawyers," I said, licking my lips. "I need to clean up."

Chapter Eighteen

Matthew spent another hour talking to his employees, and I was on the verge of calling a cab when he finally came back into the office and announced he was ready to leave. The wait and accompanying boredom had soured my mood considerably since I had given him a blowjob, and there was a palpable tension in the air on the drive back into San Francisco.

"Have I done something wrong?" he asked. "I know work ruined our date, but I just wanted to spend as much time with you as possible. That's not such a bad thing, is it?"

"No, of course not," I said tersely. "I just don't like you hiding things from me, that's all."

"I'm not hiding anything, Amy. Nothing that affects our relationship, anyway."

"So you admit there are secrets?"

"Of course there are secrets. I can't talk to you about certain work-related things because they're confidential."

"Would you tell me if I didn't work for Craig?" I asked him.

"No. Your working for Craig honestly has nothing to do with it. The secrets I keep from you are things I also keep from the majority of my employees. Why do you think the corporate team is shut away in a different building from most of the engineers? It's so we can discuss things that the other twenty thousand employees aren't ready to know yet. What's with all the questions, anyway? You have a job with Craig now, so you don't have to worry about DataStore."

"Just tell me whether I made a mistake going to work for Craig."

"Yes," Matthew blurted out. "I kept telling you not to go and work for him."

"But was that because of some petty rivalry between you two, or was it something bigger?"

"Our rivalry is not petty. I don't trust him, and I have good reasons not to."

I sighed in frustration. "This is getting us nowhere. We need to stick to that whole 'not talking about business' thing we agreed to."

"You brought it up this time. But yes, I agree. Let me just say one last thing, though—if you ever want to come back and work for me, or if you want to go work for VirtualCore, just let me know. I think we're in a place now where we can work together like adults. I was an idiot before, but we can make it work. VirtualCore is a good company to work for, as well."

"I'm fine at ITC," I replied. I should have been flattered, but it felt more like Matthew just didn't want me working for Craig than he wanted me to work for him. He was even content for me to work for VirtualCore, so long as it wasn't with Craig.

"You want to stay at my place tonight?" Matthew asked. "I am in your debt and desperate to repay you."

"You're just going to have to wait," I said. "I'm far too tired, and besides, I still had fun myself tonight."

"Tomorrow night?"

"I can do tomorrow. I'll come over to your place after work."

Matthew reluctantly dropped me off by my apartment and I walked through my door, ready to collapse in bed. Amanda's door was ajar and the crack let out light that gave the apartment a spooky illumination until I switched on the main lights.

It wasn't unusual for me to find Amanda up late at night working crazy hours, but it was unusual to find the kitchen a mess with half-eaten food strewn everywhere. Amanda was not the tidiest person I had known—at least, not in the confines of her private space—but she was a considerate roommate who always kept the kitchen clean.

I walked slower past her bedroom than I usually would and snuck a peek through her door. She was slumped forward on her desk and resting her head in her arms. Judging by the slow rhythm of her breathing, she was either asleep or close to it. The laptop screen was still awake, so she couldn't have been resting for long.

I tried to close her door so that the noise of me getting ready for bed wouldn't wake her up, but the hinges creaked, startling me and rousing Amanda from her slumber.

"Shit, sorry," I said. "I was just trying to close the door. Didn't mean to wake you."

"That's okay," she said, taking a long stretch. "I shouldn't be asleep, anyway. I have so much to do."

I always thought Amanda looked at her best when she wasn't trying. When she made an effort with her appearance, she looked stunningly beautiful, but I was more impressed with how she looked when just lazing around at home. When her hair was a mess and she was lounging around in her pajamas, she made it hard for any man to resist her. But even Amanda's natural beauty had its limits, and right now she was close to them. Her eyes gave away how little sleep she had gotten recently and she completely out of it.

"When was the last time you slept?" I asked. "Other than that little cat nap?"

"Last night, I think. It's Wednesday, right?"

"Thursday," I replied. I entered Amanda's room and picked up some of her clothes from the floor. "Why are you working so many hours? You're supposed to be a freelancer. Give yourself the night off."

"It's this story I'm working on. Kind of a tight deadline, and I have to talk to people all over the world. The time zones are messing with my sleep pattern."

"No story is worth damaging your health. You should get some sleep."

"Okay, Mom," Amanda said, holding up her hands in a gesture of surrender. "I'll go to bed. How was your night? You go drinking with your new colleagues?"

"No, I went out to dinner with Matthew."

"Oh. Where is he?"

"He's gone back to his place," I explained. "I'm seeing him tomorrow night, though, so you'll have the place to yourself."

"I'm glad to hear you two are going strong. I sure could use a distraction like him."

"If you're anything like me, then your Matthew will come along when you least expect it. You might need to leave the house, though. And shower."

Amanda stuck her tongue out at me and went back to work. Despite my teasing, I needed to develop a bit of that work ethic myself. I'd allowed all the distractions in my life to serve as an excuse for not working on my project. Tomorrow, that was going to change.

Chapter Nineteen

For the rest of this week and the next, I was still committed to working within the various groups of ITC. That meant I couldn't start on my project at work, but I could figure out who I wanted on my team. There was no time to wait for people to approach me. I was going to have to seek them out.

Any hint of subtlety went out the window and I began approaching colleagues to see if any of them wanted to be part of my team. Not surprisingly, I got a large number of "no" responses, but that was fine. It was better to know their feelings in advance.

The other responses were more perplexing. Quite a few people were polite enough to show an interest, but when I suggested they consider joining me, they were strangely noncommittal. Most just made some vague comments about how they didn't know what the future had in store for them or that they didn't think their team leader would let them go just now. One guy just admitted he was looking to cash in his stock options as soon as possible.

"They're worth a decent amount at this point, which makes for a nice little bonus, considering I have only been here for two years."

Two years? That wasn't long enough to cash in stock options, was it? "Don't you have to be here for three years before you can cash in your options?" I asked.

"Not if there's a buyout," the guy replied confidently. "That usually means you get a nice premium, as well."

If I had had options myself I might have known, but for some reason I'd never thought to demand them as part of my compensation. I was low on cash, so my only financial consideration when taking the job had been "does it pay the bills?"

Others made similar comments, although some were less optimistic about their future. A lump sum payment would only go so far, and losing their jobs was a clear concern, although no one expressly mentioned that.

I had taken a few business classes while in college but had promptly forgotten most of what I was taught. Certainly nothing to do with accounting or budgeting had stuck in my head, because I was still useless with numbers outside of a strictly mathematical or engineering context. I mainly blamed that on the professors. I assumed accountants could be dull, but they were downright lively compared to the people who taught it.

One topic had stuck in my head, though, because we'd had a guest speaker come in to teach the class. He had the privilege of teaching another boring topic—the laws around stocks and stock markets—but he had livened it up with loads of real life stories about companies doing things they shouldn't have. One of the big "no no's" was issuing more stock to employees once you had already entered negotiations to sell. It could be done, but most companies wouldn't because it could jeopardize the deal. That was how I could prove once and for all what Craig was up to.

I marched up to his office and waited outside for him to finish up a call. If Craig would refuse to give me stock options in the company, then I would know for sure that something was up.

"Hi, Amy. Come on in," he said when he was done with his call and saw me standing by the door.

"Do you have a minute?"

"For you? Of course. How can I help? You must be nearly ready to pick your team of employees."

"I'm getting there, but I'm in no rush to get started," I lied.

"Oh, really? I thought you were raring to go."

"I'm surprised myself, but I've been enjoying working as a normal employee for the firm. The things this company is doing are incredible, and I'm excited to be a part of it."

"That's great to hear, Amy. So if things are going so well, what can I help you with?"

"I want to feel more invested in what ITC is doing, and it sounds like lots of the other engineers have stock options. I'd like that to be part of my compensation package."

Craig's smile disappeared instantly. "Shit. I'm sorry, Amy, but we can't do that right now."

"Oh." I tried my best to look nonplussed. "I'm happy to sacrifice some of my salary to compensate. I'm not trying to come in here and demand a pay raise."

"It's not that. I'd love to give you stock options, but we can't do that right now."

"I don't understand," I lied. "The company does have a stock option plan, doesn't it?"

"Yes, we do, but it's on hold right now. It's only a temporary thing, though. I promise, we'll get you sorted out as possible."

"Okay, well, I don't want to cause trouble. That's good enough for me."

I saw Craig look over my shoulder and realize that someone else must be waiting to see him. There was likely a queue of people waiting by now. The CEO could never get a minute's peace.

"This is good timing," Craig said. "I want you to meet someone. I've just hired a new Chief Financial Advisor. He came highly recommend. You should meet him, because he's going to be overseeing your project and making sure you get the funds you need."

"Sounds like someone I'm going to need to charm," I said jokingly.

"That shouldn't be difficult. He's a good-looking bloke, I think. Certainly all the women here seem to think so." Craig motioned to the door for the guy to come in.

I turned around to see a tall, confident man walk into Craig's office. He should have been instantly recognizable to me, but it took me a few moments to place him. He'd aged a bit since I last saw him five years ago, but he still had that cocky grin stretched across his face.

"Chad, I want you to meet—"

"Amy," Chad said.

"You two have met?" Craig asked.

"Oh, we go way back. Don't we, Amy?" Chad asked, with a grin all over his face.

I stared at Chad, my jaw slack. I tried to speak, desperate to break the silence, but my mouth was too dry to talk. I nodded slowly. We knew each other, all right. He was the one who had drugged and raped me at college. I wasn't going to forget him in a hurry.

Part Three

Chapter One

"Are you okay, Amy?"

I heard Craig's voice and knew he was talking to me, but my brain couldn't quite interpret the words.

"Amy? You want to sit down?" Craig spoke again.

This time his words came through and I did as he suggested, taking a seat by his desk not a moment too soon. A few seconds longer on my feet and I may well have collapsed. My heart was racing. It should have been pumping blood all around my body, but my head felt starved of oxygen and my legs had no strength to them.

What was Chad doing here? He didn't look at all surprised or ashamed to see me so he must have been expecting this meeting. Did Craig set this whole thing up? It didn't seem likely. Why would he go out of his way to make me like him and then do this? Unless this was all part of some far bigger game to get back at Matthew. Have me work here and then spring my rapist on me at the last moment.

Craig didn't look like some evil genius though. In fact, he looked genuinely distressed and worried as he came round to my side of the desk to feel the temperature of my forehead.

"You don't have a temperature," Craig said, still sounding concerned. "Do you want some water?"

He didn't wait for a response and quickly summoned an assistant to go and get me a drink. The water didn't do a lot of good, but I pretended it worked like some magical elixir.

"I feel better now, thank you. I sometimes get a little lightheaded, but it's nothing serious and passes quickly."

I turned my gaze back up towards Chad. This was the real test. Could I look my rapist in the eyes and stay sane? After I found out he had spiked my drink that night, I had only seen him on a handful of occasions. The college board in charge of the matter wasn't exactly keen to put us in the same room, but they had been stupid enough to hold his hearing directly before I was due to speak to them. I saw him walk out in a smart suit and tie looking quite the respectable member of society. He had been accompanied by his mother and father. His mother had the decency to look ashamed, but the father was ranting about suing the school for smearing his son's good name.

"How do you two know each other then?" Craig asked. He sounded slightly apprehensive now and had likely picked up on some of the tension in the air.

"College," Chad replied. "We were in a few classes together, went to some of the same parties, that kind of thing."

I didn't go to those parties until you took me to them. His appearance might have changed slightly but his voice hadn't. It sent a chill down my spine every time he opened his mouth. I could still remember the first time he had spoken to me in class. I assumed he was speaking to someone else; why would someone as popular as Chad speak to me? Whenever I thought back to that moment I could remember the giddy excitement in my stomach, but it would quickly tighten and make me want to throw up.

"I hope she doesn't have too much dirt on you, Chad," Craig said, jokingly. "You're her boss now so we don't want any tales of drunken debauchery doing the rounds."

"Oh there won't be anything like that," Chad said confidently. "Amy doesn't have any dirt on me. Nothing she can prove."

If Craig had noticed my continued silence he didn't comment on it. My mouth was dry as a desert so I took another sip of water and then another. It did just about enough to stop my lips from cracking as I spoke.

"You didn't know we knew each other?" I asked Craig without taking my eyes of Chad. I hated looking at him, but I couldn't stand him being there out of my sight either.

"No, can't say I did," Craig said. "I suppose I could have figured out that you went to the same college, but you graduated in different years and it's a big place. I had to move fast to snap Chad up—he's a hot property in this area."

How the hell can he be a hot property when he's only been out of college for a few years? He's not even that bright. His parents must have hooked him up with a decent job, but even so, to get to such a high position with a company like ITC is extraordinary to say the least.

"What did you do after college?" I asked. It seemed like a sensible question—the sort of question that two former college friends would ask each other—but I felt like I was poisoning the air around me just by speaking to him.

"I've been busy," Chad replied.

His cool demeanor hadn't dropped once the entire time he had been in this room. He'd been expecting to see me, I realized. Even if he felt no remorse, he should have been at least vaguely shocked to be confronting me again, but he hadn't so much as twitched.

194

"Excuse me one minute," Craig said.

Someone was outside his office trying to get his attention so he stepped out of the room, leaving me alone with Chad.

"I do hope you don't do something stupid like spread rumors about me," Chad said as soon as the office door was closed. "I've already shut you down once; I can do so again."

Even though his words were bitter and twisted a smile remained on his face and I realized he was keeping up appearances in case anyone happened to look into the office.

"What the hell are you doing here?" I asked through gritted teeth. I didn't care so much about how I looked to anyone else. It was not like I could stay working at ITC for much longer anyway. Not with Chad as my boss.

"Didn't you hear the good news Amy? I'm your new boss."

"You know what I mean you slimy piece of shit. Why are you working here of all places. Don't try to pretend you didn't know I worked here. You're not a good liar Chad. Remember how you cried when you tried to lie about raping me?"

The look on Chad's face made all the pain I was in right now worth it. Almost. He could handle walking around having raped someone—that didn't bother him—but reminding him that he cried when I told him I had been drugged did actually illicit some sense of shame. Some, but not a lot.

"Craig recognizes talent when he sees it," Chad said smugly. "Well, not always I guess. He hired you."

"Good one Chad. The jokes come almost as quickly as you do." I held up my little finger straight and then let it droop in front of him. It wasn't exactly the height of witty retort, but fuck it, the guy had drugged me and raped me. I didn't have to be at my best around him.

"You being here is just an added bonus," Chad said when he regained his arrogant attitude. "Although

I'm guessing you won't be hanging around long now I'm here."

I opened my mouth to say something childish, but then Craig walked back into the office and we both put on grins as if we had been reminiscing about old times.

"Sorry about that," Craig said. "You two caught up?"

"Sure," I said. "But I'm going to need resources for my project soon, so I suggest we calendar a meeting for sometime in the next week. That okay with you Chad?"

Now it was Chad's turn to look bemused. His face was almost the mirror image of mine when he had first walked into the office.

"Uh, sure. Yes, let's meet up soon."

There was no way I was giving him the satisfaction of quitting. Not just yet anyway. I couldn't stay at ITC and work under Chad for long, but I was damn sure going to do so for long enough that he wouldn't think I was quitting because of him. No way was he getting that satisfaction.

Chapter Two

The afternoon passed by in a blur. I don't think I did any actual work, but I can't remember one minute of what I was doing between leaving Craig's office and heading home. Perhaps I would end up getting dismissed for not meeting productivity targets? At least that would save me having to resign.

As I walked home, I was tempted to go straight to Matthew's apartment. He wouldn't be there yet, but I could wait for him in reception and that way I could spend the evening with him. But I couldn't trust myself. If I spoke to Matthew I would tell him about Chad working at ITC and there was no telling what Matthew would do with that information. Chad had it coming to him, but I had a feeling Matthew would be pissed at Craig as well and that would be a high-profile fight the media would love to get its hands on.

I wasn't mad at Craig. He seemed genuinely perplexed by the entire thing and likely didn't have a clue who Chad was in relation to me. There was something odd going on though. Chad was way too young for a job like that. Even with help from Mommy and Daddy he shouldn't have been able to get a position that high up in a big company.

There was a pleasant surprise waiting for me when I arrived home. Amanda was sat on the sofa watching television. She looked like a changed person from the last time I'd seen her. Her eyes had regained the spark that had been there the first time I met her and she looked completely relaxed.

"What are you watching?" I asked, as I slumped down on the sofa next to her.

"I'm binge watching The Big Bang Theory at the moment and I'm also working my way through True Blood."

I nodded in approval. Not so much at her choice of television shows—The Big Bang Theory was frustratingly inaccurate for a show that portrayed itself as being about a bunch of geeks—but for her taking the time to relax. Amanda had been so caught up in her big project recently that she had stopped leaving the house and was only sleeping a few hours a night.

"Does this mean you finally submitted your story?" I asked.

"No," she said with a long sigh. "There is still a lot to do, but I decided to take your advice on board. I spotted a huge mistake in one of my drafts that must have slipped in because I was exhausted when typing. I can't function properly when I'm so tired. Also, there isn't much I can do for a few more weeks anyway. It's kind of out of my hands for a while."

"You know, I'm desperate to know what this project of yours is."

"And you will. When it is finished."

"Tease."

"I enjoy keeping people in suspense. Let me have my fun; I'm bored stiff at the moment."

"Want to help me with something?" I asked. "I could use your investigative skills. If you want to keep chilling out then that's honestly—"

198

"I'm in," Amanda said, leaping up from the sofa. "I'm not cut out for this 'laying around watching TV' thing. What do you need help with?"

"It's a little sensitive," I said. "You have to promise to remain detached and calm."

"Okay," Amanda said slowly. "I guess that's cool. Part of being a journalist is—in theory—about remaining impartial."

I told Amanda about Chad showing up as my new boss at ITC. I didn't mention how he had behaved because she seemed pissed off enough with him just being there. If I'd told her what a jerk he had been to me she would have been impossible to work with.

"Holy shit," Amanda said at last, once I had finished talking. "Holy shit."

"Still want to help me?"

"Hell yes. But what do you want me to do? I assume it's not digging up dirt on him, because you have some of that already. Want me to leak rumors that a new employee at ITC is a rapist? I could do that, but I would need to give my contacts some details. They won't spread something like that without some proof."

"No," I said firmly. "Nothing like that. His family has money and we'll all end up in court. I just want to know how the hell he ended up at ITC. There is no way it's just a coincidence."

"Why do you think that?"

"For one thing, he is way underqualified for this position. Even taking into account the fact that his family is well-connected he is at least ten years out from a position like this. ITC is a public company listed on stock exchanges; it can't just go and appoint inexperienced people to repay a favor."

"Perhaps he lied on his resume?" Amanda suggested. "If so, he'll likely get found out soon enough."

I shook my head. "No, I don't think so. Chad was not at all surprised to see me. He'd been expecting me there. Also, Craig wasn't that shocked to find out we went to college together. He remarked that we must have been a few years apart but that was it."

"So what do you want to know?"

"Let's just find out what he did after college," I said. "I want to know what and who I'm dealing with."

Amanda spent a few minutes with her laptop and then presented me with a collection of browser tabs complete with all the public information about Chad's last few years.

"It's not that exciting," Amanda said. "He went to work for an investment bank after college and stayed there for a few years. He worked for some big clients by the sounds of it, but so do hundreds of other investment bankers. I'm not seeing anything that makes him stand out as being an exceptional talent. None of his former colleagues have gone on to any positions nearly as good as this one. You're right; this does look a little odd."

"There's one notable exception to the information you found," I said. "There's nothing on here about any rape allegations. He's managed to have the record scrubbed completely clean."

"If I wasn't so disgusted I would be impressed. It's hard to make something disappear these days."

"Wait," I yelled, just as Amanda started closing the tabs. "Go back a second. Look, right there."

I pointed at the bottom paragraph on a page from his former employer. He had an employee profile that had been removed from the website but Amanda had dug up an old cached version.

"What is it that has you so excited?" Amanda asked.

"While he was working for the investment bank he was seconded to work for another company to help with their initial public offering. It says he spent two months there."

Amanda looked thoroughly confused. "That's probably quite common. It's a good way for junior bankers to get experience and build client relationships. I don't get the significance."

"It's not what he did, it's who he did it for. The company he went to work for—I've heard of them. Matthew has mentioned them a few times and said I should go work there. Chad spent two months working for VirtualCore. There's no way this is a coincidence."

Chapter Three

I called in sick the next day and stayed at home. I had been determined to go into work and show Chad that I had moved on and that he wouldn't stop me getting on with my life. In the end though, I just knew I wouldn't be able to concentrate at all. I needed to know more about Chad and it was better that I take one day off work and get it out of my system then to let it drag on all week at work.

Amanda had gone out to meet up with a friend, so I had the place to myself. Unfortunately I was nowhere near as good at online research as Amanda. As a software engineer, I had certain skills and was more comfortable in front of a computer than 99% of the population, but Amanda had a whole other skill-set. She knew places to look that I wouldn't have even considered. For all I knew, those places might not be 100% legal, but they did the job.

Without Amanda's help, I found nothing that we hadn't already seen yesterday. It wasn't entirely surprising to see a limited amount of information for someone his age, but the absence of information was still frustrating. Surely if he was good enough to get a job at ITC he would have won awards or been talked about as an up-and-coming star. There was nothing like that.

One other missing detail was intriguing. Chad's professional networking profile was detailed and contained a list of every major client he had worked on during his time at the investment bank, with one notable exception; there was no mention of VirtualCore. Why would he leave out details of a secondment with one of the biggest companies in the country? That's the sort of thing most people would scream from the virtual rooftops.

I was at least pleased to see that he had not reported any leadership positions at college. My college had completely bottled it when it came to investigating my rape allegations, but they did apparently prevent him from running any of the important clubs and community groups. Chad probably couldn't have cared less, but I knew his father would have been annoyed and I allowed myself a wry smile at the thought of his father's disappointment.

My sick day had turned out to be a waste of time, so after lunch I went to work on my project just so I could have something tangible to show for the day's lack of pay. It was coming along painfully slowly and not helped by the sporadic way I would pick it up and put it down again for short periods. I knew I was losing sight of my main goal, but it was hard not to lose focus with all the distractions around.

There was a knock on the door; I froze in position on the sofa. Could that be Craig checking up on me? The thought of my boss visiting me at home after calling in sick should be ridiculous, but he had been here once so it wasn't beyond the realms of possibility.

I yelled out "Who is it?" while trying to sound like I had a sore throat. I added a little cough just to be sure.

"It's me," came Matthew's unmistakable voice.

I sprung up from the sofa and let him in, quickly shutting the door behind him in case there was someone

203

out in the hall who might see. I was surprisingly paranoid about being busted considering I might soon quit.

"What are you doing here?" I asked and then kissed him firmly on the lips so that he knew I was pleased by his visit in addition to being surprised.

"I heard you called in sick today and I wanted to see how you were."

"How did you know... you know what, never mind. You seem to know most of what goes on at ITC it seems." But he didn't know about Chad. If he knew that then he would not be looking so calm right now.

"You also seemed a little distracted when we were talking last night," Matthew added. "I haven't done anything wrong have I?"

"No, no, nothing like that."

"Well you don't look ill, so that means you don't want to go into work for some reason. What has he done?"

"What has who done?" I asked. He was referring to Craig, but I wanted to hear him say it.

"Craig. You don't seem like the type to take a sick day unless you are laid up in bed and even then you would probably just work remotely. If you're calling in sick then there must be a damn good reason and I'm betting it has something to do with Craig."

"It's not Craig, I promise. I actually did wake up feeling like shit, but I'm better now. I could go into work, but it doesn't seem worth it just for a few hours. Stop giving me grief and come chill out in front of the television with me."

"What are you watching?" he asked, sitting down next to me and wrapping his arm around me.

I lay my head on his chest and grabbed the remote. I hadn't been watching anything, but there were plenty of shows I had recorded ready to watch. With Matthew to myself all afternoon I didn't want to watch much television anyway.

"You know," Matthew said as he took the remote. "Your taste in TV is almost as bad as your taste in music. How about we just switch this off and make our own entertainment."

"Hmm," I said, pouting my lips and pretending to think. "I did want to catch up with Scandal, but I suppose you could persuade me otherwise."

Matthew grabbed hold of my arm furthest away from him and pulled me in close. I quickly straddled him and pressed my lips against his just as I heard Amanda's key in the door.

"Shit," Matthew muttered as I clambered off his groin as quickly as I had jumped on.

"You'll never guess what I found out today," Amanda said, as she fumbled with her shoes. She didn't seem to have noticed that Matthew was home so I had time to resume a more natural and innocent position with him. "It turns out that Chad is much more of a creep than we had realized. While in college he—"

"Amanda," I yelled, to both Matthew and Amanda's surprise. I hadn't been quick enough. She had mentioned Chad and Matthew was bound to pick up on it.

"Calm down Amy, I—" Amanda froze as she saw Matthew sat next to me on the sofa. "Shit. Sorry."

"What is it?" Matthew asked. He likely wouldn't have noticed anything if I hadn't yelled out. "Who's Chad?"

I shared a look with Amanda but neither of us spoke.

"Amy, what the hell is going on? Who is Chad?"

Chapter Four

"I'm going to give you two some privacy," Amanda said as she disappeared into her bedroom.

I considered lying, but I wasn't sure I had any lies that would convince Matthew. If I hadn't yelled out in panic I could have just pretended that Chad was a boyfriend or love interest of Amanda, but that was hardly going to work now. I couldn't pretend Chad was ex-boyfriend of mine either because Matthew knew about the only boyfriend I had ever had.

"Amy, tell me what is going on here," Matthew said, rearranging himself on the sofa so that he could look me in the eyes. He knew I couldn't stare into those eyes and tell a lie.

"Chad is my new boss at work," I explained. "Well, not my direct boss as such, but Craig brought him in to oversee the finances for my project. He will be the one to determine how much I can spend and that kind of thing."

"What else?" Matthew asked. "There's clearly more to it than that. Everyone has someone to keep an eye on their spending. Hell, within the company even I have to answer to my CFO sometimes. Why has this new boss of yours led to you taking the day off work?"

"We don't get on," I said calmly. I wasn't showing any emotion on my face, but I knew I wouldn't be able to finish this conversation with dry eyes.

"Amy, please tell me everything. You're far too nice a person to fall out with your new boss that quickly. Unless he did something to really..." Matthew trailed off and the look on his face went from sympathy to anger. "Amy, did he touch you or act in anyway inappropriate because if he did—"

"No," I said quickly. "He didn't." I had to tell him. Matthew's imagination was running wild and soon he would either guess correctly or think up something even worse. He should hear it from me. "I never told you the name of my ex-boyfriend. The one who raped me."

"Oh Jesus, Amy."

"His name is Chad Mitchell and he is now my boss."

I stared at Matthew and kept the tears inside. I had to keep Matthew calm and that meant being as strong as I possibly could be. Matthew was trying to remain calm and sympathetic, but I could see the anger behind his eyes and feel it as his hand held mine tighter than was comfortable.

"You told me he wasn't an engineer," Matthew said after an uncomfortably long silence.

"He's not," I replied. I knew why Matthew had asked the question.

"So what is he doing working for ITC?"

"He got a job in finance," I replied with a forced shrug.

"He's too young and vastly underqualified for a job at a place like ITC. If he got a job working at the same company as you it was no coincidence."

Matthew leaned over and kissed me on the cheek. I turned to meet his lips with mine but he was already standing up and walking towards the door.

"Where are you going?" I asked.

He paused with his hand on the door knob, not turning to look back at me. "I have to take care of something."

"This is not Craig's fault." I walked over to Matthew and tried to pull his arm away from the doorknob. I may as well have tried to pull the door off the hinges for all the good it did.

"There is no way this 'Chad' just happened to get a job as your boss. This was deliberate and the only one at ITC who can make a recruitment decision like that is Craig."

"Craig has no idea," I argued. "You should have seen the look of surprise on his face when he realized Chad and I knew each other."

"He faked it," Matthew replied, his hand still on the doorknob. "Besides, he would have seen that you went to the same college."

"It's a big college and we graduated in different years remember. And don't say that Craig could have found out about Chad from background checks. Somehow Chad has wiped the slate clean. Besides, if there was something there you would have found it when you were doing background checks on me."

"You're really not going to let me forget that one are you?"

"I plan to bring it up whenever it's convenient for me," I replied. "Come and sit back down and snuggle up with me on the sofa." I gave his arm a final pull and he let go of the doorknob.

We resumed the same position on the sofa with me resting my head on his chest, but I could tell Matthew was in no mood to relax.

"I just don't understand how you can be so calm about this," Matthew remarked after a few more minutes of silence.

"I'm calm because I have to be," I replied. "But if you think I'm sitting back and ignoring this then you are very much mistaken."

"Oh?" Matthew sat up straight forcing me to lift my head from its comfortable position listing to the beating of his heart. "What have you found out?"

"Not a lot so far," I explained, grabbing my laptop from the table. "But I'm sure it's not Craig's fault so as much as I know you want to blame him you are going to have to get past that."

"I'm blaming Craig until you convince me otherwise."

"Answer something for me first," I said. "Why did you keep telling me to go and work for VirtualCore?"

Matthew shrugged but not before swallowing and looking somewhat guilty. "It's a good company. And more importantly it isn't run by Craig."

"You know the CEO there?"

Matthew nodded. "Vaguely. What has all this got to do with VirtualCore?"

"I don't know yet, but I do know that Chad worked there for a bit. Just a couple of months on secondment from the bank. He doesn't mention it on any of his profiles, but it was on the website of his former employer. Doesn't it seem a little odd to you that he was working for VirtualCore and now he has shown up at ITC?"

Matthew was silent, the only noise the sound of him drumming his fingers on the arm of the sofa. I was about to continue speaking when he finally spoke up. "I hate to ask you this Amy, but do you think you can lay low on this for a few days?"

"What do you mean by lay low?"

"Go to work if you can, but you don't have to speak to Chad. In fact, try to have nothing to do with him if at all possible. And don't keep investigating VirtualCore. Can you do that?"

I considered it for a few moments and then nodded. I was planning to go to work anyway so that was no problem and I had no choice but to keep it quiet. There was no more information about Chad and VirtualCore online for me to find.

"What are you going to do?" I asked.

"Nothing drastic, I promise. Just give me a few days."

Chapter Five

When I went back to work the next day I half expected Chad to be waiting around every corner ready to jump out at me. It took me a few hours to relax and put him to the back of my mind. Chad wasn't even working on the same floor as me so I could just pretend he wasn't there.

I was about done with my little tour of all the different departments so that morning I started speaking to people about being part of my team. Jason had been right about meeting the other engineers before trying to recruit them. Having worked alongside people meant I knew who would be a good fit and nearly everyone I approached was at least interested in being part of the team.

Craig had restricted me to five engineers on the project, but the response had been so positive that I ended up with six people agreeing to work with me. I sent an email to Craig asking him to approve one extra person on a trial basis. I figured that one of the team was bound to drop out after a few weeks and then I would be left with five.

For a CEO, Craig was usually quick at responding to email, but I went the rest of the day without hearing anything from him. My inbox had plenty of emails coming in, but none of them were what I wanted to see. Finally I saw a response to my email, but it came from Chad not Craig.

Craig had forwarded my email to Chad for financial review and Chad had taken it upon himself to respond to me directly. He had never been one to mince his words and that hadn't changed. Chad told me in no uncertain terms that I would not be allowed to pick six engineers. In fact, I would not be allowed five. According to Chad, the budget for a project like mine was three engineers, all of whom would be part-time only.

I should have just waited for Craig to respond. He had already authorized five engineers and he would probably have sorted it out if I had given him the chance. That's what I *should* have done and if the email had come from anyone else I undoubtedly would. Instead I replied instantly asking Chad what the hell he was playing at.

The next email didn't come from Chad; it was from Craig and he was calling me into his office. I looked down the email chain and saw to my horror that I must have hit "reply all" when sending my message to Chad. There were no references to our past in the email, but to a neutral observer like Craig it looked like Chad had sent a calm, rational email about my budget and I had responded with a string of f-bombs. This would not be a fun meeting.

I knocked sheepishly on Craig's door and walked in.

"Amy, what the hell was that about?" Craig asked. "You can't go sending emails like that to people at work, especially people who are your boss. Chad has every right to go to the board and ask for you to be fired and I'm going to have a hard time coming up with a reason to keep you. Just because you knew him at college doesn't mean you can act like you are still there."

I could either stand there and get told off or I could fight back. I'd had enough of cowering in fear because of Chad and what he did to me.

"Why did you hire Chad?" I asked.

Craig looked taken aback by the sudden change in the topic. "What has that got to do with any of this?"

"Please," I said. "Just tell me why you hired him. I know it's not just because of his experience. There are plenty of people out there who have worked in investment banks and have financial backgrounds. Chad has never worked for a company this size and he is in way over his head. Why did you hire him?"

Craig leaned back in his chair and stared at me. I knew he was trying to figure out where I was going with this line of questioning, but in the end he decided to answer me.

"You're right," Craig said, sitting forward now and inviting me to take a seat. "He is an unusual appointment and it wasn't easy to convince the board. I own most of the company but I'm not allowed to just do as I please unfortunately. Chad came highly recommended and that's why I hired him."

"That was it? A recommendation? Who from?"

"I can't tell you that, Amy. I'm sorry, I know it's tough to see people like Chad come in above you, but that's largely how the world works."

"What do you mean 'people like Chad?' " I asked.

"Believe it or not Amy, I'm actually a lot like you. I came from a poor family as well. My parents worked hard just to keep me in clothes and put food on the table. You know what that's like, so I won't give you the sob story. I hate that rich kids still get all the advantages and breaks in life, but that's just the way things are."

"I don't hate Chad because he's rich," I said. "I hate Chad because of what he did to me in college."

"Amy, I don't think I want to hear this. I'm still your boss; if you had a crush on Chad or if he messed you around in college that's really none of my business. This

213

is a professional place of work and we have to put what happened in college behind us."

"I can't put this behind us," I said. "Chad didn't 'mess me around' in college. He spiked my drink at a party and then raped me."

Craig's face went from mild frustration and annoyance to shock and then sympathy. He quickly moved around the desk and sat down next to me, placing his hand on my back.

"Amy, my God, I... I don't know what to say."

"It's okay Craig, honestly. I don't want to go into the details, but it happened and he was never punished."

I thought it might get easier to talk about the more I told people, but I still found myself welling up inside when I said the 'r' word. The was no emotional attachment between Craig and me which did help a little, but I still couldn't talk about what happened.

"Let me guess, his rich family had influence in the college whereas your family had none because they were poor? The case got dropped and no more was said about it?"

"That's about the gist of it," I said. "I'm sorry Craig, but I can't continue working here while he is around." I only made my decision as I spoke the words. "I'm going to have to quit."

"No," Craig said instantly. "That is not how this goes down. He's the one in the wrong, not you."

"I'm not naïve Craig. I know that he is on a huge contract and he will get a substantial pay off if you fire him. Call your legal counsel if you like."

Craig leaned over to the phone and dialed the lead attorney at ITC. "Adam, I have a quick question for you. Are you someone private?"

"Sure," Adam replied. I could hear a click as he took the phone off speaker.

"How watertight is Chad's contract?" Craig asked. "Could we fire him if we wanted to?"

"Already? Jesus Craig, he's only just started. What's happened?"

"I can't say," Craig said. "But let's say he did something bad—reprehensible—a few years back. Could we fire him?"

"No," Adam said. "Not unless it was fraud or something related to financial misconduct. He insisted on a very generous severance package and you told me to give it to him when my team drafted the contract."

"Shit. Okay, thanks Adam." Craig hung up the phone and looked back at me. "I can still fire him. We would just need to make a big payout. I'm happy to do that. He doesn't deserve this job. Hell, he deserves to be in prison."

"No," I said. "Don't do that. It's bad for the company and besides, I don't want him to be rewarded with a huge payout. At least if he stays here he will have to work for his money."

"Are you sure?" Craig asked. "I could arrange for him to have an unfortunate accident."

I laughed, but I wasn't sure if Craig was joking. "You really are so much like Matthew sometimes."

"That hurts Amy," Craig replied, pretending to be offended.

I rolled my eyes and not for the first time wished that these two could put their feud to one side. "Look, don't worry about me. I have other opportunities lined up already and long-term this might not work out anyway. I think I need a little more time to put my past behind me."

"I'm sure Matthew has already said the same, but if you need any contacts I can help. I know everyone there is to know in this business. You've worked your way up from nothing and I can relate to that so please do let me know if I can help."

I said goodbye to Craig and walked straight home. It had been a rather surreal day, but there was no feeling of shock or regret. Deep down, I think I always knew ITC wasn't for me and seeing Chad join was just the final straw. Something did bug me all the way home though. On two occasions Craig mentioned that I worked my way up from a poor family. How did he know that? I

215

had never told anyone and it wasn't obvious from my resume. I did get a scholarship to offset some of my college tuition but that was based on merit, not family income. Somehow Craig knew about my background and I was going to find out how.

Chapter Six

I devoted an afternoon to investigating myself. I couldn't use my own computer, because of all the cookies and information already stored on there about me. I wanted to do a search as if I were a complete stranger, so I went to the library and sat at a computer in the corner where no one could see my screen.

The whole thing with Craig had freaked me out more than I realized. It wasn't just the comments about my upbringing that seemed a little off; I remembered Matthew saying that Craig didn't really like manga and was just trying to impress me with the books on his shelves. I had never told Craig I liked manga so why would he do that?

After three hours of searching I had found nothing about myself that indicated I came from a poor family or that I liked manga. Other than some mildly embarrassing photos, there was not much information that I wouldn't happily put on my résumé or share in a conversation with friends. I did use a website that kept track of the books I had read, but I never recorded my manga books on there. As far as I could tell, there was no way Craig could have known those things about me just from online research.

Matthew had confessed to snooping on me in the past, but even then he had never found out those details. I suppose if Craig really went to extreme lengths he could investigate my friends and ask them questions, but I liked to think that if my friends had been questioned by a stranger they either wouldn't say anything or would at least tell me someone had approached them. Besides, people like Craig and Matthew assumed everything they needed to know was online. So how did Craig know?

I gave up my own investigation and decided to ask Amanda for help. I hated having to rely on her so much, especially when she was so busy, but she had a knack for thinking of places to look that never occurred to me.

First I just asked Amanda to research me online and see what she could find out. It turned out she had already done that before accepting me as a roommate. There was nothing I hadn't already found.

"Okay," I said. "Now I want you to specifically look for information about my family. Can you find out anything about my upbringing?"

"You mean if you are rich or poor that kind of thing?" Amanda asked.

"Yes, exactly."

I paced back and forth in Amanda's room while she typed furiously and skimmed through the content of websites quicker than I thought possible.

"I've got nothing," Amanda said finally. "I can see the geographic area you were brought up in, but not exactly where you live. The county you grew up in had a wide variety of rich, middle class, and poor people, so there's no way to tell which group you fit into."

"Now see if you can find out about my reading habits. Specifically I want to know if there is any information online about me being a fan of manga."

Amanda found. "Are you going to tell me what this is about?"

"I will, but let's see what you find first."

Amanda spent fifteen minutes searching online but once again came up blank. "Okay, I give up. You keep your online presence cleaner than most people—which is a good idea by the way—and I cannot find any information about your reading habits beyond the books you list on your open profiles. Can you let me in on the mystery now?"

"Things got really weird at ITC today just before I quit."

"With Chad?"

"No, with Craig actually. He seems to know things about me that I have never told him and it is kind of freaking me out. He definitely knows I came from a poor family and Matthew thinks he pretended to be interested in manga just to build a connection with me."

"So you think he's been spying on you?"

"I did, yes, but now I'm not so sure. It's looks like that information is not out there to find."

"Let's look past the information online," Amanda said closing her laptop. "What other ways are there to find out that information? Start with the information about your family."

I closed my eyes and took a few moments to think. Not many people knew about my upbringing, because I didn't like to talk about it. People I went to school with would have known; kids always knew when other people were poor just by the clothing they wore. However, once I went to college that kind of thing became easier to hide and I didn't make a big deal about it. I wanted to make my parents proud of me, but that was my internal motivation and I always made an effort to leave it out of interviews and personal statements that were submitted as part of job applications.

"I honestly don't know, I never..." I trailed off. There was one time I had talked about it recently. "I mentioned it in a meeting. One of the support meetings for abuse victims I go to occasionally. I talked about how tough my upbringing was and how I wanted to be a success to repay my parents for what they did for me."

"I hate to say this, but do you think one of the women there could have leaked the information to Craig?"

I shook my head vigorously. "I really doubt it. Even if some of the women there are untrustworthy, they wouldn't know who I was or that I work for Craig. And Craig didn't know I went to meetings so it's not like he could have placed someone in the crowd."

"All right, what about the manga thing. How many people know about that?"

"Very few," I replied. "It's not that I'm embarrassed about it as such, it's just I don't know anyone else who likes it so I don't talk about it."

"What about people seeing you buy it?"

"I mostly read e-books. I suppose a couple of men might know," I added grimacing. I told Amanda about the tattoo on my inner thigh. Once she had stopped laughing we agreed that none of my embarrassing one night stands were likely to talk to Craig about it.

After an entire afternoon of searching, I was none the wiser about how Craig was getting this information. I was fed up and frustrated, and there was only one way to cheer me up right now. Matthew would probably still be working, so I sent him a message to see if he wanted dinner. He said he was too busy for dinner, but didn't mention why. Before I had time to be annoyed or suspicious, he sent me another message that would more than make up for missing out on dinner.

Chapter Seven

"I had planned for this to be a surprise," Matthew said, as I stepped into the passenger seat of his car on Saturday morning. "But you seemed a bit down when you messaged me so I figured I would let you in on the secret."

"I'm so glad you did," I replied. "Although you still haven't told me everything. All I know is that we are spending the day somewhere and that I should bring warm clothes."

"I guess you'll find out soon enough. We're going to Monterey to wander around Fisherman's Wharf and eat good food. There's another little treat there for you, but I'm keeping that close to my chest."

Despite having lived within a two hour's drive of Monterey for the last five years I had never actually been. I had always assumed it was expensive because the people I knew from there were rich. I don't know why that stopped me visiting though. The trip was worth it just for the drive down there. Most of the drive involved sweeping down the coastal roads with gorgeous views of the best of what California had to offer. This was much better than the concrete jungle that San Francisco had become.

The traffic was slow the entire way there, but it became gridlocked when we got close to our destination. Matthew took some side streets and parked in a random driveway.

"Um, Matthew, I know you're rich and cute and all, but some people don't like strangers parking in their driveways." Especially people who own houses like this, I thought. Nothing in this location cost under a $1 million and this house had three stories and a pool that I could smell from the driveway. We were parked in front of a $2 million property at least.

"The owner is a friend," Matthew replied, taking my hand and walking towards the streets.

"You own it, don't you," I said, as the pieces clicked together in my head.

"Yep. You like it?"

"Looks alright," I said with a shrug. "If you like big houses and swimming pools."

Matthew laughed. "I haven't spent much time here yet because work keeps me up in the city, but I intend to move down at some point. It's so much more relaxed here. Plus—as much as I enjoy doing yoga in my playroom—it's so much better doing it outside in the fresh ocean air."

Matthew wasn't exaggerating about the fresh air. Smelling the slight saltiness of the ocean did more to wake me up than three cups of coffee ever could. I walked with a spring in my step and forgot all about my problems with Craig and Chad. I'd told Matthew about quitting, but after that he hadn't asked questions and I hadn't volunteered any information. There was time for that, but this day was just for us.

Monterey was not at all like what I had expected. The people were relaxed and if they were rich they at least didn't give off that vibe. We headed straight towards the wharf, but I soon got distracted by all the stalls selling jewelry, sea shells, and assorted knick knacks that I didn't need but wanted desperately all the same.

"I warn you, I have a weakness for candles," I confessed, as I held up a huge square candle in two hands and took a deep smell of its fragrance.

"That one is designed to clear the mind," the lady selling the candles said. "Those are real seashells in there."

I held the candle in front of my eyes and saw three seashells inside the soft wax of the candle. "I sure could use something to clear the mind right now," I said, more to Matthew than the woman.

"It's ten dollars, but you can get two for fifteen."

I picked up another candle that the woman told me would act as an aphrodisiac, "not that you need it with him," she added with a wink.

"Will you ever actually use these?" Matthew asked as he took the bag for me.

"Nope, but they look pretty." I had a collection of candles at home, but rarely ever lit them. Even when there had been a power cut, I refused to use the good ones and just burnt the small cheap ones like those on tables in Chinese restaurants.

"You should feel free to buy whatever you want," Matthew said. "My house down here is looking rather sparse and could do with a woman's touch. How about you spruce it up a bit."

Matthew would soon regret that request. We went round buying cushions, sheets, lots of pictures and paintings, and more candles. We even had to make a trip back to the house to drop off the goods before our arms gave out. Well, my arms anyway.

I only got a quick look inside, but I liked what I saw. The kitchen was surprisingly modern for a house that looked quite old from the outside, and the hardwood floors were shiny enough to skid around on like a kid. Matthew had barely made any effort with the interior, but he had made his mark in the living room. There was a big screen television and a collection of video game consoles and controllers scattered around.

We headed back out to the wharf and stopped at the edge to admire the collection of sea lions. They weren't doing anything; just lazing around on rocks and making a ton of noise. They seemed to be a tourist attraction in and of themselves, so we took a few pictures as well. I didn't need a photo to remember this day, but it would give me a way to share the day with friends online.

"Alright, I'm getting hungry," Matthew said.

"Me too. Shopping always makes me hungry. Let's go to one of the seafood restaurants we walked past earlier. It seems crazy to be here and not eat some of the local fish."

"I agree, but we aren't going to one of the restaurants."

"You want to get take-out at your place?" I asked. I knew he didn't have enough in the kitchen to cook anything.

"You remember how I said there was one more surprise?"

"Yes," I said anxiously. I liked surprises, but not where food was concerned. I was hungry and just wanted to eat.

"Follow me," Matthew said as he pulled me along by the hand. We walked to another of the wharfs and stopped by the edge. "What do you see?"

"The ocean," I replied with a frown. "Seagulls. What else am I supposed to see."

"Look a little closer," Matthew said, motioning to my left.

"Oh shit, are you kidding?" Matthew was pointing at a luxury yacht anchored to the wharf. There were so many boats around I hadn't paid too much attention, although this one certainly did stand out.

"Step aboard, ma'am. We are going out into the ocean."

Chapter Eight

Matthew powered the boat far enough out into the ocean that we could barely see the wharf. If there was anything sexier than a man like Matthew holding the wheel of a powerful yacht, I didn't know what it could be.

The boat had a full complement of seats on the deck and a kitchen inside. Matthew disappeared to the kitchen and came out just minutes later with freshly grilled fish and vegetables.

"I had someone put food on the boat just before we left," Matthew said when he saw the look of confusion on my face.

There was a rail around the edge of the boat and the ledge was easily large enough to sit on, so Matthew and I perched up there and ate our food. I had expected it to be windy out on the ocean, however the sun was out and with no shade to be found I had to take off my sweater to keep cool. Matthew went one better and removed his shirt. His chest glistened in the sun and out of habit I looked around for any women who might be staring at him. This time I had him all to myself. There were no other boats anywhere near us, so I stripped down to my underwear.

"Wow," Matthew said, his eyes running up and down my body. "Just when I thought the scenery couldn't get any more beautiful."

"I never even wear a bikini at the beach, but I feel like we have the entire place to ourselves."

The surface of the ledge was cool to the touch so I placed a towel down and laid out on it. I looked over the side and stared at the waves as they rippled against the side of the boat. The water was relatively clear so occasionally I would spot a fish near the surface. It was absolutely mesmerizing.

Matthew's fingers lightly moved the hair from the side of my face and planted a kiss on my neck. I murmured with pleasure and a shiver went down my spine. His other hand moved down my back before coming to a rest on my ass. The fingers teased at the lace of my panties and I knew Matthew wanted to pull them off.

I turned on my side to face Matthew and pressed my body against his as we kissed. He still had his shorts on but I could feel him stiffening already, desperate to get inside me. It had been too long.

"Shall we go inside?" I asked. It felt like a strange question to ask on a boat, but I thought I had spied a bed in there by the kitchen.

"Let's stay here," Matthew said, pushing me onto my back.

He got down off the ledge and stood on the deck in front of me between my legs. My body yearned for him to grab hold of my legs and thrust himself inside me. I pulled off my bra and threw it onto the floor of the boat while Matthew did the same with my panties. The breeze felt liberating between my legs. I reached my hand over my head to grab hold of the rail while Matthew removed his pants. He stood there naked in front of me with his cock throbbing; I couldn't take my eyes off it until Matthew dropped to his knees.

He buried his face between my legs and ate me greedily. His tongue moved slowly up and down my lips, but stopping agonizingly short of my clit each time. When my hole was soaking wet, he slipped two fingers inside me and finally moved his mouth up to my bud, taking it between his lips and sucking gently.

My hands gripped the railing as my moans of pleasure were whisked away on the breeze. I squirmed on the towel as my hips rocked against Matthew's fingers and his mouth.

"Harder," I moaned softly, as his fingers fucked my pussy. He moved faster and the orgasm quickly took over my body. "I'm coming Matthew. I'm coming hard." My hands now gripped the rail so tight that my knuckles were white and I arched my back into the air as his fingers slipped in and out of my tunnel.

Matthew kept sucking my clit as I came in his mouth and didn't stop until my body came to a rest at least a minute later. I let go of the rail and slipped down the ledge into Matthew awaiting arms. He had already slipped on a condom and I could see in his eyes that he was about to claim his reward.

"Take me," I whimpered, still barely able to breath.

I went to lay back down on the ledge, but Matthew's strong hands grabbed my waist and spun me round so that my ass pressed against his firm cock. A hand went to my shoulder and pushed me forward. I bent at the waist and let my arms stop my fall before coming to a rest on my elbows.

"I wish you could see what I see," Matthew said. I knew he was looking down at my exposed pussy. "Your cunt is the sexiest thing I have ever seen."

I loved that word on his lips. "It'll look a lot better once you're stretching it open," I said.

"Beg me, Amy," Matthew said, planting a gentle slap on my ass. "I've never wanted to fuck anyone as much as I want to fuck you right now. I want to know you need this as much as I do."

"I'm dripping for you, Matthew," I pleaded, truthfully. I could feel my wetness trickling down my legs and knew he could see it. "I'm not complete without your cock inside me."

"I don't believe you yet."

I thrust my ass back and rubbed my sex up and down his shaft. "You can feel how wet I am. Fuck me, Matthew. Grab my ass and have your way with my pussy."

"More," Matthew groaned through gritted teeth.

His fingers were digging into my skin; I nearly had him, but would have to completely let go first. I had to surrender all inhibitions and let him know what I needed. There was something I wanted to say, but my brain said I shouldn't. It felt wrong, but I had to say it to get his cock.

"I want you to thrust your thick cock into my tight wet *cunt*." The word felt wrong on my lips, but also felt so right. "Fuck my cunt Matthew." It was even easier the second time. "I want you to have your way with me and ruin my cunt for all other men." Now it was almost like a normal word, but it still had a power that felt intoxicating on my lips.

"You are a naughty little girl, Amy," Matthew said as he placed the head of his length inside me and pushed forward.

I moaned as he filled up my insides until his balls brushed against my legs. His hands had a tight hold of my hips as he withdrew and then slammed back inside me. I was so wet he almost fell out of me each time he pulled back and I got wetter each time his balls slapped against my lips.

With each forward thrust my head was forced out over the edge of the boat giving me a view of the ocean waves crashing into the boat with almost as much vigor and aggression as Matthew's cock pounding into me.

"I can't believe how tight you are," Matthew moaned. "And so wet." One of his hands left my hips and grabbed hold of my hair, pulling me up towards him. My pert breasts pointed up into the air as Matthew nuzzled at my neck. A hand squeezed my breast hard enough for me to cry out. There was some pain, but I held his hand there and urged him to keep going.

Being on a boat in the ocean with a gorgeous billionaire was driving my mind crazy, like it couldn't possibly be real. Something in my head told me I was about to wake up from this dream. My mind had no place in this moment so I closed my eyes to focus on what Matthew was doing to my body. He pushed me forward again and I perched my ass into the air waiting for his orgasm that I knew was coming soon.

His cock left my pussy and a few seconds later I felt his juices crash against my back. Three heavy streams covered me and started collecting in the crevice of my spine. I turned round and dropped to my knees to collect the last few sweet drops as his member shrunk in my mouth.

Matthew used the towel to wipe his essence off my back and we finally made it to the bed. The motion of the boat combined with the slow rising and falling of Matthew's chest sent me into a deep and relaxing sleep. It didn't occur to me until the next morning, but I had gone an entire day hardly thinking about Craig and Chad at all. Right now they felt a world away and I wanted it to stay that way as long as possible.

Chapter Nine

Going back to San Francisco was a painful return to the reality of life as an unemployed engineer. Matthew had offered to help me out with money and pay my rent, but I didn't want to start taking his money. Day trips on a boat were one thing, but he shouldn't be paying for my entire lifestyle.

The first night I was back in the city I decided to attend another support meeting. I didn't feel the need to go this time, but enough people had told me over the years that it is as important to attend meetings when things are going well as when they are going badly. Something to do with not associating meetings with pain all the time. Karen had asked if I would be attending one and I agreed to meet her there.

The turnout was low for this meeting which was likely because it was associated with a local church group. Some people erroneously assumed they wouldn't be welcome if they weren't a member of that local church or weren't religious. It was unfortunate because the church always welcomed me with open arms even if I wasn't exactly a practicing member. There was the usual assortment of coffee and light snacks by the side, so I grabbed myself a cup and took a seat next to Karen.

I never knew what to say to most of the women I met at these meetings, but conversations with Karen were always easy; it was like catching up with an old college friend in a coffee shop. She remarked on the last speech I gave a few weeks ago and suggested I go up and speak again. I had to politely decline; I had nothing to add tonight and while going to a meeting in a positive mood was a good idea, I found it almost impossible to make a speech without a particular issue on my mind to talk about. I could have gone up there and spoken about Chad, but that was too risky. If someone knew where I worked they could find out who Chad was and that would be a mistake.

Matthew had offered to come with me again and I was tempted to say yes, but something about having him join me here didn't quite feel right. It felt unfair to the other women to bring a man into the meeting, although I had seen it before on rare occasions. Not only did I have to trust Matthew for myself, I had to trust him on behalf of all the other women here as well and I wasn't quite ready to make that leap just yet.

Usually I dashed out of meetings as soon as they were over, but tonight I decided to hang around for a bit to see if I could help any of the women who were at a worse stage than I was right now. I didn't approach anyone—that often just scared people away—but I tried to look friendly and inviting in case anyone felt the need to speak. No-one did. I stood in the corner for about ten minutes but eventually decided to call it a night. The one problem with meeting in a church is that the heating barely worked and the building was starting to get cold.

I placed my now empty cup of coffee back on the table and headed towards the grand church entrance. I was nearly out the door when something caught my eye. There were two women talking near the exit in hushed tones. People whispering was hardly unusual here given the context of the meeting but my brain wasn't happy with something about this image. The woman nearest me, whom I could only see side on, looked distinctly familiar. I'd seen her before, but that in itself wasn't odd. Many of the women here had been to other meetings. I'd seen this woman in another context entirely.

My brain played around with the image the entire way home and it wasn't until I walked through the door that I had my "eureka" moment. The woman at the meeting was the same one Matthew had gone to the charity function with recently. I'd seen her with him outside a shopping mall. What was her name? Francine Mahoney, that was it. Francine had looked familiar when I'd seen her with Matthew; I must have seen her before at other meetings.

The whole situation made sense, so why couldn't I shake the feeling that something was wrong. Matthew and Francine had been attending an event for victims of domestic abuse. Francine might well have been a victim herself at some point which was why she attended meetings. I felt emotionally shaken, but had no idea why so I did what I always did when confused—burdened Amanda with my problems. I told Amanda what I had seen and pulled up some pictures of Francine to confirm.

"Yep, that's her," I said confidently. "She was at the meeting tonight. I don't want to sound like a stalker girlfriend, but something doesn't feel right to me about this. What do we know about Francine Mahoney?"

"Not a lot," Amanda replied. "We didn't bother doing much research on her last time, but I can poke around a bit. She looks kind of ordinary actually," she continued, after doing a few online searches. "She's obviously proud of her charity work and she sits on the board of a number of similar organizations. It's not clear where she gets her money from, but judging by her choice of outfits she has a fair chunk of it."

"How far back do Francine and Matthew go? Are they old friends?"

"Not as far as I can tell. She's not in any photos with Matthew that are any older than a year. Oh, what do we have here…"

"What is it?" I asked when Amanda trailed off into a frustrating silence.

"I've actually found Matthew in photos with the same woman on multiple different occasions. Looks like he was once in a steady relationship."

My curiosity got the better of me and I took a quick peek at the photos which must have been at least five years old, if not more. Matthew looked notably younger although that was largely due to the lack of stubble around his face in those days. The woman was younger than him, early twenties, and petite with a grin that lit up everything around her. That was an image of a girl who had never been happier than when Matthew's arm was around her waist.

"Before you go reading too much into this," Amanda said, "remember that they are no longer together. There's likely a good reason for that."

Amanda closed the browser, but it was too late. Those images were ingrained in my memory and it would take many sleepless nights before I could shake them off.

"Oh God," Amanda said, closing her laptop and spinning round to face me. "I think I know what's troubling you about Francine. But it doesn't make any sense…"

"What is it Amanda?" I asked tersely.

"Amy, how much do you really trust Matthew?"

Chapter Ten

How much do I really trust Matthew? That was a question I had asked myself many times already. I trusted him enough to tell him about my past, but not enough to take him to one of the support meetings with me. That was probably expected given though; we hadn't known each other that long after all.

"What is it?" I asked Amanda again. "What have you found out?"

"Okay, but I'm probably wrong. In fact, I'm fairly sure I am, because this doesn't make a lot of sense and—"

"Amanda, just tell me."

Amanda took a long, deep breath and exhaled slowly. This was either big news or she was being overly dramatic. Both were possible. "We've established that Matthew knows someone who attends your meetings."

"There's nothing particularly unusual about that given how many people go to the various events hosted around the city."

"Sure, but you were also asking me how Craig knows certain information about you. The manga thing and you growing up with a poor family. The manga tattoo is, uh, well-hidden from most people and you said the only time you had talked about your family recently was at a meeting."

"Oh shit," I said, sitting down on Amanda's bed. "I really don't like where this is going."

"Is there a chance Francine Mahoney told Matthew about your family?"

"There's a chance," I replied. It would be a complete breakdown of the trust required at those meetings and a perfect example of why my online project was so essential, but where human beings were concerned anything was possible.

"And I'm guessing Matthew knows about your tattoo?" Amanda asked.

My cheeks went red even though it was hardly a big secret that Matthew and I were sleeping together. I gave a quick nod.

"He knows about both of your secrets then. But the mystery is why the hell would he tell Craig? Don't those two hate each other?"

I nodded again. I had a bigger concern than the possibility that Matthew had for some reason shared my secrets with Craig. There were *three* particularly unusual things—too unusual for mere coincidence—that Craig had done or said that worried me. Him knowing about my enjoyment of manga and my poor family were two of them, but there was also Chad. I refused to believe that Chad showing up at ITC as my boss was a fluke.

Matthew didn't know about Chad; that much I was fairly certain of. If he had, then Chad would likely be black and blue by now. I was missing something and there was only one person who could give me the answers I needed right now.

"I going over to see Matthew," I told Amanda. "And I'm not leaving until he comes clean."

—

The worst thing about being unemployed—other than the lack of a paycheck—was the fact that everyone else still operated on normal schedules. I wanted to go straight round to Matthew's and demand an explanation, but when I left the apartment I remembered that he would still be at work. I killed a few hours wandering around the shops and treated myself to some workout clothes, although I stayed well clear of the expensive designer brands I usually went for. I passed some time in a coffee shop with my book although I found it difficult to concentrate.

My brain wouldn't let me switch off. Why would Matthew have told Craig those things about me? They were such minor issues that there didn't seem to be a lot of point. Once I had finished my coffee I decided to give up the pretense of reading and headed straight to Matthew's apartment even though he was almost certainly not home yet.

I buzzed his door at the entrance and looked up at the camera so he could see who it was. After a few seconds without a response, I turned to walk away when I heard the distinctive buzz of the door unlocking.

I used every available second in the elevator to compose myself while remembering that I was mad. Curiosity was the prevailing emotion at the moment because the puzzle was driving me nuts, but if I was right then Matthew had betrayed me once again and he would have some explaining to do.

Matthew was waiting for me in the doorway. He was dressed in jeans and a shirt, with the sleeves rolled halfway up. He never dressed that casual at work, so must have worked from home today.

"To what do I owe this honor?" Matthew asked.

I let him kiss me on the cheek, not wanting to cause a scene in the hallway, and then stepped inside. His laptop was open on the table and I could see he was composing an email. When I worked from home there was usually a semi-circle of mess around me—food wrappers and empty mugs of coffee in particular—but Matthew had nothing other than his laptop.

"Craig knows I like manga and he knows I come from a poor family," I said to Matthew once the door was shut.

"Okay. Does that bother you?" he asked, clearly confused.

"It bothers me that he somehow has information about me that I never told him. Do you have any idea how he might have come across those details?"

"No," Matthew said quickly. "I didn't find that out when I did background research on you, so I doubt he could have done either. Unless he went even further with it than I did. Perhaps he spoke to friends of yours or something like that. I did tell you not to trust him."

"Don't give me that fucking lecture," I snapped. "It's not him I'm having the problem trusting right now."

"Amy, what the fuck are you talking about?"

"You knew that information about me. I think you told Craig although for the life of me I cannot figure out why."

"I haven't spoken to Craig since I met you," Matthew said, sitting down on the sofa and pulling me down next to him. "And anyway, I don't know anything about your family. You mentioned you weren't well off, but I had no idea you grew up poor."

"You spied on me," I replied, my voice shaking. I had no conviction in what I was accusing him of. When I imagined coming over here it was easy to picture myself yelling at him. But with him in front of me, it was impossible to imagine Matthew doing something so creepy. "You had someone spy on me."

Matthew blinked and shook his head in confusion. "Amy, you need to backtrack and explain what has happened. Tell me everything from the beginning."

Chapter Eleven

I told Matthew how Craig had pretended to like manga and how he had known about my family. The accusations sounded petty when spoken allowed, but my issue wasn't Craig knowing those things, it was *how* he knew those things.

Matthew took a few moments to process everything I had told him. The fact that he didn't instantly dismiss my concerns was reassuring. The last thing I wanted right now was for Matthew to tell me I was overreacting and to just ignore it.

"First of all Amy, I definitely did not tell Craig those things. We haven't spoken in a while. I have not mentioned your manga tattoo to anyone and frankly I doubt anyone is all that interested. Like I said before, I don't really know much about your family so I couldn't tell anyone that."

"You could have found out by paying some of you 'researchers' to investigate my past."

Matthew gave a slight shrug of the shoulders. "Probably," he admitted. "But my research stopped when I found out you had misled me about your time at college. As your employer, that was far more interesting to me than whether your family was poor."

"If it wasn't you then who was it?"

"I'm going to assume you've already looked yourself up online to see if there are any obvious clues that could be found on your social media sites?"

I nodded. "I checked and Amanda helped me. She's a journalist; if there was something there she would have found it. Besides, I'm not one of those who posts every detail of my life online anyway."

"I'm going to help you figure this out," Matthew said, taking hold of my hand, "but I need you to start trusting me. *Really* trusting me. You can't keep accusing me every time something strange happens that you don't understand."

"I will," I said, "*if* you open up to me. Tell me about your ex-girlfriend."

Matthew frowned. "What ex-girlfriend?"

"The one you were with up until about five years ago. She's quite short and slim. Very pretty."

"I've never had a steady girlfriend Amy. I honestly don't know who you are talking about."

"This is why I can't completely trust you," I said, feeling frustrated. "I don't even care that much about you having an ex-girlfriend; it just seems weird that you would keep her as some big secret."

"I'm assuming you found photos of me and this girl online?" Matthew asked. "Where were we?"

I thought back to the images I had seen on Amanda's laptop. Most of them were too close up to identify the location, but in quite a few of them they had both been wearing football jerseys. "I think you were at football games in quite a few of them. Perhaps tailgating."

Matthew let out a long sigh and looked up at the ceiling. Without saying a word he stood up and walked to the kitchen to grab a glass of water which he finished before he had rejoined me on the sofa.

"That wasn't an ex-girlfriend in the photos," Matthew said, as the silence was beginning to get unbearable.

"Please don't tell me she's your ex-wife?" I asked. He had never mentioned being married and that would be one hell of a secret to have kept from me.

"No, not a wife. Not a girlfriend. Nothing like that."

"You two looked pretty cozy," I said.

"We were," he replied, with a nostalgic look in his eyes. "That girl you saw is my sister. Her name's Rachel."

I let out a loud sigh of relief. He'd still kept a secret from me, but it didn't relate to a former relationship which somehow felt better. "I didn't know you had a sister. Why didn't you say something?"

"We don't talk a lot any more," Matthew said quietly.

"I'm sorry. Listen, if you don't want to talk about this we don't have to. Not right now at least."

"It's okay, we should talk about it. If you can tell me what happened to you then the least I can do is tell you about my sister."

Matthew looked as somber as I had felt just before I told him how Chad had raped me in college. Whatever he was about to tell me it wouldn't be easy to hear. Matthew and his sister had looked inseparable in those photos, so anything that meant they were no longer speaking must be serious.

"Rachel is a few years younger than me so of course I was the typical overprotective brother during her teenage years. I didn't have much to be concerned about though; she was almost *too* well-behaved. I teased her a bit for not going out and drinking with friends enough."

"Why didn't she go out much?" I asked. "Was she shy?"

Matthew shook his head vigorously. "No, not at all. She lit up every room she was in and I'm not being biased when I say that. She had loads of friends, but she studied too hard. She did that in high school and kept it up in college. I had hoped that when I made my millions—and then billions—she would relax a bit, but if anything she just intensified her work ethic. I think she was trying to compete with me. Stupid really, because my parents never played favorites and she had nothing to prove."

"We all just want to make our parents happy."

Matthew smiled. "Yeah, that's true. When you make a billion dollars, your only thought is how happy they would be if you make two billion. Anyway, DataStore had a particularly good year and the company threw a massive party. I pleaded with Rachel to come along for a few hours and finally she relented. There was a big test the next day—every test was a big test to her—but she agreed to show her face."

"I shudder to think how messy those parties get. All those young men with too much to drink must mean a lot of work for the cleaners the next day."

"Yeah, that's about right. As soon as Rachel arrived she was ready to leave again, but after about an hour I saw her getting into the spirit of things. She has the same awful taste in music as you, so when Taylor Swift started playing she got up to dance. I tried my best to keep an eye on her, but people kept dragging me away and introducing me to important strangers I would never see again. A few hours later I went looking for her, but was told she had left. With a guy. I actually laughed when someone told me. I pictured a guy thinking he was going to get lucky and Rachel saying goodbye to him without so much as a kiss on the cheek. She was completely oblivious to how attractive she was to guys."

I had a horrible feeling I knew where the story was going. This had all the signs of a sexual assault, but if that were the case wouldn't Matthew have mentioned it when I told him about my past?

"Did he... attack her?" I asked.

"He tried," Matthew replied. "He 'escorted' her to her apartment and then made his move. He didn't stop when she said no."

I had my hand over my mouth and could barely breath. I'd heard stories like this too many times at the meetings. Everyone's story was different but there were common threads in all of them.

"What happened?" I asked, although I was fairly sure I knew.

"She killed him," Matthew replied. "He tried to rape her and she killed him."

Chapter Twelve

She killed him? Matthew's sister had killed someone who tried to rape her? My initial reaction was "good for her," but I didn't dare say that out loud. Rapists had it coming to them, but Matthew did not look pleased at the outcome. He said they hadn't spoken in a while. Was she in prison?

"What happened?" I asked.

"He made his move, but she rejected him. Apparently it was almost playful at first, but then he started grabbing her and getting violent. They were in the kitchen and she reached for the only thing to hand; a knife. The wound wasn't that deep by all accounts, but it struck an artery. He died before the medics could arrive."

"Did she get in trouble?"

"No," Matthew said, with a shake of the head. "There was plenty of evidence supporting her version of events. Bruises on the skin for example, and some of the neighbors overheard what happened."

How did I not know about any of this? Amanda and I had done a number of searches for Matthew online and had never come across any story about his sister.

"How did you keep it quiet?" I asked.

"That wasn't too difficult. Some of the police officers botched the investigation and treated her like a criminal. When the true story came out it was in the interest of all parties, including the dead guy's family, to keep the events under wraps."

"Where is she now?"

"She's in law school actually," Matthew replied, the smile of a proud brother appearing on his face. "The fiasco of her initial arrest inspired her to go. She wants to become a public defender."

"That's brilliant. You must be really proud."

"I am," he said, although he did not sound at all certain. "There's no money in that career mind you, but she's less materialistic than I am anyway."

"I'm sure you can help her out financially," I said, thinking how easy it would be for Matthew to get his little sister set up for life.

I was surprised to see him shake his head. "I wish I could, but she won't accept my money. She insists on going it alone. We still speak occasionally, but it's strained. I think she partly blames me for the whole thing."

"Because you encouraged her to live a little?"

"Partly. Also because the guy was one of my employees. I brought him into our lives."

"That's silly," I said, giving Matthew's hand a squeeze. "I have some idea of what your sister went through and I can tell you one thing; she will get past this. There's nothing to forgive you for—she's just mad and confused right now. By the time she's finished law school this will all be over."

"I wish I could believe you, but you should see how she looks at me now. It's not hatred, but there's a constant sadness there whenever she is around me."

I rested my head on Matthew's shoulder and he rested his head on mine. We just sat there in silence for fifteen minutes. Nothing needed to be said; we were just there for each other.

I had almost drifted off to sleep when Matthew lifted his head from mine. The muscles in his shoulders tensed under my cheekbones and his grip on my hand tightened.

"Everything okay?" I asked, not opening my eyes.

"I know," Matthew said quietly. "I know who told Craig about you liking manga and coming from a poor family."

"Who?" I asked, opening my eyes and lifting my head up from his shoulder. I had to blink a few times to clear the sleep from my eyes. Naps always ended up making me feel more tired afterwards than I had been before them.

"Shit, this is all my fault. I don't understand yet, but it has to be her."

"Who?" I asked again impatiently.

"Rebecca. The woman I came home with the day I first met you. She's the one responsible for all of this."

Rebecca? I'd forgotten all about her. I'm not sure whether it was because of the hangover I was suffering from that morning or just my brain trying to block out the embarrassment, but I had barely thought about that morning at all since it happened. Once Matthew and I became an item it didn't seem so important any more.

"I thought she was just a one-night stand," I said eventually.

Matthew shook his head. "Not exactly. Didn't you ever wonder why we both came home at seven in the morning?"

"I've tried not to think about it too much to be honest. But yes, I remember you being in an immaculate suit and she looked like she was dressed for the Oscars."

"We weren't hooking up," Matthew said. "She's not my type at all."

"She's stunningly beautiful. How can she not be your type?"

"Quite frankly, she's a nightmare to be around. Rebecca treats people like dirt, especially those with

245

less money than her—which is most people—and I couldn't wait to be rid of her."

"But I remember how offended she was to see me in your bed. She said something about how you were planning a threesome with me and her."

Matthew smiled. "Yeah, that was a lie. She panicked because we weren't supposed to be seen together and that was all she could think of."

"So you brought her back to your apartment, but you weren't going to sleep with her. What were you going to do?"

"We had just come back from a business trip on a red-eye. We couldn't talk in public so she came back here to iron out a few final details."

I couldn't hide how pleased I was to hear that Rebecca was not one of Matthew's former flings. She was intimidatingly gorgeous to look at and I felt Matthew looked better with her on his arm than me.

"As pleased as I am to hear all this," I said, "why would Rebecca know those things about me and why would she tell Craig?"

"Rebecca is the owner of VirtualCore."

"That company you kept telling me to join?"

Matthew nodded. "Rebecca and I have been talking about a possible merger between our two companies recently. At first it seemed like a great deal, but I've been suspicious for a while. Her company is huge and it makes little sense that she would want to merge. I think she's up to something, but I don't know what?"

"I'm glad I didn't go and work for her," I said.

"Yeah, good job you never listen to me."

"How did she know about me liking manga and about my family?" I asked. Matthew had explained a lot, but I still didn't feel any closer to knowing what was going on.

"Well, you gave her a good viewing of the tattoo when you dropped the towel," Matthew said, as his finger circled the inside of my thigh where the tattoo was under my pants.

"Oh yeah," I said with a grin. I didn't feel nearly as embarrassed about flashing Rebecca know I knew she was only a business associate of Matthew's. "What about my family?"

"That is still a mystery, but this whole thing has Rebecca's fingerprints all over it and I'm going to figure out what the hell she's up to."

"*We're* going to figure it out," I said. "If this woman has been fucking with my life I want to find out why."

Chapter Thirteen

That night I slept for a solid ten hours for the first time in years. Partly that was due to sheer exhaustion—going to bed with Matthew always left me with little energy by the time we were actually ready to go to sleep—but my mind also felt more at ease. I felt frustrated thinking about how Rebecca—a woman I barely knew—was trying to sabotage my work and personal relationships, but that was more than canceled out by the good news from that talk with Matthew.

By confiding in me about his sister he explained a lot more about his behavior than he probably realized. It had always seemed unusual to me that a guy who was so modern and liberal would be so concerned at me sleeping with strangers once a year. He didn't seem like the type to judge someone for having casual sex. Now I knew why. He wasn't judging me, he was just legitimately concerned for my safety and after what happened with his sister how could I blame him.

Matthew had seen what could happen in extreme circumstances and he didn't want to see history repeat itself. Deep down I think he knew that his approach was illogical, but logic has a funny way of seeming irrelevant where people we care about are concerned. After all, sleeping with a stranger on the anniversary of my rape is hardly logical, so I wasn't about to be overly judgmental.

Matthew left for work in the morning, but he was happy for me to hang out at his place for as long as I wanted. He even gave me express permission to snoop around, although he needn't have bothered because I was going to anyway. His playroom—I still sniggered at the name—contained an impressive mixture of fitness equipment and video games. There was a surround system in place which must make this the go-to place for movie nights among his friends.

There wasn't a lot else that I hadn't already seen. Matthew was frustratingly tidy and organized and despite his huge apartment he lived a very minimalistic lifestyle. Apparently when you have enough money to buy whatever you want it's easier to exercise a degree of control. The one place in the apartment where my jealousy really kicked in was the closet. Or rather *closets*. They were huge walk-in spaces which—in my opinion—were wasted just being used for boring suits. The space for shoes was largely unused; I would have to change that if I started spending more time here.

After I had seen everything there was to see, I settled down at my laptop to do some work. I wasn't in the mood to be overly productive so I wasted time browsing through all my bookmarked websites until I was confident that I was up-to-date on everything there was to know. Just when I thought I was out of ways to waste time, I decided to see how Matthew's sister was getting on at law school.

If she was like every other law school student she would have a well-developed professional profile to show herself off to potential employers when they did the inevitable background check that was now common-place in most professional industries. According to Matthew, she now went by her mother's maiden name in an attempt to disassociate herself with Matthew. I could tell he was hurt by that, but he seemed to understand. She wouldn't be treated like a normal student if everyone knew she had a billionaire brother and from what I had heard, law school was tough enough without people thinking you were a spoiled rich kid.

Rachel certainly had been busy the last couple of years. While in college she had joined a number of societies aimed at providing legal services to the poor and was part of a project to provide legal aid to inmates on death row. I didn't notice any particular affiliation to domestic abuse groups though; her focus seemed more aligned with ensuring everyone had access to legal representation. Right now her resume looked perfect for a job as a public defender and based on what Matthew had told me, that was her dream job.

Rachel attended law school in New York which Matthew believed was another attempt to put as much distance between the two of them as possible, although the law school was ranked as one of the best in the country. Sure, she could have gone to Stanford, but other than that, most of the best law schools were on the East Coast.

Nothing I saw about Rachel contradicted what Matthew had told me which validated my decision to place my complete trust in him. I hadn't been looking for anything to the contrary, but I was still pleased to see he had told me the entire truth. Even knowing her full name, there was little information I could find online about the incident which led to Rachel killing her attacker. She might not be close to her brother anymore, but he had definitely done her a huge favor there; one day she would hopefully appreciate what he had done for her.

Once I had read all there was to read about Rachel, I went to the kitchen to make some coffee and grab a snack. Now I had no excuse not to start working. I waited until the coffee was cool enough for me to take a sip and then got some caffeine into my system. The snack bar provided protein for natural energy. I didn't need any of it; after ten hours sleep I had more than enough energy, but the chemicals tricked my mind into getting some work done.

No sooner had my fingers touched the keys on the keyboard than my phone rang. It was Matthew.

"Hey what's up?" I asked, placing the phone on speaker, and relaxing back into the chair.

"I can't stop thinking about Rebecca," Matthew said.

"That's not really something I want to hear darling," I joked.

"Not like that," Matthew replied seriously. "I don't know what is going on and I hate being in the dark."

"Why don't we just ask her?" It seemed like the best way to find out, although everything I knew about Rebecca suggested she would just lie to us.

"I don't want to approach her without any information. She'll just spin us a load of BS and then we'll look like idiots."

"Well, what do you propose?" There was silence on the other end of the phone. "Matthew?"

"I can't believe I'm going to say this, but I don't think we have any other choice. I've already called his secretary to set up a meeting. Meet me by the ITC building tonight at seven o'clock. We're going to have a meeting with Craig."

Chapter Fourteen

"Don't you think this is all a little over-dramatic?" I asked Matthew, as we waited for Craig in the corner of a loud and dark dive bar.

I was supposed to meet Matthew by ITC, but he and Craig had exchanged a few messages and agreed to meet at a sleazy bar instead to avoid being seen. I neglected to mention to Matthew that this bar was the same one I had been in when I hooked up with his friend James. From where we sat I could see the table where James had first made his move. I'd insisted on leaving when his hand had been so far up my leg his fingers were grazing against my panties.

Now I was in here with Matthew and would have loved to get a little frisky with a man who knew what he was doing. Matthew, however, was too caught up in avoiding eye contact with the handful of people who were in the bar this early in the evening.

"We need to be somewhere no-one will recognize us," Matthew said. "Places like coffee shops are full of software engineers and there's a good chance we will be spotted. This place on the other hand, well I can't imagine many of my employees coming here, put it that way. It's also loud, so we won't be overheard."

"Is it that bad if people think you and Craig might be friends who can hold down a civilized conversation?"

"Yes. An impromptu meeting like this could cause a huge swing in our stock price. All it takes is one person to see this meeting and report it to a technology website and before you know it there will be rumors swirling around about mergers and the like. That will in turn affect our stock price. It's serious stuff."

I doubted a couple of friends having a drink could cause that many problems, but perhaps I was just being naïve. Either way, I didn't want to have that particular argument right now.

"Here he is," I said, pointing to the door and giving Craig a quick wave so that he could see where we were sat.

"Matthew," Craig said with a nod as he sat at our table.

"Craig," Matthew replied, returning the nod.

I rolled my eyes, although in the dim light of the bar I doubted either of them could see it.

"Hello Amy, I wasn't expecting you to be here as well."

"Hi Craig. Matthew should have told you I was coming. It's kind of about me as well."

"Okay," Craig said, calling over a waiter to order some drinks.

We kept the conversation to pleasantries while waiting for the beers to arrive which meant I had to do most of the talking because Matthew and Craig were incapable of being pleasant towards each other. Craig was genuinely interested in how I had been getting on and I could tell he was still racked with guilt for what had happened with Chad.

"I don't know if this helps," Craig said, "but I have made sure Chad is swamped with work. That guy has not left the office before ten o'clock in the evening since I found out what happened between you two. I know it's not much, but I take some moderate satisfaction from it."

"Me too," I said, as the waitress brought our beers. "Thank you."

"Okay, let's get down to business shall we?" Matthew asked after taking a long sip of his beer.

"Yes, let's do that," Craig said. "If you just want to lay into me for hiring Chad then go ahead, but I promise you I feel bad enough as it is about that."

"We know you've been getting information from Rebecca," Matthew said, ignoring Craig's comment. "She has been feeding you information about Amy, but I'm confused as to *why* she would do that?"

Craig didn't respond immediately and seemed to be weighing up whether or not to come clean. He took another long swig of his beer and went to rest his arms on the table before noticing how sticky it was and thinking better of it.

"How do you know?" Craig asked.

"You knew I liked manga and that my parents were poor. I keep that information close to my chest. Rebecca knew about the manga thing—I won't say how—and I think she might have known about my family as well."

Craig grimaced and nodded. "Yeah, she fed me that information. She's been feeding me information on you ever since that first time we met in the pitch presentation."

"She was the one who convinced you to withdraw the job offer," I said, as that piece of the puzzle finally clicked into place.

"Yes, that was her doing. I won't bother repeating what she said, because it was a lie anyway, but she recommended I withdraw the offer. She was then the one who convinced me to offer you a job after you left DataStore."

"Are you two fucking?" Matthew asked bluntly. I slapped him on the arm, but he didn't even seem to feel it.

"No, we certainly are not. She tried to initiate something, but I don't want that woman anywhere near my personal life."

"But you don't mind if she gets involved in your business affairs?" Matthew asked.

"She seemed to be helping at first."

"At first?" I asked. "She's not anymore?"

Craig shrugged. "She doesn't get the chance. I've stopped returning her calls. After that thing with Chad I want nothing to do with her. She's the reason I hired him. The two of them worked together at some point and Rebecca said he was a genius. Apparently she wanted to hire him herself, but couldn't because there was a conflict of interest."

"This is too weird," I said. "Why has she been leaking all this information to you about me? I don't see what purpose it serves."

"I have an idea," Matthew said quietly, barely audible among the noise blaring from the bar's lousy speakers. "I'm going to say something and you cannot spread a word of it outside this room."

Craig nodded. "You have my word."

"Rebecca and I have been talking a lot lately. About business," he added, when he caught me glaring at him. He looked around to make sure no-one was within earshot even though someone would need to be sat at the table to hear what was being said. "Rebecca has proposed a merger of VirtualCore with DataStore."

Craig raised his eyebrows and leaned back in his chair, clearly stunned at the news. He moved forward about to respond, but then closed his mouth and leaned back again.

"I have to admit, I was tempted by her proposal. Her offer would have generated quite the windfall for our shareholders and was incredibly generous. Knowing what I know now though, she can get stuffed. I'm not risking my business and employees by merging with her company."

A merger between DataStore and VirtualCore would have created one of the biggest companies in the world. ITC would have been left in the dust. Those two companies would have been able to destroy any competition put in front of them.

"I don't know what to say," Craig said when he finally spoke.

"Like I said, I'm not going through with it."

"No, of course not. She was playing you Matthew. There was never a deal on the cards. She never planned to merge her company with yours."

"Jealousy is not an admirable quality Craig," Matthew said with a smug grin that I planned to admonish him for in private. "I assure you her offer was genuine."

"No Matthew, it wasn't."

"Why do you say that?" I asked. Craig had a certainty about his voice that did not sound like jealousy.

"Because there was a reason Rebecca was feeding me all that information. She wanted ITC to get an edge over DataStore and she thought Amy could help with that."

I sincerely doubted one person could make any difference in huge companies like ITC and DataStore, but it fit in with Rebecca's weird obsession over me.

"And why would she want to help ITC?" Matthew asked.

"Because she has proposed a merger of VirtualCore and ITC," Craig said. "While she was negotiating with you she was doing the same with me. She's been playing us all along."

Matthew banged his fist down on the table, shaking the glasses and snapping me out of my confused gaze.

"What next?" I asked Matthew.

"I don't like being played for an idiot. Let's go speak to Rebecca."

Chapter Fifteen

If I had let Matthew have his way he would have gone straight to see Rebecca right there and then. In the mood he was in, that seemed like a terrible idea and Craig agreed. We both convinced him to take some time to calm down and set up a meeting for a few days later.

Apparently Matthew wasn't in the mood to go into work either so he insisted I pack a small bag with clothes while he whisked me away for a few nights. We were traveling by car, so I had assumed we were going down to Monterey again to spend some time on the boat, but when I saw signs for Nevada it became fairly obvious Monterey was not our intended destination.

"We aren't going to Vegas are we?" I asked, trying not to sound ungrateful. "I'm not a huge fan of that place."

"That makes two of us," Matthew replied. "I guess I can tell you, because it will become obvious soon enough. We're going to Lake Tahoe. I have a cabin there and it is gorgeous at this time of year."

I loved Lake Tahoe. I'd been once before when my college organized a ski trip during winter. I had always wanted to go skiing, but it was an expensive hobby and far beyond the reach of my family. When organized through college it had been a little cheaper and I had student loans to spend, so I splashed out on some equipment and the basic ski passes. By the end of the four day trip I could just about move around in the skis, although I was far from competent.

Lake Tahoe during the summer couldn't have been more different than in the winter. The place was barely recognizable. There was no snow to be seen—even on the peaks of the mountains—and people were sat around in shorts and t-shirts having picnics and soaking up the sun.

Matthew looked instantly more relaxed as soon as we walked into his cabin, which was located just outside of the areas populated by tourists. He forget all the work issues and problems with Rebecca that had been weighing him down since yesterday's meeting with Craig.

The cabin was secluded enough to be romantic, but didn't feel completely in the middle of nowhere either. With the log fire and rug in the middle of the floor, it looked just like you would imagine a log cabin in the woods to look like—except without the stuffed animal heads on the walls.

"I hope you like barbecue food," Matthew said, as he dragged some coal outside and dumped it beside a large grill.

"I do usually," I replied. "But I'm slightly nervous because it looks like you are going to be the one cooking it."

"This isn't cooking, it's grilling. Grilling I can handle."

He wasn't exaggerating. Watching Matthew grill ribs was worth the trip up here by itself. The sun was still beating down so Matthew removed his shirt while I lay on a chair with a glass of wine, staring at his chest as it glistened in the summer sun. I had no idea what I had done to deserve this, but I fully intended to enjoy the moment while it lasted.

The smell of the meat and spicy marinade made the wait agonizing. Once the food was on a plate in front of me I wasted no time in stripping the meat off the bones with my teeth.

"That is so sexy," Matthew remarked. I hadn't noticed he had been watching me eat. "I love a woman who isn't afraid to get her hands dirty."

We stayed outside for a few hours after eating with me snuggled up on Matthew's lap while we watched the sunset.

"Not that I want to spoil the mood or anything," I said, "but you have the grill, fireplace, sunsets and everything else a girl could want up here. It's impossible to resist. Is this where you would bring women if you ever had trouble 'sealing the deal?' "

"Nope," Matthew replied. I gave him a disbelieving look. "It's true. I've never had trouble sealing the deal, so didn't need this place. In fact, you are the first woman I have ever brought up here. The first person, period. This cabin was always supposed to just be for me. A place of seclusion for when I just needed to get away from it all."

"Then why am I here?"

"You know why you're here, Amy."

"Because you want to make me feel better after everything that has been happening lately?"

"I do, but no, that's not the reason you are here."

"You feel guilty about Rebecca messing me around?"

"Nope, although I do feel a little guilty about that. Mainly just angry with her, but yes, slightly guilty as well."

"So why bring me here?" I asked. I felt sure this was some trick or that he had been keeping another secret from me and this was all part of some plan to butter me up.

"I thought it would be obvious by now, Amy."

"It's not."

"What do you *think* makes you different from all the other women I have dated?"

I thought for a few moments. There were lots of differences. I wasn't glamorous. I wasn't after Matthew for his money. I never wore elegant dresses.

"You first met me when I was lying naked in your bed," I said at last.

Matthew laughed. "Yes, that is true. That morning seems like an eternity ago now. I must admit, I didn't see this coming. But that's not what makes you different from all the rest. Amy, I never loved any of those other women. Never even close. But I love you."

I felt light-headed and put the wine down before I dropped the glass. My stomach clenched up tight and my heart was fluttering in my chest. I didn't realize a heart could beat so fast and I wasn't sure it was healthy, but there was little I could do about it. *I love you.* I'd never heard anyone say those words to me. I'd dreamed of hearing them, but even in my imagination I couldn't have pictured a moment as blissful as this one.

"Amy?" Matthew asked looking concerned. "Are you okay?"

I tried to speak, but my mouth was too dry and I just made a strange noise instead.

"I shouldn't have said anything," Matthew said. "You don't have to say it back. We can just—"

"I love you too." The words came out much easier than I thought they would. When I switched off my brain and just spoke the words they came as easily and naturally as ordering a drink in a bar.

"Let's go inside," Matthew said, standing and lifting me up in his arms as he did so.

He carried me inside like a bride on her wedding night and placed me down on the bed. I lay on the silk bedspread as he stripped me and kissed every inch of my naked body.

"Let me just go get a condom," he said, standing by the bed with his erect penis eager to enter me.

I shook my head. "We don't need one. I'm on the pill and I trust you."

"Are you sure?"

I nodded and pulled Matthew down onto the bed. He went to lay between my legs, but I pushed him down onto his back and straddled his groin. My pussy was wet and ready to take his length inside me. I held his shaft in my hand and maneuvered the head against my opening, before sliding myself down so that he filled my insides. The feeling of his flesh against mine without the thin plastic barrier was surreal and I came quicker than ever. Matthew grabbed my thighs and we both rocked in a slow and steady motion, never taking our eyes off each other until he finally dug his fingers into my skin as he came hard.

His essence filled my sex and I felt more complete, more whole, than I ever had done before. I collapsed down on top of him, resting my head on his chest, and didn't move all night.

Chapter Sixteen

I was starting to get used to these secretive meetings and maybe even enjoying them as well. Once again, Matthew insisted on meeting in a location that would provide a degree of cover and allow him to blend into the background. I tried explaining to Matthew that he was not the type of guy who could easily blend into the background, especially with women around, and eventually he agreed to rent an office space for the meeting instead of using some sleazy dive bar.

Matthew didn't do things by half measures, so the office space was located on one of the top floors of a skyscraper providing glorious views over the city. The office was empty with not even a chair in sight, so Matthew and I had to stand around waiting for Rebecca like we were in a spy film.

"Isn't this all a little dramatic, Matthew dear," Rebecca said as she walked into the office. "We could have just met at my office, no-one would have—"

She froze when she saw me. "Hello, Rebecca."

There was a long pause while Rebecca tried to regain some composure. "Do I know you?" she asked.

Her face looked stern, but her voice carried little conviction.

"Don't play games, Rebecca," Matthew said. "I've had quite enough of them."

"Oh yes," Rebecca said, "I remember you. You were that naked slut in Matthew's bed. Good lord, Matthew, don't tell me you've ended up dating this thing. I know you are no angel yourself, but I reckon this one's been around the block a few times even by your standards."

I knew Matthew would never hit a woman, but looking at the white knuckles on his balled fists, I could tell he wanted to right now. I wanted to hit her myself, but I needed to remain calm for Matthew. If he saw me losing my cool then he would want to protect me and this whole thing would unravel.

"You know who I am," I said. "You know a lot about me actually. You know I like manga and you know that Chad raped me when I was in college. You also know that my family is poor, although I must admit to being a bit confused as to how you know that. Care to share the details?"

Rebecca's face remained stern for a few more seconds before it finally soured and she crumbled before our eyes.

"Why, Rebecca?" Matthew asked, when she remained silent.

"I'm just trying to help this deal go smoother between us," she confessed. "That's all."

"I don't believe you," I said. "If that was the case then why all the focus on me."

"Oh I'm sorry, dear, did you think you were some special snowflake? This has nothing to do with you. You just put your naked body in the middle of it."

"I don't understand."

"No, I don't suppose you do. Look, when you showed up in Matthew's apartment I was confused and I panicked. I had you followed and when I found out you were going to be pitching your business to Matthew I

263

knew the opportunity was too good to pass up. Originally I wanted you to work for Matthew. I figured it would prove a nice distraction."

"Which is why you fed false information to Craig so that he wouldn't hire me. And then you decided it would be even more distracting for all concerned if I went to work for Craig so you helped him lure me in."

"I admit, I made mistakes."

"How did you know about my family?" I asked.

"You spoke about it at one of those pity meetings you go to."

"You spied on me?" I asked. I sounded surprised, but at this point I probably shouldn't have been. Rebecca had no apparent idea of what was right and wrong and I would wager she'd done a lot worse to get where she was today.

"I had a friend do it for me, but yes, that's about it. What gave the game away?" Rebecca asked.

"Chad," I replied. "That was one step too far."

"I don't know how you thought you'd get away with this, Rebecca," Matthew said, "but the deal is most definitely off. There will be no merger and I would be willing to bet Craig will feel the same way once I have spoken to him."

"What?" Rebecca yelled. She seemed genuinely surprised by the news that Matthew wouldn't want to continue with the deal. Rebecca was nothing if not confident in herself. "You can't do that. We're too far along. Do you have any idea how much I have spent trying to get the company ready for this deal?"

Matthew frowned but didn't say anything. Something wasn't quite right. Matthew's company, while huge by any normal comparison, was smaller than Rebecca's company. He had more to benefit from the deal than she did in theory.

"There's been something bothering me about this for a while," Matthew said, speaking slowly and calmly. "You've been far too eager to get this deal done. Why? Your company doesn't need DataStore."

Rebecca bit her lip and turned her eyes up to the ceiling before letting her head sink to face the floor. She took a deep breath and looked back to Matthew.

"We're in trouble," she said. "Nothing has been made public yet, but we are looking at some huge fines for overseas bribery issues and there's been a security breach. We can keep it quiet for a few months, but eventually news will get out.'

"Jesus, Rebecca, what were you playing at? How big a problem is this?" To his credit, Matthew sounded genuinely concerned although that was likely for the tens of thousands of employees that might lose their jobs if VirtualCore were to go under.

"I got in over my head. It's tough to get respect as a woman. I would lead meetings and find that men—my subordinates—were taking over the conversation because no-one thought I had anything to add. I had to start making big decisions to win people over."

"That's not how you bring about change," I said. "Now you are going to make people think women really can't lead technology companies. You've done more harm than good."

"Amy's right," Matthew said. "You have no excuse. Our deal is off."

"Don't do this, Matthew," she pleaded. The hard edge had returned to her voice. "You'll regret making me an enemy. I still have people I can turn to. If you reject me now, DataStore will be history within a year."

"Goodbye, Rebecca."

Rebecca gave a fleeting look in my direction as if I would stick up for her. I shook my head and she disappeared out the door.

"Now what?" I asked when she was in the elevator.

"Now we wait for her to make a mistake. It shouldn't take long."

Chapter Seventeen

"I hadn't expected her to be so desperate," I said to Matthew after Rebecca had left. "I knew she would be mad, but she *really* needed this deal."

"That took me by surprise as well," Matthew said, pulling out a laptop from his backpack. "But it makes sense. I should have known her offer to me was too generous. She must have been hoping the terms were so good I would take the bait with minimal due diligence."

Our plan to catch Rebecca out rested on getting her angry enough with us that she would go and speak to Craig to convince him to do a deal. Craig was ready for her and would record the entire conversation. With any luck she would say something she shouldn't and we would have enough evidence to report her to the Securities and Exchange Commission. Rebecca would likely avoid prison, but the fines would be substantial and she would never run a successful company again.

We had certainly managed to make her mad, but above that I think we had scared her as well and neither of us knew how she would react when scared.

"How long has it been now?" I asked. "Since she left?"

The office we had rented was only a five or ten minute walk from Craig's building. With any luck she would go straight there and say something stupid before she had time to regain her composure.

"Fifteen minutes," Matthew replied. "No need to panic yet. It'll take her a while to make it over to his office in those outrageous heels she's wearing."

"Good point." I sat down on the floor and played around with my phone to try and pass the time. It didn't work; I couldn't concentrate on anything else and neither could Matthew.

Thirty minutes passed. Why would it be taking her so long? If she has time to think things through then she might get away with everything she had done to me. I barely knew Rebecca but I knew enough to know I hated her with a passion.

Matthew's phone vibrated on the hard floor. "It's from Craig. Rebecca's just turned up at ITC and is being escorted up to his office now."

Matthew opened a few windows on his laptop and soon had a black and white video feed streaming a live image of what was going on right now inside Craig's office. We also had an excellent audio link courtesy of a microphone on Craig's desk. The microphone was always there because Craig liked to use voice-recognition technology so it shouldn't look too suspicious.

I felt voyeuristic watching Craig as he sat as his desk pretending to work. He knew we were watching him—it was Craig who set up the video feed in the first place—but it still felt odd until Craig gave a sly wink towards the camera. I even caught a smile on Matthew's face although it quickly disappeared when he remembered he supposedly hated Craig.

"Here we go," I said, as I saw Rebecca walk into Craig's office. Even on a black and white image she looked red-faced and angry. Craig acted concerned and sent an assistant to go get her some water.

Rebecca said something that we couldn't quite hear, so Matthew turned up the volume on his laptop.

"Why do we need Chad here?" Craig asked Rebecca.

"Because I'm not here to mess around today," Rebecca replied as she sat down on the chair opposite Craig's desk. She had such a strong physical presence that anyone would think it was her office, even though she was sat on the wrong side of the desk. "I want to talk numbers so let's get your finance guy in here."

Craig put a call through to Chad and asked him to come to his office.

"This is interesting," Matthew remarked. "Why is she bringing Chad into this?"

"Maybe it's to remind Craig who is in charge," I said. "She recommended Chad to Craig so this is a reminder of how well they could work together."

"Maybe," Matthew said, but he clearly didn't think I was right.

Neither did I, but I had a feeling Chad's presence would work in our favor unless Craig slipped up. I knew Craig hated the sight of Chad almost as much as I did so I just hoped he could keep cool and stick to the script. Chad walked into the office and took a seat next to Rebecca.

"I want to do a deal," Rebecca said. "Quite frankly, I'm getting tired of messing around. Let's agree on a number and our two companies can merge within the next month."

"A month!" Craig yelled, loud enough to make Matthew and I cringe and lean back from the laptop. "That's nowhere near enough time. The due diligence alone will take at least three months. Does your legal team know you are in here making this offer?"

"I don't have to get permission from my own employees. Unlike you, I run my company personally.

What I say goes. We can get this deal done in a month if we both have the desire."

"You'd have to make one hell of an offer," Craig said. "And even then I'd still have to think about it."

So far, things were going roughly as we expected, but Chad's presence had me worried. He hadn't said a word since he sat down and barely moved in his seat. He was a loose cannon, but I wasn't sure if that would work in our favor yet or not.

"Our two companies will merge," Rebecca said. "Same cash terms as before, but you will be a 49% shareholder in the newly created entity. We will buy out all the smaller shareholders, so it will just be me and you. I will hold the 51% of course."

"She's desperate," Matthew said. He spoke quietly as if they might be able to hear us. "That's a crazy offer based on the current stock prices; she's practically giving her company away."

Craig sat silent for a few moments. He had heard our entire conversation with Rebecca, so he wouldn't take the bait, but he had to act as surprised as he would have been if he didn't know.

"ITC doesn't need this deal," Craig said finally. "We're in a strong position; never been better in fact. Your offer is incredibly generous, but I have enough money as it is and could do without the stress. Chad, since you're here, tell Rebecca how strong our financials are."

Chad turned to Rebecca. "The company is..." He paused and turned back to Craig. I could barely see Chad's face but I knew he was grinning. "The company is still going strong in some historical sectors, but it is bleeding money in research and development for products that are unlikely to ever succeed."

"Chad, what the hell are you doing?" Craig said, raising his voice and clenching his fists as if he were mad.

"It's working," Matthew said. "Chad's going to play right into our hands."

269

I went to speak, but closed my mouth so I could hear Chad continue his speech.

"He's going to have to accept our offer," Chad said to Rebecca. "The company's share price is only going down from here."

"*Our* offer?" Craig said, doing a great job of looking bemused. "What are you doing, Chad?"

"Didn't you get the least bit suspicious when I placed him right into your lap?" Rebecca asked. "He's been reporting back to me all this time. You even kept him busy with extra work, so he obtained a phenomenal amount of data in a short space of time. Didn't you dear?"

Rebecca turned to Chad and placed a hand on his as she leant over and appeared to kiss his cheek. The image wasn't clear, but whatever they did made Craig grimace.

"You placed a spy in my finance department and stole my data?" Craig asked.

"Yes, and it wasn't even particularly difficult. You're too trustworthy, Craig."

"Do you think that's enough?" Craig said, raising his voice.

"What?" Rebecca asked. "Who are you talking to?"

Matthew pressed a button on his computer and spoke into the built-in microphone. "That's more than enough. We've got her. And Chad. They're both going down."

There was a slight delay as the message was fed through to Craig's speakers and I heard some of Matthew's speech come back to us through the laptop. Rebecca recognized Matthew's voice instantly. She might be a lot of things, but she wasn't stupid. She put the pieces together in seconds but before she could leave Craig's office his security team was in there to take her and Chad away.

"What happens now?" I asked.

"Honestly, I don't really know. But they will be punished, you don't have to worry about that."

"We did it," I said, wrapping my arms around Matthew's neck. "After all these years, Chad is finally going to pay for what he did to me."

"How does it feel?" Matthew asked.

"You know how some people say revenge feels empty and isn't worth it? They're lying. This feels great. It's the second best feeling I've ever known."

"What's the best?"

"This," I said, as I opened my legs and pulled Matthew down on top of me.

Chapter Eighteen

The weeks following our nail-biting operation to catch Rebecca in the act were a huge anticlimax. Rebecca and Chad weren't arrested because there wasn't enough evidence yet for criminal charges. That would probably happen later down the line when the SEC had finished its investigation. They weren't allowed to leave the country though and the internet was abuzz with discussion of the investigation.

Matthew spent more time at work than I would have liked. He explained that ever since Rebecca had first proposed the merger he had been distracted at work and hadn't been on top of things as much as he should have been. Apparently I hadn't helped matters either, although I liked to think I had served as a more pleasant distraction.

I used the time to finally get my business off the ground. Unlike all my previous attempts, I actually succeeded. Once I had put my mind to the problems I faced they turned out to be far from insurmountable. Matthew encouraged me not to focus on getting things perfect and to start asking for users to test the program and see how it worked. Amanda's friend Emily helped put me in touch with women who were sympathetic to my cause and would test the product. They weren't victims of abuse, so I felt comfortable having them test the program's security features. Emily even promised to pay some friends of hers to hack into the system—or try at least—and report back on any vulnerabilities.

With Matthew's help, I came to terms with the realization that the software was never going to set the world alight, but that was fine. In fact, that was preferable. It was best that no-one knew about the software until the moment they needed to use it. If I could stay under the radar then that would be best for all concerned.

One evening, I was about to leave my apartment to go see Matthew when I received a message telling me to head to a bar instead. The message was short and to the point, but that was just the way Matthew seemed to communicate over texts. The bar was nearby so I headed straight over there and asked to be taken to Matthew. I had long since stopped looking for him in bars, because he would always be secluded in some VIP area. Sure enough, he was tucked away in a corner behind a velvet rope when I met him. This time, he was not alone.

"Craig, hi," I said, kissing Matthew and sitting down beside him. "I wasn't expecting to see you here."

"It came as a bit of a surprise to me as well," Craig replied. Whatever the surprise was he was clearly happy about it judging by the smile on his face.

"I got some news today," Matthew said. "From a contact at the SEC. This won't be made public for weeks yet so you can't say anything."

"Is this about Rebecca and Chad?" I asked eagerly, as if it could be anything else.

Matthew nodded. "They're going to sign a plea agreement."

"Oh," I said, disappointed. "So they're going to pay a fine and get away with it?"

"Not in the slightest," Matthew continued. "They will both be spending some time in prison for what they did. Rebecca will serve a year behind bars, but Chad will get three months as well."

"Chad was not involved in any of the overseas corruption activities," Craig explained. "That's why he isn't facing such a hefty prison sentence."

"He also gets off lightly with the fines," Matthew said, "but that's because he doesn't have as much money. However, I can assure you, his career is ruined. No self-respecting business will touch him. His only skills are in finance and he won't be working there in the near future. The SEC is restricting what positions he can hold in companies. If you ever see him again—and I hope to God you don't—he will be serving you fast food. And that's if he gets lucky."

"Wow, that's...I don't know what to say." A smile took over my face and I felt deliriously happy, but for some reason I broke down in tears and cried on Matthew's shoulder. Matthew had already seen my cry, but Craig hadn't. I felt like an idiot, but I couldn't help it.

"Amy? Are you okay?" Matthew asked, running his fingers through my hair.

I nodded into his shoulder, but a minute passed before I was able to sit up and wipe my eyes dry. "I'm sorry, I don't know what came over me. I just... I never expected Chad to get any kind of punishment. It feels like he is finally being punished for what he did to me. I know he's not, but I'm going to pretend he is anyway."

"People like him always get what's coming to them Amy," Craig said. "You handled yourself impeccably this entire time and this is your reward. Nothing will ever bring back what he took from you, but hopefully this heals some of the damage."

"Actually," I said, looking up into Matthew's eyes, "I'm feeling better than ever. And thank you Craig for all your help with this."

"Yeah, thanks," Matthew grunted. The words had to be forced out, but they were sincere. Craig nodded at

Matthew and raised his glass slightly in a gesture of appreciation.

"You two are practically best friends now then," I joked.

"Are you going to tell her or shall I?" Craig said to Matthew.

"Tell me what?" I asked.

"Craig and I have been here for a few hours discussing business," Matthew said. "With VirtualCore facing some troubling times ahead, we thought maybe now would be a good time to consider a merger between ITC and DataStore."

"You're kidding?" I asked. "That would be amazing. I can't even imagine how powerful that company would become. What would you call it? Oh, can I help name the new company?"

"No," Matthew said firmly. "I'm afraid not."

"We *talked* about merging," Craig said, "but ultimately decided it would be a bad idea."

"Nonsense," I said. "The two companies compliment each other perfectly. You are practically a textbook case for a merger. I can't think of a reason why the two of you wouldn't go ahead and do it except for the fact that you both fight like a couple of..." I trailed off as I saw the grin on Craig's face.

"We decided it's much more fun to have a friendly rivalry," Craig said. "A bit of competition keeps us on our toes."

"I do like the distraction of having to worry about a competitor," Matthew said. "If you can call ITC a competitor. More like an occasional nuisance really."

I rolled my eyes and let out a loud sigh that would have been heard by others in the bar even over the noise of the music. "If your face weren't so good damn pleasant to look at," I said to Matthew, "I would knock both your heads together. You're like a couple of kids."

I tried my best to convince the two of them to change their minds, but soon gave up. I had no chance of succeeding and I wasn't sure I wanted to. Listening to

Matthew and Craig bad-mouth each other it was obvious that they both needed this and if Matthew was happy then so was I.

And I *was* happy. For the first time since Chad had raped me in college I was happy without any reservations. I'd been happy when I graduated college or whenever I was with Matthew, but there had always been something there in the back of mind. Something dark, that sat in the corner waiting to reappear when I least expected it. Not anymore. I was happy and so long as I had Matthew, I couldn't foresee a day when that wasn't true.

Epilogue

"I can't believe this is our last night together," Amanda said, as we tapped our glasses of wine together in a toast. In a strange twist of fate, Amanda had chosen the same dive bar that I had hooked up with James in and where Matthew and I had met with Craig. For some reason, this horrid bar was home to many important moments of my life.

"I'm only moving out," I said. "It's not like we're never going to see each other again. I'm not even leaving the city."

"I know, I know, but it's so easy to lose touch. I'm going to be busy with work and I can't imagine you will ever want to leave the house when you have Matthew around to keep you amused."

"I think I can tear myself out of the bedroom once a month to meet you for drinks," I joked. "It is a little odd though. I've never lived with a man before. What if he has lots of bad habits?"

"This is Matthew. I can't imagine a habit so bad that it would make you want to leave him. Seriously though, are you worried this is all happening a little too fast?"

I only needed a few seconds to think before answering. It was a question I had asked myself many times already. "No, I don't think so. I know it is quick compared to a lot of people, but we went through more in those first few months than most couples do in five years. We're going to be just fine."

"You remember what I said about his friends?"

"Yes, Amanda. I will endeavor to meet as many of his friends as possible and warm them up to the idea of dating a journalist. Do you really want to date some billionaire though?"

Amanda glared at me as if I had just asked her whether the sky was really blue.

"Alright," I said, holding up my hands in defeat. "I'll be on the lookout. Most of them are probably jerks, but if I find a nice one I will try to reel him in."

"That's all I ask. Speaking of good-looking billionaires; yours is here to pick you up."

I looked behind me and saw Matthew approaching. All the women in bar turned their heads to watch him walk past; I still hadn't gotten used to that.

"Hi, honey," he said, kissing me on the cheek. "Evening, Amanda. You girls ready to leave? I have the car waiting outside."

"I know I was supposed to go back to yours tonight, but would you mind if I stayed with Amanda? It's only proper that I spend one last night in the apartment."

"I suppose," Matthew grumbled. "I'll have the driver drop you both off at your old place then." He leaned down to whisper into my ear. "You better not have any plans for tomorrow," he said softly. "Because I have plans for you."

I bit my lip and tried to hide my grin, but Amanda saw it. We carried on drinking when we got home and didn't stop until we exhausted our supply and crashed out on the sofa.

—

"I'm going to be home late tonight," I explained to Matthew at lunchtime. "I'm going to a meeting tonight and it won't end until eight."

After moving in with Matthew I couldn't imagine life would ever get any better and I was tempted to stop going to meetings. It felt wrong to watch other people suffer when my life was so good, but I knew that was what I had to do.

When I had been at my lowest, other women had been there to pick me up. They didn't just listen to my problems; they showed me there was a way out. That if I kept going my life could pick up and get back to some sense of normality. Now it was my turn to repay the favor. It sounded arrogant, but I could serve as inspiration to some of those women and I owed it to them to try.

There had been false dawns before, but this time I knew I had turned a corner for real. I would never go back to being frightened. I would never need to fuck a stranger on July 26th just to feel in control of my body.

Matthew had been incredibly supportive. I knew he wanted to be the one I spoke to about all my problems, but he understood how important those meetings were to me.

"I'll have dinner waiting for you when you return," Matthew said. "Let me know if you stay late and need a ride home."

"Thanks." I was about to say goodbye and hang up when something else occurred to me. Something that, for the first time, felt completely natural. "Matthew?"

"Yes?" He sounded suspicious.

"I want you to come with me. To the meeting."

There was a long pause and I checked my phone to make sure he was still on the line.

"Are you sure?" he asked finally.

"I'm sure. I want you to be there in the audience when I tell those women they should never give up and that wonderful things can happen when you're least expecting it."

279

"I'll be there. I love you, Amy."

"I love you too."

Author's Note

Keep reading for a free preview of my Crash series.

Thank you so much for reading my book and for supporting an independent publisher. I really hope you enjoyed it—I know I loved writing it.

If I may be so bold, I would like to ask a favor of you. Most people do not leave reviews, but if you enjoyed the book (or even if you didn't and have some feedback for me) please do consider writing a review at the online store where you obtained this book. Independent publishers like myself are entirely dependent on reviews—we cannot sell books without them.

Thank you!

Now, here's a free preview of Crash

CRASH
MIRANDA DAWSON

Chapter One

I took a peak into the conference hall to look at our audience. There were hundreds or people out there. Mainly men, but with a token scattering of women in power suits. Soon they would all have their attention fixed on me. Was I ready for that? I'd never been the subject of attention like this before.

"Do you think we should do one more run through of the presentation?" I asked John. "We did slip up a little in the middle when talking about the historic financial data."

John smiled at me. "Relax, Emily. We've got this. That slip up was entirely my fault and it won't happen again. The more we stress about every little detail, the more likely we are to make a mistake."

"I can't help it," I said. "You do realize that everyone out there is going to be waiting for me to screw up?

"Not this again, Emily," John sighed. "No one in the audience even knows about your leg."

"Actually, smartass, I was referring to the fact that I am a woman. I've checked out the list of speakers for this conference, and only three women are scheduled to speak. And the other two look like they could be part-time supermodels."

John sighed again, but he didn't argue. He couldn't disagree with me on this one; Silicon Valley was still a boys club, and the vast majority of women who did make it here were attractive or had other connections. I had neither.

"The fact that you are a woman gives you an advantage, not a disadvantage," John said. "Besides, I guarantee you that most of the men in this audience would do anything to get you in the sack."

"Oh, please," I said. "I'm hardly beating men off with a stick."

"That's because you won't even let them get that close. I'll let you in on a little secret, Emily—when men think about what they like in a woman, the lower half of one leg features pretty low on the list. Now stop sulking and get ready for this presentation."

John was right. I needed to get my head in the game and stop worrying about things that were out of my control. This presentation could make or break our startup, so it had to be a good one. My paranoia about having a prosthetic leg would have to wait.

John was on fire. He spoke with a confidence I had not seen in him before as he wowed the audience of investors with the business plan for our start-up venture. LimbAnalytics had started as just an idea—something I had dabbled with in my spare time while pursuing my biology major at Stanford—but with John's help, I had made it into a business.

With the right investors, LimbAnalytics might revolutionize life for people with artificial limbs like me. To say I was excited would have been an understatement.

I scanned the room and picked out a few faces I recognized. Silicon Valley was a close-knit community, so the same people appeared at most of these events. Every face in the crowd represented cash, the lifeblood of my business.

But one face stood out from the crowd. A man stood at the back of the room whispering into a woman's ear. I saw her giggle as he handed her a business card. Based on her body language, they would be having more than a networking lunch.

I kept an eye on him as he pulled his mouth away from the woman's ear. He was captivating. I was standing on stage next to my business partner as he gave a presentation and yet all I could do was stare at this man. He wore a fitted, light gray suit that hugged his muscular arms and bulging chest. I'd never mentally undressed a man before—heck, I'd never undressed a man period—but I already had him shirtless and was unbuckling his belt in my mind.

My eyes followed him as he left the room. His tight trousers left me with a detailed view of his rear and I couldn't help but imagine sinking my teeth into it. The man was a walking Greek God—an Adonis. I ached with longing and found myself eager to get back to my hotel room and spend some time between the sheets.

"Emily?" John said next to me, sounding a little agitated.

I looked toward him and could hear the crowd murmuring and snickering at me as I stood there under the lights. I looked at our presentation and realized it was my turn to speak. Judging by the sweat glistening on John's forehead, he had been trying to get my attention for some time.

"Uh, sorry. Um..." I muttered, kicking myself for daydreaming at the worst possible time. "As John has explained the business plan, please now let me explain a little more about how LimbAnalytics works and how it will revolutionize medical treatment for people with—"

As I spoke, my fake leg hit the back of my other calf and I went flying into the podium. I tried to grab hold of it, but only succeeded in pushing it over on my way down to meet the floor. My knee took the brunt of the fall, but that wasn't my concern right now. My trouser leg had crept up and my prosthetic limb was showing to all and sundry. The gasp from the audience washed over me as John picked me up.

"At least now I have your attention," I said, rearranging my clothing. It was a bad joke, but the audience gave a polite laugh.

The rest of the presentation went surprisingly well, given that little incident. I did have to apologize to John for leaving him hanging. Apparently he had called my name at least five times with no response. I gave him some excuse about seeing an old college friend in the audience and he seemed to buy that.

It didn't matter anyway. After the presentation we were inundated with people who wanted to speak to us about our product. Intriguing people had never been a problem, though; it was getting them to invest that had caused many sleepless nights. LimbAnalytics had a great business model, but we required huge capital investment with little chance of return for five years. I had every belief we would succeed, but I couldn't blame potential investors for getting cold feet after looking at our accounts.

John and I spent the rest of the afternoon and into the early evening networking with nondescript men who all started to look alike after a while. They were all white, middle-aged, and dressed in a suit, but without the tie, which was about as formal as it got in the Valley.

The only way I could tell them apart was the way they acted with me. There was Niles, the skinny guy who kept trying to peer through the gap in my blouse. Preston kept putting his hand on my knee or on my arm whenever he made a bad joke. Richard and Wilson treated me like an idiot and assumed I wouldn't understand any of the financial aspects of investment.

None of them were ideal investors, but at least they retained my vision for the company. They were not the real problem. The problem that kept me up at night was PharmaTech, the world's largest pharmaceutical firm that had been sniffing around our company for months. They would make an offer sometime in the next few months, that much I knew. It would be an offer that would make us millionaires overnight and likely mean we would never have to work again for the rest of our lives. But they would also destroy my dream.

PharmaTech would buy the company and then immediately dismantle it because our product threatened their profits. PharmaTech made big money under the existing system and we worried them. I couldn't let them buy the company. I started LimbAnalytics to help people, not to make a rich company even richer.

"You going to call it a night, Emily?" John asked when he had finally managed to shake off the last hanger-on.

"I'm going to grab a bite to eat at the bar," I said. "I haven't eaten since breakfast and my stomach is growling. Want to join me?"

"No, better not. I promised Tom I would give him a call. He always worries that these networking trips are just orgies in disguise."

I smiled and said goodbye. John's boyfriend was a little clingy, but it was nice to see John settling down in a serious relationship. He'd spent all of college sleeping around, so a boyfriend was a big lifestyle change for him.

The hotel restaurant was small and all the tables were taken. I considered heading out into the city for food when a few people got up from the bar and vacated their seats. I grabbed a stool and skimmed the menu before settling on a large burger. It was hardly an original choice, but I needed comfort food right now.

The burger arrived quickly and I immediately set about destroying it. I didn't look entirely ladylike, but at that point I couldn't have cared less; it'd been a long day. Not a lot could have taken my attention from my dinner right then, but someone walked into my line of vision and stopped me mid-bite.

In through the hotel entrance walked the man I had seen earlier while I gave my presentation. He strolled through the door in the same gray suit, although I would never have guessed he had spent the day in it. The only change to his appearance from earlier was the rough stubble around his face. Other than that, he looked immaculate.

The man stopped to finish up a phone conversation, giving me a great opportunity to take him all in and store him in my memory for later. He held the phone in his hand; elbow bent to reveal a large bicep that seemed eager to escape his suit. His tailored shirt did not leave a lot to the imagination either, and if I had to guess, I would have imagined he had the beginning of a six-pack on his stomach.

He put the phone down and I quickly looked away to avoid getting caught, then went back to picking at my food. Just a few moments later, someone pulled out the stool next to me and took a seat.

My peripheral vision took in a gray suit. I chanced a quick look to the side as he picked up the menu. It was him. He was sitting right next to me. I could smell a faint whiff of subtle aftershave and it sent my hormones into overdrive. Suddenly I felt drunk and giddy like a schoolgirl.

The bar had emptied out somewhat while I had been eating, and there were now plenty of tables free. He did not have to sit next to me, and yet here he was. If I were to move slightly to my right, my arm would brush against his.

Why had he sat next to me? Surely he wasn't planning to hit on me? One-night stands were hardly unusual in hotels, but that sort of thing didn't happen to me. Just a few seats to my left a stunningly gorgeous woman in a red dress was drinking alone, practically screaming for a guy to buy her a drink, and yet this man, this god in human form, had chosen to sit next to me.

Maybe he had a thing for broken women? Or he could detect my innocence and wanted to teach someone "pure?" I wasn't technically a virgin, but I felt like one and I was sure I gave off that vibe.

I made an effort to eat slowly and finish my drink. Hopefully he would take note of the empty glass and decide it might need a refill.

"Hi," came a soft voice from the seat next to me. "Can I buy you a drink?"

Oh my God, it had worked. It was really happening. No one like this had ever hit on me before except at college, and that was usually as a joke.

I tried to act cool. "Sure. I'll have a vodka tonic," I said, turning my head to smile at him. But he had his back toward me. He turned and looked at me over his shoulder, staring into my eyes and looking confused. My heart sank as I saw a stick-thin, beautiful woman in a silver dress on the other side of him. It was the same woman he had been talking to during my presentation. He wasn't asking me for a drink; he was asking her. The woman snickered and made little effort to hide her amusement.

"Oh, I'm sorry," the man said, looking at me with pity. "I was asking this lady. But please, allow me to buy you a drink anyway."

I quickly rummaged around in my purse for some cash, then threw it down on the bar and ran as fast as I could with only one working leg. A few strangers cast worried looks in my direction, but I ignored them and headed straight for the elevators. Unfortunately, they were all on their way up to other floors.

I looked back over and saw them both still looking at me. The elevator took an eternity to arrive and by the time I arrived back in my room I was a hot, sweaty mess. What a fool I had been. Men like that did not buy drinks for women like me. I lay on the bed and cried myself to sleep.

Chapter Two

I couldn't face going downstairs to breakfast the next morning. It took me nearly an hour to shower and make myself look presentable, and by the time I was done, the breakfast buffet was probably just down to the dregs anyway.

My phone had a few missed calls from my mom. I'd promised to update her on how the day went and she tended to panic when I forgot to call. I contemplated just sending her a text, but I really needed to speak to a comforting voice right now.

Mom always answered the phone with a generic, "Hello?" as if she didn't know exactly who was on the other end. It usually drove me nuts, but right now I found it kind of endearing.

"Hi, Mom."

"Oh, hello, dear. How are you? How did the big day go?"

"I'm fine, mom. Sorry for not calling last night. John and I were networking into the early hours, and by the time I got back to my room I was just exhausted. I fell right to sleep." I could never outright lie to my mother, so I just kept to statements that were technically true.

"Networking?" Mom said. "I am impressed, dear."

Mom was impressed with most of what I did. I was the first in the family to go to college, so when I graduated Stanford University with a major in human biology, it was a pretty big deal. Mom didn't entirely understand my business or the amounts of money that were being bandied around, but that was probably for the best.

"It's not as exciting as it sounds, I'm afraid," I said. "Just talking to lots of rich men about money."

"Sounds exciting to me dear. I wouldn't mind spending my evenings talking to rich men who want to give me money."

"Mom!"

"What? I'm just saying that perhaps things aren't all that bad. Any chance one of these rich men wants to buy you dinner?"

"Hardly, Mother," I said. "I doubt I'm their type."

I heard my mother sigh on the other end. "Not this again, darling. You are a beautiful young woman, and when you project a little confidence, I doubt any man can resist you. No man worth having is going to care about your leg."

"I know, I know," I said, just to keep Mother happy. I didn't want to get into that discussion right now. "This is just not a good place to meet men, that's all."

293

"I thought it was a sausage-fest over there," Mom said. "You should be able to have your pick."

I cringed at Mom's choice of words. No one wanted to hear their mother talk about "sausage-fests." Her and Dad had started drifting apart after my brother died and Mom seemed determined to regain her lost youth. That meant talking to me like she was still twenty, and it was painful.

"I'm trying to keep it all business while I'm out here," I said. That should keep her happy. She wanted me to find a man, but she also wanted me to be successful, so work had to come first sometimes.

"Anyway, can we talk about that on your birthday? I assume you can still make it over for that weekend? I've booked a restaurant for us." It wasn't a cheap one either, but then it wasn't every year your mother turned fifty. With Dad unable to get out of work this weekend, she would only end up spending it with other couples. She hated that, so we'd arranged for her to come and spend the weekend with me in the city.

"Oh, yes," Mom said. "I'll be there. Can't wait to get out of this place, actually. The weather is getting up into the hundreds, so it's too hot to even go outside."

"All right, well, I'm going to buy your plane ticket when I get home tonight. I've got to dash now. I have one final bit of networking to do."

"Okay, dear. Do see if you can snare a man while you're at it."

"I've told you, Mom. I'm not interested in these guys."

"Not for you. For me. Have a good day."

Mothers. I checked myself in the mirror and decided to try and take Mom's words to heart. I was the founder of a popular start-up company and people were interested in me. I wasn't unattractive. When I wore trousers or a long skirt to hide my leg, I attracted a lot of glances. Bigger tits would have been nice, but the ones I had were pert and went well with my slender frame.

I pulled on a professional pair of trousers and paired it with a blouse that opened low, revealing a hint of bosom. I didn't have a lot to work with, but I was damn sure going to make the best of it. Time to go charm some investors.

Chapter Three

After two days of mingling with investors, I actually found it rather challenging to return to work. Whereas I usually leapt out of bed in the morning ready to change the world, I now found myself lingering between the sheets and reluctant to even switch on my computer.

I spent Saturday at home, but it was not exactly productive. I answered some emails and made a few minor tweaks to the code, but nothing exciting. John didn't like it when I fiddled around too much with his code, because more often than not, I broke it and he would spend days fixing it. Still, given that only a year ago I had known nothing about computer coding, the fact that I could do anything at all was an achievement.

Unfortunately I made the mistake of streaming TV shows on Netflix, and from that point, the day was over in terms of productivity.

John apparently had the same problem. "Want to work at the SF Station tomorrow?" he asked in a message. "Can't work at home with Tom around."

"Sure. See you there at 10 am."

The SF Station was our go-to coffee shop located roughly equidistant between John and me. They served excellent coffee but were criminally underrated, which meant John and I could always find a table to sit down and work.

"Usual, Emily?" Jane asked as I approached the counter.

"Yes, please, but could you drop a second shot of espresso in there today?"

"One of those days, is it?" Jane asked with a smile.

"Something like that."

John had already claimed a table in the corner that was big enough for four people. Or it was until we pulled out laptops and chargers and spread ourselves out.

"Morning," I said, sitting down adjacent to him.

"Hey," John replied. "Thanks for coming here today. I was just getting so much grief from Tom for working at the weekend. I had to get out."

"But he doesn't mind you working at the coffee shop?" I asked.

"He might," John said. "But I told him I was visiting my brother down in Palo Alto."

"Ah. Well, I would likely have come here anyway. I barely got a thing done yesterday."

"*How I Met Your Mother*?" John asked.

"*Frasier*, actually," I replied. "Haven't watched it in years, and you know what it's like once you get started."

"Only too well," John said.

We had a quick catch up on where we were with the business and then divided up a couple of important tasks. LimbAnalytics had started with us working like this in the coffee shop, so being back here with John helped me forget about the investors and really knuckle down to work.

"I'm going to need another coffee," John said after we had worked in silence for at least two hours. "You want one?"

"Oh, yes," I replied. "Soy milk latte, please."

John left the table and headed over to order the drinks. I should have asked him to grab me a snack as well. As soon as I stopped working I realized how hungry I was.

"Do you mind if I join you?" asked a man with a strong accent. Was he English?

I hated sharing a table, but the two of us could hardly justify taking up a large table if the place was busy.

Except it wasn't busy. I looked up and saw a number of empty tables in front of me. It was too late to say anything now; the stranger was taking a seat opposite me and next to John.

"Thank you," the man said.

"No problem," I muttered and took a quick look up at the man.

It was him; the guy from the bar at the conference, the man in front of whom I had completely embarrassed myself.

"Hi," he said with a grin. "Remember me?"

How could I forget him? In shock, my lungs expelled the air from my body and I saw a tiny bit of spittle escape from my mouth and land directly in front of him. He pretended not to notice. His appearance was different from the night before. The stubble had gone and a polo shirt and jeans had replaced the tailored, slim-fit suit, but his face was not one I was likely to forget in a hurry.

"Yes," I said, finally able to form a word. "I'm sorry about what happened. I hope I didn't spoil your evening."

The man looked puzzled. "Why are you sorry? That was all just a misunderstanding. These things happen."

He kept staring at me, his eyes looking deep into mine as if he were trying to read my mind. What should I say next?

The silence stretched on while he waited for me to speak. With impeccable timing, John returned to the table with my coffee.

"Oh, hello," John said to the stranger, assuming I knew him from the way we were looking at each other. "I'm John, Emily's business partner." John held out his hand to the man while I looked on, still not entirely sure what was happening.

"Hello, John. I'm Carter. Pleasure to meet you."

"Is that an English accent?" John asked, his eyes lighting up. He was a sucker for an English accent almost as much as I was. Knowing my luck, the two of them would be talking about *Doctor Who* any minute now.

"Yes," Carter replied, glancing back at me. "I'm from Winchester. It's near London," he added when John glanced at him with a confused look on his face.

"I met Carter at the conference the other night," I said, trying to take some control over the situation.

"Ah, you want to invest in LimbAnalytics?" John asked.

Carter lifted his cup to his lips, his bicep flexing under the tight shirt as he did so. God, this guy was a dream. Better, in fact. Even the men in my dreams were grounded in reality. This guy should not have been real.

Two Chinese girls at the table next to us were clearly talking about him. I didn't need to know Mandarin to recognize sexual desire when it was that obvious.

"No, no," Carter said. "I'm afraid I know nothing of technology. Not my thing at all. I just popped by to ask Emily for a favor."

It all fell into place. The other night was no doubt an illicit liaison that needed to stay secret. He had come here to ask me to keep my mouth shut. How romantic.

"How can I help you, Carter?" I asked.

Carter smiled. "You can accompany me to dinner on Friday."

Chapter Four

I saw John mouth the words, "holy crap!" He looked as excited as I should have felt.

"I, uh, I've just remembered I need to make a call outside," John said, standing up from the table so quickly he banged his knees and nearly tripped over the power cord connected to his laptop. I thought he mouthed, "go for it," as he left, but I couldn't be sure.

"You want to take me to dinner?" I asked.

"Yes, if you would be so kind." Carter leaned back in his chair and crossed one leg over the other, never losing eye contact with me.

"Look, I get that the other night was embarrassing for all concerned, but you don't need to make it up to me."

"I know," Carter said. "I'm not trying to make it up to you. I just want to buy you dinner."

"Why?" I asked. "I'm not exactly your type, am I?"

I caught a hint of confusion in Carter's face, but he did a good job of hiding his emotions.

"What is my type, exactly? I wasn't aware I had one."

"I saw the woman you were with the other night. She was stunning. Don't tell me you are interested in someone like me."

"You don't really think a lot of me, do you?" Carter asked, each word coming out soft in his English accent. "I don't have a type. I just like beautiful women, and you, Emily, are very beautiful."

He must have been lying, but what for? Did he just want to sleep with a disabled girl for a laugh? Maybe he hadn't noticed my leg? I'd assumed he'd noticed as I tripped on my way out of the restaurant, but it was possible he'd been too fixated on Miss Big Tits to notice.

"Why are you in the US?" I asked, changing the subject.

"On business," Carter replied.

"So you are only here for a week or so?"

"A couple of months, actually."

"And then you go home. I'm not looking for a short fling, I'm afraid. I suggest you stick to women who are only looking for a night of fun."

"Ouch," Carter said. He looked genuinely offended. "All I want to do is take you for dinner this Friday. Is that really so much to ask? I think I could show you a good time, and if you don't want anything else to happen, then it doesn't have to."

Carter wasn't used to people telling him no, and I must have been crazy to be doing that. I could see

John staring through the window and egging me on. Was I mad to be turning him down? Carter looked genuine enough, but something didn't quite fit in this situation, and there was no way I could let myself fall for someone like him. In a few months he would head home and leave me here where no man could ever measure up.

"I don't mean to sound rude," I said. "I'm sorry. I just don't like jumping into things so quickly, and knowing that you're going home in a few months just makes this the sensible decision. Besides, I have a disability that isn't exactly conducive to having passionate flings."

Carter smiled. Was that a nice smile or a condescending one? I couldn't decide.

"You have an artificial leg, Emily. That hardly makes you incapable of going to dinner with me. Do you always do the sensible thing? Because life would be a lot more fun if you let your hair down once in a while."

"Unfortunately, yes," I replied. Every decision in my life was based on being sensible. "Anyway, it's my mom's birthday on Friday and I'm taking her for dinner."

"Okay," Carter said, standing up. "I'm not going to try and force you to do something you don't want to do. It's a shame, though, because you seem like a remarkable woman."

"Wait," I called out as Carter walked away. "How did you know I would be here?"

"Easy," Carter replied. "I saw your company name on your name badge at the convention. That company has an office nearby, according to public records. I assume it's just a PO box, or something like that?"

I nodded.

"You're a start-up. Start-ups like to work in coffee shops. I looked in a few ones nearby and bingo, here you are."

"Impressive," I said.

"Like I said, I really want to take you to dinner, and I always get what I want. Goodbye, Emily. I will see you again soon."

I gave a weak wave as he left the coffee shop. He had gone through all that effort to find me. Why would he do that for a girl who made a fool of herself in front of him?

"Are you crazy?" John yelled at me as he sat back down. "You turned him down? Are you blind?"

Everyone in the coffee shop was staring at us now.

"He just wanted a one-night stand," I said. "And yes, I know he is attractive—"

"No, he's not attractive," John said. "Brad Pitt is attractive. Carter looks like he was personally sculpted by God and then given an English accent. What were you thinking?"

"Come on, John. Doesn't this all sound a bit weird to you? He could have anyone he wants, but he decides to invite me out to dinner? He just wants to have a bit of fun with a cripple and then ditch me. Maybe he just wants to brag to his friends that he slept with a one-legged girl."

"Don't be ridiculous," John scolded. "Anyway, so what if he just does want a bit of fun? What's wrong with that? I don't mean to sound rude, Emily, but you really need to let someone in one day. And not just in your heart, if you get my meaning."

"He's not my type, John, okay? Now just leave it."

John dropped it and we got back to work, but he looked baffled and acted a little off for the rest of the day. I kept typing away, but couldn't get Carter out of my mind. Those eyes. Those arms. I just couldn't shake them.

As soon as I got home, I took some time to myself between the sheets. I shuddered to a climax imagining Carter's strong arms lifting me up and throwing me onto the bed before making me into a woman.

Every time I masturbated, I told myself that I would loosen up and get a man for real. I'd allow him to breach my sex and fill my insides with flesh in a way that my fingers just couldn't do. But then I would meet men and clam up; all the negative possibilities would take over my mind.

What if he freaked out when he saw my leg? What if I was crap in bed? Logically, I knew thinking this way was stupid, but that didn't help. I couldn't change the way I was, but didn't seem to be able to accept it either. Until I did, men like Carter would only be fucking me in my fantasies.

Chapter Five

Mom insisted on staying in a hotel even though I offered her my bed. She said she didn't want to cramp my style, but I had a horrible feeling she just didn't want me to cramp hers. My mother made no secret of her newfound lust for life, and I dreaded to think of the ways she might occupy herself with a hotel room in a big city.

On Friday night, we met at the expensive restaurant I'd picked for her meal—La Table. John and I ate here the night we first got some seed funding for the company. It was a reckless way to blow through a couple of hundred bucks, but we'd both been living on noodles for months and John convinced me that we deserved a treat.

The business was generating a bit of cash now, but this night would still represent a noticeable blow to my bank balance. Still, my mom wouldn't be turning fifty every year, and without Dad around I felt like I had to make an effort.

The restaurant was one of the few places in San Francisco that actually had a dress code, so I wore a dark blue, full-length dress with thin straps and a somewhat risky low neckline. This dress was one of the few that gave me a bit of confidence in my figure, mostly because it completely covered my leg but also because it hugged my figure, pushing my breasts up and out. The maître d' at La Table seemed to approve, judging by the lusty look he gave me.

"Good evening madam," he said, reluctantly tearing his eyes away from my chest. "Do you have a reservation?"

"Yes, table for two under the name Emily Saunders."

"Ah yes, your other guest is already at the table."

He walked me over to a little two-seater table at the back of the room. It was in the middle of an aisle and near the restroom, so we would have people squeezing past us all night. I'd been lucky to get a table at all and couldn't afford to be picky about its location.

"Happy birthday Mom," I said, wrapping my arms around her thin frame. She lost a little weight over the last few months and looked damn good. If I looked like her at fifty, I would be very happy.

"Thank you, dear. I cannot believe how fancy this place is. You really didn't need to bring me somewhere like this. Have you seen the prices?"

I smiled. Mom was used to the dirt cheap food they served in Phoenix, so the prices in San Francisco were bound to be a bit of a shock to her. "Don't worry about that, Mom. It's my treat for your birthday. Just order whatever you want."

"I'm glad you said that, because I have taken the liberty of ordering us a couple of cocktails. Ah, here they are."

Over the next hour we sampled a bit from the cocktail menu, usually ones with rude names that seemed to titillate my mother, and got through our appetizer and main course. The courses had been quite modest in size, so I contemplated squeezing in dessert.

"Mom, you getting anything?" I asked.

No reply. My mom stared into space, deep in thought. "Mom?"

"Huh? Oh, sorry, dear. Did you say something?"

"I was asking if you wanted anything for dessert?"

"What I want for dessert has just walked in through the door. Goddamn, what I wouldn't give to devour that fine specimen."

"Mom!" I exclaimed. "I don't want to hear things like that."

"Look behind you at your five o'clock and tell me you wouldn't do wicked things to that man."

I sighed, but swiveled slightly in my chair to get a better look at the object of my mom's desire. I couldn't see anyone at first, but then noticed the man with his back to me. He was pulling out the chair for his date, a stunning leggy blonde who must have come straight off the catwalk. This man certainly had a nice ass, I agreed with my mom on that point. Rich as well, judging by the location of the table which had a view out over the bay and by the fact that staff were hovering around to see to the couple's every whim and desire.

Finally the lady took her seat and the man turned round to take his own. He was stunning, all right. Stunning and familiar.

It was Carter.

About the Author

Miranda Dawson is a 25-year-old Californian who can't find the man of her dreams and so writes about him instead. She likes reading romance novels and watching scandalous television shows. Her writing is influenced by both!

You can contact me at miranda.dawson@sfpublishingllc.com or check out my Facebook page.